THE FOURTH FONTANA BOOK
OF GREAT GHOST STORIES

The Fourth Fontana Book of
Great Ghost Stories

COLLECTED BY ROBERT AICKMAN

Collins
FONTANA BOOKS

First published in Fontana Books 1967
Second Impression December 1968

The arrangement of this collection is copyright
© *Robert Aickman 1967*
Printed in Great Britain
Collins Clear-Type Press
London and Glasgow

CONTENTS

ACKNOWLEDGMENTS

Acknowledgment is made to the following for authority to include the stories named: Messrs. A. D. Peters & Co. for *The Accident* by Ann Bridge; The Richards Press for *Not on the Passenger List* by Barry Pain; Messrs. G. Bell & Sons Ltd. for the translation by T. Keane of Pushkin's *The Queen of Spades* from *The Prose Tales of Alexander Pushkin*; Mr. Michael MacCarthy for *Pargiton and Harby* by Sir Desmond MacCarthy; Sir Rupert Hart-Davis for *The Snow* by Sir Hugh Walpole; Mr. Eric Ambrose, F.R.I.B.A. for *Carlton's Father*; Messrs. Edward Arnold (Publishers) Ltd. for *A School Story* from *The Collected Ghost Stories of M. R. James*.

Despite considerable inquiry, it has unfortunately proved impossible so far to trace the owner of the copyright in *When I was Dead* by Vincent O'Sullivan.

INTRODUCTION

"Judge a man by his questions," advised Diderot, "not by his answers." This is at once useful guidance for any interviewer; and deep wisdom.

Answers are almost always insufficient. (There is, in fact, a famous ghost story which bears that very name.) They are almost always misleading. To go through life believing the common answers is to walk through a minefield in blinkers. The main reason why science has not made people happier is that the scientific approach asks the wrong questions and then gives incomplete answers. The more you know in that way, the less you know: as many of the wiser scientists have always acknowleged, and occasionally still do.

This is not merely a paradox. Every scientific answer raises more doubts than existed before the asking of the question; leaves the questioner even nakeder and chillier than he was before. It is in this way that science will end the world, rather than with a big bang. Even if there is no big bang, we shall destroy the world in no time, if we go on as we are. We shall crowd ourselves out; starve ourselves out; bore ourselves to bits; choke with protest against all the wrong things.

Knowledge lies within us. It is to be found nowhere else. It is a matter of delight and of inaccessible horizons, rather than of question and answer. Truth can be found only through the imagination, and those whose imaginations have been cramped with answers will never find it.

The so-called ghost story, the story of rare sensations, gives access to a modest, but extremely significant, section of the truth. As the scientist and his alter ego, the bureaucrat, close in the world around us, shutter by shutter, poetry and religion, which represent a fundamentally different way of life, seem to lose much of their authority. People abandon the quest for their own truth, in favour, at the best, of selecting or building up an external truth from ingredients offered by specialists, much of whose impressiveness lies, as they are the first to say, in their incomprehensibility to non-specialists. It is a curious road to truth for the common citizen. Ghost stories, believe it or not, are one of the last outposts of the spirit of man. Hence, undoubtedly, the quite remarkable rise in their popularity. Hence, equally, the great difficulty of finding new ones that qualify; that really *are* ghost stories.

The essential quality of the ghost story is that it gives satisfying form to the unanswerable; to thoughts and feelings, even experiences, which are common to all imaginative people, but which cannot be rendered down scientifically into "nothing but" something else. In a world of meaningless fact and meaningless violence, people shrink from admitting that they still harbour entities of the imagination. The element of form in the ghost story is, therefore, crucial. Hence the fact that so many of the best ones derive from the period, at the end of the last century and beginning of this, when form was a particular and conscious literary preoccupation. In the present collection will be found a *conte* by Oscar Wilde which is almost nothing but form, and which manages to carry suggestions going far beyond its precise ironical details and narrative. There is often something curiously extra-terrestrial about Wilde's style of mockery: something much more poetical than satirical (even in the proper use of that vulgarized word). It is this innate, smiling concern with two worlds at once that largely accounts for the unique charm, going beyond standards of customary literary criticism, that so many, here and abroad, have always found in his ostensibly rather casual opus. "Under the common thing, the hidden grace," as Lord Alfred Douglas put it, in one of the most beautiful sonnets ever written. No one can hope more from life than to find that particular grace, even occasionally. From Wilde it seldom absented itself, even through all his troubles.

The ghost story, like poetry, deals with the experience behind experience: behind almost *any* experience. Often, alas, as often as in life, the experience is of guilt; as here perhaps in *Pargiton and Harby*, *The Accident*, and *When I was Dead*. The first of these, by one of the greatest of English literary (and dramatic) critics, relates to the frenzy so often encountered in the community of professional letters, as excess sensibility and the compulsion to self-expression encounter little public interest and less comprehension. In all of us the passion of guilt is terrifyingly autonomous: related at once to everything we do and to nothing we have done; strong or weak in us by virtue of forces which have little connection with our actions or conscious thoughts: expressed, more often than not, so indirectly and obliquely as to build up rather than diminish in the seeming release. *The Accident* depicts this mystery against an apt and proportionate geographical background, most adroitly and compellingly portrayed; thus it was, we feel, utterly realistically, in every detail. *When I was Dead* is a very rictus or spasm of guilt; sudden and shattering. Vincent O'Sullivan was a master of this dyeing and soaking in guilt. The curious should try to find a copy of his novel, *The Good Girl*. The quest is difficult, but the product distinctive. O'Sullivan, having lived a longish life as a more or less well-to-do rentier, in latish middle age found himself ruined, wrote his last book (*Opinions*) under terrible conditions, and, dying in Paris, ended anonymously in the common pit for the cadavers of paupers.

But guilt is not the only human experience which has a soul. Vulgarity and parvenuism has a soul, and in several stories Saki bleached it white, but never whiter than in *The Wolves of Cernogratz*. The fancy that ancient lineage has no meaning is here deftly cauterized. So too in Pushkin's immortal *Queen of Spades*: on the face of it, redbrick finds retribution, but the curiously mechanistic, matter-of-fact, man-of-the-world telling of the wild tale, offers little hope to the impure hearted of any persuasion. Modeste Tchaikovski, in adapting the story for his brother's opera, widened the field of sympathy by working up the sentiment between Hermann and Lizavetta. This was quite legitimate, and the splendid *Pique Dame* would not have lasted with audiences as it has, if he had not done so; but people have become so familiar with the opera, and also with Mr. Thorold Dickinson's, in its way, almost equally excellent film, that they may be taken by surprise at the dry-boniness of the original.

Not on the Passenger List appears to concern itself, indeed does concern itself, with something warmer and more positive, something almost cordial; though it is wholly typical of Barry Pain's work in this field that he conveys to the reader at the same time a *very* faint feeling that the author himself is not unreservedly convinced by the soft rosiness of the message. *The Snow* relates to the inadequacy of good intentions. As we all know, we have to be right as well as more or less good. (And that is impossible?) Sir Hugh Walpole has been objected to, since his death, both as an artist and as a man; but in many stories, written from the far side of the fireplace, he excelled in depicting the more horrible injustices of life by projecting them slightly beyond the edges of this world. *Carlton's Father* really deals, as much as does *A School Story*, with the cosmology of the schoolboy; with, that is to say, a world of the imagination from before the prison-house has closed upon him, which, if not fed and fostered by the grown man, brings about the man's death with its own, and be the man never so assured and apparently in social demand. To my mind, certain of M. R. James's stories contain an element of patronage: one becomes aware as one reads of the *really* great man, the Provost of Eton, the engineer of the inscription on the Unknown Warrior's grave, relaxing; all too consciously descending a little, to divert, but also still further to edify, the company. *A School Story* I find free from this defect. The Provost knew about schoolboys.

And that leaves *Mad Monkton*; which by concentrating upon some very peculiar and exceptional events, has more to say about life as a whole, about the non-appearing aspects of life, than, possibly, any of the others. Wilkie Collins felt himself to be a man at variance with his epoch. This made his work very uneven, and his life very arcane. To this day, surprisingly little seems dependably to be known about him. Both in writing and in living, he hid his tracks; though perhaps leaving occasional toeprints detectable by the discerning. At its best, his work is so garishly penetrating that he seems to write by the light of gas flares. If he had lived at another time, he might have escaped the inner conflict that produces this effect. But art is so dependent upon conflict, that though he might have gained, we, his readers, would have lost.

I cannot pretend that these tales were not first called ghost stories because they were regarded as stories that dealt with the dead who returned. I should like to suggest that now the word "ghost" should be seen more as the German "geist"; that ghost stories should be stories concerned not with appearance and consistency, but with the spirit behind appearance, the void behind the face of order. Ghost stories inquire and hint, waver and dissemble, startle and astonish. They are a last refuge from the universal, affirmative shout.

ROBERT AICKMAN

It was Goethe himself, when I visited him one day in his garden-house, who gave me the following account of how it came to be haunted: "I have invisible servants who always keep the landing swept clean. Very early one morning I had what I supposed was a dream, but it was exactly like reality: upstairs in my bedroom the door leading to the stairs was open, and I saw an old woman with a young girl leaning against her. She turned to me and said: 'We have been living here for twenty-five years on condition that we must be gone by daybreak; now she has fainted and I can't go!' When I looked more closely she had vanished."

JENNY VON PAPPENHEIM
May 1831

THE ACCIDENT

Ann Bridge

The grey-haired man sitting on the wall opposite the Hotel
Monte Rosa at Zermatt folded his copy of *The Times*, knocked
out his pipe against the cement parapet on which his feet
rested, and, groaning a little, hoisted himself up out of
his wicker chair. " The wall " at Zermatt, it should be
explained, is not really a wall at all, but a narrow terrace
raised a foot or so above the narrow street, with just room
on it for a single row of chairs. There, since the earliest
days of mountaineering, Englishmen with skinless noses,
wearing baggy trousers and shabby tweed coats, have sat
during the months of August and September—smoking
pipes, reading *The Times*, or discussing routes up Swiss mountains, propping their feet on the narrow ledge in front of
them; watching other climbers enter and leave the hotel, and
above all, gossiping as only Englishmen of the more learned
professions on holiday know how to gossip. This sin besets
climbers in particular: a small class of men, somewhat a
race apart, the interest they take in the exploits and even
the personal idiosyncrasies of each other is something of
a portent.

Now, as the grey-haired man went over to the door of
the hotel, tapped the barometer, and then took his large,
powerful, and slightly heavy figure off down the street, two
much younger men, drinking an early tea at one of the little
green-painted iron tables by the hotel doorway, looked after
him with interest. They were climbers, too—the button of
the Alpine Club adorned their jackets; nailed boots their
feet; in the afternoon sunshine the wall was now deserted,
and the grey-haired man disappearing past the bootmaker's,
the only subject of interest or speculation in sight.

" Who's that? " the younger asked.

" That's old Allard. The alienist chap."

" What *is* an alienist? " the very young man inquired,
pouring out another cup of tea.

" A loony specialist, my dear Billy. He's a great swell.

13

Runs that big asylum in Hampshire. He climbs with old Franz Leukerbad. He did that new route on the Pretzelhorn last year."

Dr. Allard meanwhile wandered on down the small street. He was taking an off day, and was filling in the time as one does fill in off days at Zermatt. He went into the Wega bookshop and found a new French volume on dementia praecox, which he bought. It was still too early for tea, and he pottered idly up into the little cemetery and stared, as two generations of mountaineers have stared, at the monument commemorating the four climbers who perished on the first ascent of the Matterhorn. The imagination cannot resist the dramatic quality of that episode—success at last, after years of undaunted and fruitless struggle on the part of Edward Whymper, darkened in the very hour of triumph by an unexpected and still inexplicable tragedy. "Lord Francis Douglas," Dr. Allard read. He turned away, sighing a little ; poor old Whymper, he remembered him the last time he came to Zermatt—the little stocky man, old and shabby, with a square face rather like Lord Beaverbrook's. He looked across to the Matterhorn, an obelisk of brown and silver, dominating the end of the valley ; plastered with new snow, it was, and lovely to see—but no hope of doing the Zmutt ridge for days yet. Well, Whymper was dead now—but when Lord Beaverbrook and his papers and his wealth were forgotten, the Matterhorn would still stand there, he thought, and Whymper be remembered ; no one could look at the Matterhorn for ever without remembering Whymper—the man who had made the mountain his monument. And his courage and tenacity, and selfless devotion to that shape of ferocious beauty.

There were two newly made graves in the cemetery, and drawn by some curious fascination he went and stood by them, and read the names on the small temporary wooden boards set up at the foot of each mound of raw earth: "James Bull, July 16th, 19——" ; "George Henry Whitelegg, July 16th, 19——." Just a month ago. Poor chaps—no one would ever know why they had fallen either ; they were alone, climbing guideless, when they were killed. There was nothing much wrong with the north-east face of the Weisshorn—it had been done at least four times before, and once by a girl of nineteen. Bull—well, one ought not to speak ill of the dead, but he was rather a nasty bit of work. Unscrupulous, jealous, touchy, always on the make, Allard thought with distaste ; crabbing other climbers, puffing his own exploits, writing himself up. The best thing about him was his passion for mountaineering ; but even that he sullied—everything turned to journalism at his touch. Poor young Whitelegg was quite under his spell—he had that power of dominating another person, almost of possessing them.

Sometimes one's own thoughts give one a start. When Dr. Allard got as far as " possessing them," he pulled up short. No, he didn't really mean that ; not even of Bull. The word " possession " had for Dr. Allard a perfectly definite technical meaning ; that form of mental derangement when the personality is invaded by some alien intruder which, in its attempts at domination, wrecks the delicately adjusted mechanism of the human reason. He specialised in this little-studied branch of psychiatry ; he had written a book about it.

As if his thoughts tired him, he sat down on a bench in the sun. His poor Rose! So eager, so beautiful, so good —and struck down, just six weeks before their wedding, by that appalling malady. He could never forget the days when, gentle and amiable as she still seemed, she had begun to look at him with the eyes of a stranger ; that memory clung more hauntingly even than the shocking moment when she attacked him with demoniac fierceness. She had been certified, and died shortly after in an asylum, but she had turned Allard into a mental specialist. All his spare time had since been spent in investigating this special form of derangement. For years he had never come to Zermatt—he had met her here; but latterly he had begun to do so again—it was so long ago, and time blunts the edge of even the most passionate memories. This time, however, it had all been brought back to him vividly by the presence of that nice child, Phyllis Strangeways. She reminded him strangely of Rose. Not in person—she was smaller, fairer ; but in her ardent love of mountains and the beauty of mountains, her tireless enthusiasm for climbing them. They could never be still, she and that brother of hers ; they must be doing something every day of their precious three weeks. Yesterday they had gone off, on his advice, to do the Bieshorn, the only thing which might conceivably be expected to go with these masses of new snow; their guides, the young Kaufmatters, were in his opinion rather too frivolous and reckless to be entrusted with such a pair of babes. Dr. Allard had an almost tender feeling, half parental, half something more wistful, connected with memories of his own youth and another's, about those two; he felt that they wanted looking after. And eagerly, sweetly, deferentially they accepted any advice he gave; they had even begun to come and seek it, and his company too.

He glanced at his watch. The 4.05 from Randa would just about be in; they ought to have caught it. He would go and see. Hoisting himself up out of his seat—this beastly rheumatic stiffness!—he left the cemetery.

He met them in the street. Yes, they had done the Bieshorn all right—a frightful plug, though, in all that snow. But he missed their usual accents of joyful enthusiasm. The girl looked tired, and rather white; she was unusually silent while he gave them tea at one of the little green tables. Something in her aspect troubled Dr. Allard, and when she went in to have a bath he detained the boy. "Roger, what's wrong with your sister?"

The boy frowned. It was that fool Christian. On the way down he had insisted on making a detour across the Bies-glacier to show them the place on the Weisshorn where the accident was, a month ago—and that had upset her.

How like guides, Dr. Allard thought, with their morbid love of horrors! Still, he was a little surprised at its having so much effect on her; she had seemed a person of considerable nervous stability. "I'm sorry, Roger," he said. "Still, there was nothing to see, was there, after all this time, and this new snow?"

The boy said nothing—he still frowned, with a puzzled, uncertain look. "Roger, what is it?" Dr. Allard asked him now, sharply.

"Well . . . I think I'd better tell you, sir, though you'll think us all fools," said the boy, flushing at his tone. "As a matter of fact, we did see something. It was as we came away. We'd left the foot of the face, and got right out on to that flat snowfield that lies below it, when suddenly we came on tracks in the snow." He stopped.

"Well, what of that?" said Dr. Allard, a little testily. "Some other party might easily have been there. Where were they coming from?"

"That's just it," said Roger. "They weren't coming from anywhere. They just began, right out in the open. We didn't somehow notice at first how odd it was, and we followed them, because it was easier going. But then the guides began to talk between themselves, like they do, discussing how on earth those tracks could have begun just from nowhere, right out in that huge open space—and Phyl caught the drift of what they were saying, and just as they began to go down-hill she turned all white and said to me: 'Those are *those men's* tracks!'" And nothing would make her go that way any more."

Dr. Allard pulled at his pipe. "And what did the guides say?" he asked.

"Oh, Christian laughed and said: '*Es war nur Spuren*'; but he and Hans didn't much like it either, because unless somone was dropped from an aeroplane, how *could* they begin like that? It was . . . *nasty*," said the boy, wriggling his shoulders, as if to throw off some oppression. "So we branched off to the left and came down the rocks by the side of the ice-fall, and back that way. But that's what has upset Phyllis."

II

Dr. Allard pondered this information all the evening. When he had sent Roger off to change, he sought out the guides and questioned them. They confirmed Roger's story in every particular; the footsteps had begun, quite suddenly, in the snow, right out in the flat open space below the N.E. face of the Weisshorn, as if the makers of them had dropped from a *Flugmaschine*. But the men were not at all anxious to talk about it, and from their rather foolish and giggling manner, more than from anything they actually said, he divined that they shared Roger's discomfort about the whole matter. In fact, Hans and Christian Kaufmatter had got the wind up. That was the one thing which emerged clearly. Why, they would not or could not say.

After the children had gone to bed—Dr. Allard always thought of them as children, though Phyllis was nearly twenty and the boy at least seventeen—the doctor strolled a little way up the valley road in the warm starlight, smoking. In front of him rose the Matterhorn; barely visible, a shadowy, almost transparent shape of sky-colour, which held no stars. He began to set the facts in order in his head. No aeroplane had crossed the valley, so Alois, the porter, said, " within the last thirty-six hours—since the last snow fell, in fact." Therefore that explanation of the phenomenon was ruled out. But four people had seen it. Were they all four mistaken? Possibly—Dr. Allard knew too much about hallucinations to exclude that possibility. But even if they were mistaken, the problem remained ; four people experiencing the same hallucination, and all, though in varying degrees, feeling precisely the same sense of discomfort about it. Phyllis had felt it most, Roger next most—and Phyllis alone, he noted, had connected it with the two dead men. H'm. It wasn't very nice, however you looked at it. He dallied with the thought of going up next day to the Bies-glacier, to see what was to be seen for himself, but on further consideration he decided against that plan. He would do better to stay with the children, keep them amused, and talk to Phyllis. He knew the importance, in any case of shock or disturbance, of making the person talk it out—suck the poison from the wound, as it were, and prevent an injury to the subconscious. He would get on to that in the morning.

Dr. Allard had reason, next day, to be extremely glad that he had not gone off to the Bies-glacier, for the afternoon brought a fresh and far more disturbing shock. The morning passed quietly enough. He and Phyllis went for a stroll, into the meadows beyond the town—the hay was cut, but small bright flowers bloomed in the stubbly grass and on the ledges of the scattered rocks ; the air was aromatic with thyme. Sitting in those sweet and peaceful surroundings, Dr. Allard had his talk with the girl. It was not very satisfactory. Phyllis, to his surprise, took a rather superior line about herself. She had been tired ; she must have been fanciful. No, she didn't really mind it a bit now. It *was* odd, but it didn't worry her, really, Dr. Allard. This disconcerted the doctor a good deal. She would not come out into the open—and why wouldn't she? There were two possible reasons—either that she really had got over the shock, and thought herself silly; or that she was so profoundly frightened that her mind was shying away from the subject. The latter was the more likely, but so long as she would not talk about it, he could not be positive; and more important, he could not help her.

All he could do was to keep the pair of them occupied, and with this end in view they went up to the little restaurant at the Corner Gorge for tea. Phyllis seemed really merry up there, which made the shock when it came all the greater. The post had come in when they got back, and Dr. Allard took his letters from fat old Alois and sat on the wall with them; absorbed, he was vaguely conscious of the children sitting close by, chattering over their own mail, when he heard Roger say . . . "What's this card, Phyl? Who on earth is J. Bull?"

The name hit the doctor at once, with a little sharp tap like a hammer. He looked up quickly at the pair. Phyllis was turning a picture postcard over in her fingers, with a puzzled look on her face. "I can't imagine," she said. "Stresa . . . I don't know anyone at Stresa ; and I didn't think I knew anyone called Bull. Why should he want to climb with us? And yet the name is familiar, somehow—I know I've seen it lately."

Dr. Allard got up and went over to them. "Some mistake?" he said . . . "let me see, may I?" He did it all very gently and naturally, like a person moving up to a wild bird ; whatever was on that card, he wanted to know it before Phyllis remembered where she had recently seen the name J. Bull —on the wooden board at the foot of that new grave in the cemetery, where he himself had seen it, only yesterday. But even as he went to take the card from her, the girl's face blanched ; she put one hand over her mouth with a curious gesture, and stared at him with darkened eyes. "James Bull," she said, almost in a whisper, from behind her hand, " he . . . he was one of *them*!"

" My dear child, that's got nothing to do with this post-card," said Dr. Allard, firmly and heartily. " Let me see it, will you?" She gave it to him, and he read it through. It was written in pencil, which came out rather faint on the glossy surface on the card, below a picture of Stresa. " George and I are making our way over to Zermatt, and hope to find you and your brother there. We mean to climb with you. Yours . . . J. Bull." That was all. The doctor turned it over. It was addressed, correctly enough to Miss Phyllis Strangways, Hotel Mont-Rose, Zermatt, and bore the Stresa postmark of two days before ; just one day, Dr. Allard noted, before the children had seen those strange footsteps on the Bies-glacier. George—that was young Whitelegg's name. It wasn't very nice, it was a horrible practical joke to play on anyone. Before he could think of the next thing to say, young Roger of course must needs do the silliest thing he possibly could. " George Whitelegg was the other chap's name, surely?" he blurted out.

Dr. Allard had to control his irritation with the boy. " Yes, it was," he said quietly and rather sternly, " and that shows that someone is playing a very stupid and heartless practical joke on your sister. I can't conceive of anything in worse taste." He turned to Phyllis, who still sat staring at him with those fixed and darkened eyes. " You're sure you don't know the writing?" he asked in a very everyday voice. " Look at it again."

But neither Phyllis nor Roger could recognise the writing in the least. So Dr. Allard took the card, promising to institute inquiries about the practical joker ; he was so firm about this person that presently he saw the girl's colour restored, and a more natural expression come into her face.

But his inquiries did not take the form that a listener to the foregoing conversation might have expected. It is true that he did, from the post-office, ring up the office of the small local journal which published the visitors' lists at Stresa, and ascertained that no one within the last week had registered in the name of Bull at any of the hotels or pensions there ; he hardly expected to find that they had ; but when the children were out of the way he went and looked up James Bull's signature in the hotel register. Written with the usual deplorable Swiss nib, in the usual gluey hotel ink, it was mostly a purple blot, hardly legible, and quite useless for purposes of comparison with the faint pencilling on the postcard. He further ascertained at the bureau that Bull had paid his bill in notes, not by cheque. Finally he was driven to inquiries among the few English climbers in the hotel, as to whether any of them had known Bull well enough to recognise his writing. But none had—Bull was not generally popular. Dr. Allard was obliged to admit himself stumped in this direction.

Next day they did a climb on the Riffelhorn. The children appeared to have swallowed the practical joke theory fairly

easily, and if Dr. Allard's own thoughts took a rather
darker turn he kept them to himself. Phyllis climbed well,
and after a huge tea at the Riffel-alp they ran down the
path through the pine woods in the usual happy spirits of
descending mountaineers. At the door of the hotel Dr. Allard
met an old friend, just come in from traversing the Matterhorn, and stopped to exchange greetings with him—he was
interrupted by Roger, who came out from the hall and touched
his arm, with a disturbed face. " Could you come to Phyl a
moment, sir? She's had another."

The doctor hurried in. Phyllis sat, white and frightened, on
a chair at the foot of the stairs, holding a postcard. It bore
the postmark of Ornavasso, and a similar message to the
first ; the date was twenty-four hours later. Dr. Allard took
the girl up to his room—the hall was full of people—and
there talked to her. Now she *did* come out into the open ;
half crying, she admitted that she was frightened, and with
just the same fear as she had felt on the Bies-glacier. " I
don't believe it is a joke—I believe it's *them*. I have a feeling
—I don't quite know how—that they're trying to get *at* me!"
she said, staring at him with terrified eyes.

Dr. Allard mixed her a sedative, and talked to her reas-
suringly. She mustn't give way, he said, to those ideas ; she
must at least think of it as a practical joke, till they had
proved whether it was or not. " Spirits don't write postcards,"
said Dr. Allard. He gave her a new Tauchnitz novel and
sent her to bed for supper—but he went down to dinner very
ill-at-ease. No—spirits didn't write postcards, but they did
cause the hands of others to write them. He had seen that.
It looked—well, to Dr. Allard it looked very nasty indeed.
" We mean to climb with you "—what could that imply but
a determination to climb most intimately with them, in their
persons, possessing them? If, that is, it wasn't a joke. And
the doctor didn't really believe it was. The whole thing hung
together too well. Ornavasso was almost at the mouth of the
Val Anzasca, which led up to Macugnaga and the Monte
Moro—mountaineers would come that way if they came on
foot. No, he didn't like it—didn't like it at all.

He took the only precaution he could—of telling Alois to
keep all postcards for Miss Strangways and give them to him.
So Phyllis escaped the one which arrived next day—from
Bannio, as the doctor expected, half-way up the Val Anzasca,

with a still more recent postmark. The day after that there wasn't one—and he took the pair out step-cutting on the Findelen glacier. But on the afternoon of the fifth day, when they came in for tea after a walk, Alois, the porter handed the girl a note. A party, he said, had given it in on their way down from the Regina Margherita Hutte on Monte Rosa, an hour before. Phyllis opened it—turned white, and handed it to the doctor without a word. It bore the date of that very day, and contained only the words: " See you in Zermatt this evening. . . . J.B."

III

Dr. Allard's first thought was to trace the bringers of the note. But here Alois could give little help. They were Italians, *Führerlosen* (guideless climbers)—they had handed in the note, asked the time of the next train to Visp, and gone on to the station, where a train actually left within half an hour. They would, it was clear, be gone some time since.

But these inquiries and considerations were soon cut short by concern for Phyllis's state. Roger, very sensibly, had taken her up to her room; but he presently sent a chambermaid down to request the Herr Doktor's presence immediately. Allard went up. The girl was sitting huddled in a chair, staring in front of her; she started violently at his entry, sprang up, and then stood, trembling all over. "They'll get me," she said, in a low vibrating voice; "they'll be here to-night and they'll get us." Dr. Allard spoke soothingly to her, putting his hand on her arm: "Phyllis, I will take care of you—you mustn't get so excited."

"You can't—you can't keep them off. They've been coming, and coming, and coming—and now they'll be here —this *evening*!" she said, her voice rising almost to a scream. "Oh!" She sank down in the chair again, covering her face with her hands, while shudders shook her body.

Dr. Allard was thoroughly alarmed. Whether there *was* any reality in the menace he feared, or whether it was merely a horrid practical joke, the effect on the girl was the same —she was nearly frantic. He began to fear for her reason—if this state of panic terror went on, anything might happen. In such cases argument, he knew, was useless; the only chance was some definite action which would relieve the tension. He took a sudden resolution.

"Roger, go and get hold of Franz and Christian and tell them to be ready to start the moment after tea," he said decisively. "And tell Marie to put up some food for to-morrow. We're going up to the Trift to do a climb." The boy ran off and the man put his hand firmly on the girl's shoulder. "Phyllis!" he said. She looked up, and he held her eyes with his, steadily—a trick he had long since learned to use in his piteous profession.

"Listen to me, Phyllis," he said. "If anyone does comes, they won't find us here. We're going up to the Trift for the night, and if the weather holds we'll traverse the Rothhorn to-morrow, to the Mountet hut." He saw that he had caught her attention—she had heard; she was taking in his meaning, and the trembling lessened. He went on, pursuing his advantage. "As for all this business, it's very nasty and mysterious, my dear; but if you will trust me, and do exactly what I tell you, I will keep you safe, you two. Do you understand?"

"Yes," she said faintly, but a little more naturally.

"That's right," he said. "I can take care of you, if you will obey me—but you must do what I say. Now, put your things together for two or three days—we might even go over the Dent Blanche, if the weather is good and you don't get too tired. Have you got spare unders? and your woollies? Well, put them all in, and then come down and have tea, and we'll start the moment after."

He waited, while she began to collect her effects in heaps on the bed—asking her where her rucksack was, commenting on items of her outfit, keeping her attention on these practical details, till Roger came back. "When you've done your things, help Roger with his," he said, and grasped the boy's arm till he winced, to check his protest. The boy, startled, looked at him and understood, thank goodness. "Try and be down in ten minutes," he said, and left them.

Walking up through the narrow gorge which leads to the Trift Hut, after tea, Dr. Allard took the opportunity of having a talk to Roger. He had got hold of old Franz, his leading guide, and put a little of the situation to him. The Fräulein, he explained, had got an *idée fixe* as the result of being taken to the scene of the accident—it was very unfortunate, but these things did happen. "Ja-Ja"—Franz nodded acceptance of the statement. It was therefore most important to keep her mind occupied, Dr. Allard pursued, and he,

Franz, was to come up to her on the path and enter into conversation with her, and keep her talking. But he was not to mention accidents, or death, or *Gespenster* (ghosts), or any such thing—nor Herr Whitelegg, or Herr Bull, naturally. " Ja-Ja "—Franz nodded again. (His style, Dr. Allard reflected, would be greatly cramped by cutting out two of the Swiss guides' favourite topics ; but Franz was an old friend, and absolutely trustworthy.)

So while Franz amused the young lady with anecdotes of Wills and Whymper, Davidson and Coolidge, Dr. Allard talked to Roger. He wanted to ascertain what Roger himself felt about the whole business—worried as he had been over Phyllis, he had given little thought to the boy ; besides, he could be a most useful ally in dealing with his sister, if he could be got to grasp the situation. The doctor was careful to begin by being very medical, explaining the danger to Phyllis's mind and nerves involved in the strain of such terrors ; the importance of keeping her attention occupied, and of not leaving her alone. (He remembered that point afterwards.) On what justification there might be for her fears he did not touch, at first. But Roger did. After listening thoughtfully to Dr. Allard's injunctions, he put a question on his own account : " Phyl thinks—she's convinced—that those men want to go on climbing, and haven't bodies to climb with now, and want to use ours. That seems pretty fantastic, but "—he paused—" is it possible, sir?"

Dr. Allard chose his words carefully before replying. There was a form of mental illness, he said, for which the word " possession " was used ; but generally it was, so to speak, by some attribute of personality, like violence or cruelty, rather than by a whole personality itself, that the sufferer was enslaved. " And even then we are guessing, really ; judging the cause by the effects."

" So you *don't* think it possible?" the boy said, looking at him.

Dr. Allard stopped, and took off his grey felt hat. They had emerged from the gorge, and the open upper valley where the Trift Hunt stands, lay spread out before them, the mountains round it catching the last sunlight ; a cool wind off the snow touched his damp forehead gratefully.

" I simply don't know," he said at length, returning the boy's look, steadily, with his grey eyes under the jutting brows.

" All I can say is that in a lifetime on this job I have never known a case of direct possession by a personality newly dead." He wiped his forehead—finding those words and saying them had made him as hot as the steep pull up through the gorge. But Roger seemed satisfied. " Good! " he said.

" Are you frightened at all, Roger?" the doctor then asked.

The boy in his turn paused before replying. The doctor saw him look at his sister's figure, slender and trim in breeches and shirt, walking lightly across the rough valley ahead of them beside old Franz—then he ran his eyes round that group of noble and lovely mountain-shapes enclosing the valley. " Not much," he said at length, ". . . apart from Phyl, that is. And not so much up here. It *was* getting rather beastly down there "—he nodded towards the Zermatt valley over his shoulder—" but I always feel safe among these chaps " ; he swept a hand round the circle of mountains.

The Trift hut is really a small inn, stone-built, with bedrooms and a *salle à manger*, and quarters for the guides. There the party had supper—the usual *Maggi* soup, thickened with cheese ; coarse bread, stringy veal, and compote. Soon afterwards the doctor sent the children off to bed. He gave each of them a strong sleeping-draught, and went in, paternally, to tuck them up. Drowsy with the Dial, Phyllis smiled at him from her pillow. " Sleep well, child," the doctor muttered, stirred by the childish face. " I'll take care of you." And went out.

But he did not go to bed. He had a curious feeling that he would be better awake and on the watch that night. One by one the few other climbers went off to bed and the doctor remained alone in the little *salle à manger*, propped in a wicker chair. He had a book, but he did not read ; he would reserve that till he began to feel sleepy. Instead, he ran over the affair in his mind from the beginning. That matter of the writing was curious. The doctor took out a pocket-book and extracted from it three postcards, a note, and a letter ; he spread them on the bare wooden table and examined them. Oddly enough old Morrison, the friend who had turned up after traversing the Matterhorn the other day, *had* been in correspondence with Bull on some debated point of topography, and had actually had a letter of his by him—it was his which the doctor now compared with the three postcards

and the note which had been sent to Phyllis. No—the
writings were not really the same; and yet there was a likeness—just the sort of likeness you would expect if someone
was trying to imitate a handwriting, under whatever compulsion. It was rather uncanny. And why had that phrase,
" under whatever compulsion," suddenly come into his mind
in connection with it? No—the more he looked at it, the
less he liked it. The door rattled suddenly; the doctor started,
rose up, went and opened it. There was no one there—the
moon was rising behind the inn, and its light just touched the
summits of the Wellen-kuppe and the Gabelhorn, opposite,
with silver; from the gorge below rose the strong voice of
the stream. Peaceful and still the valley lay; Dr. Allard
remembered the boy's remark about the mountains. Soothed,
he went in again, shutting the door. His thoughts now ran on
Phyllis and her symptoms; poor child, if this expedient
failed she would be in poor case. That huddled staring
which his entrance had interrupted in her room at Zermatt
had frightened the doctor more even than her trembling and
her cries; it was a bad sign. He thought of Rose, his lost
Rose; so she too had sat, with far less apparent reason,
nerveless, sunk together, gazing before her. Eh dear! how
that child's face brought it all back. A bad business—a
horrid business. Were they asleep, he wondered? Removing
his old leather slippers the doctor stole upstairs and peeped
into each room. Yes—sleeping sweetly, the pair of them. He
went down again. But his anxiety returned, and remained
with him all night. The shutters outside the windows, the
door, the stairs, made faint sounds, creaked, and were
still. And ever and again, more stiffly each time, at some
particularly loud and alarming sound, Dr. Allard hoisted
himself out of his chair and crept upstairs to listen outside the
children's room; or went to the hut door, opened it noise-
lessly, and looked out. But ever and again, nothing was
to be seen save the grey shape of the moraine in the shadowed
empty valley, and the mountains white under the moon.

IV

The traverse of the Zinal Rothhorn is one of the pleasantest
climbs round Zermatt. The peak itself stands, like a great
canine tooth of reddish rock, on the high ridge forming the
watershed between the Val d'Anniviers and the Zermatt

valley—a watershed which runs almost throughout its length above the snow-line. The Rothhorn cannot compare for beauty with its neighbour the Weisshorn, that lovely pyramid whose exquisite outline is so completely satisfying from all sides; but it has a splendour of its own, a tilted curve, at the summit, as of a breaking wave—so that he who will may fling his prune-stones between his boots sheer down to the snow hundreds of feet below. The ascent on the Zermatt side is on the whole easy: a walk up the Trift valley to the little glacier-fed tarn at its head, a long weary grind up the Trift-glacier moraine—that curious geological formation, long and curved as a snake and pointed as a roof, into which the fallen stones from the surfaces of glaciers are loosely piled up; on and upwards over the easy snow-slopes above, bearing always to the right, till at last—how thankfully!—the climber takes to the rocks. This first part of the climb is what Roger called "a plug"—the rest is pure pleasure. Above the first easy rocks a snowy ridge leads upwards till it merges into the steep slabs of the final peak; slabs of hard red rock, sound and firm, so that the smallest holds for toes or fingers give a sense of absolute security.

Up this route the party from the Trift inn made their way next morning. It was dark when they started at 3 a.m., and the lights from the lanterns carried by the guides winked like a procession of wandering stars as they plodded up the faint path and floundered painfully over the loose stones of the moraine. It was warm—a thing not only unpleasant in itself, but ominous as indicating a change in the weather; climbers like a cold air at dawn. Dr. Allard perspired freely. At the foot of the rocks they halted to put on the rope; the breather was welcome to the doctor, who found that a "white night" in a wicker chair is not a helpful preliminary to a first-class expedition. The sun by now had risen, and they were already high enough to look out southward over the peaks beyond the Zermatt valley; they glowed a furious rose, beautiful to see but threatening for the future; the guides spat and muttered at the sight. The Matterhorn was visible, looming up over the gap in the ridge between the Ober- and Unter-Gabelhörner; distinct, among so many others, by something wild, almost savage, about its shape. Refreshed by a good night, the children were in tolerable spirits; Phyllis had made a poor breakfast down at the inn, but Dr. Allard saw her munch biscuits and chocolate with alacrity while she identified the various summits and discussed the ways up them.

And how she loved climbing! Long afterwards Dr. Allard was to remember her happiness that day on the Rothhorn. For after they had roped up and proceeded on their way, up the rocks and along the snow arête, she seemed to forget all her fears, and her spirits to mount within her as her body, triumphing over gravitation, mounted towards that sky of intensest blue overhead. When they reached the steep rocks of the final peak, she went up the slabs like a cat —hardy, fearless, and strong ; pausing in some exposed and airy situation, where ordinary people are wont to cling with concentrated attention to their holds, to look back at the doctor, and call down some gay remark or a question. Old Franz was delighted with her, and exchanged flattering remarks on her performance with the Kaufmatters in guttural Swiss. On the top, when they reached it at 10.30—slow time, but Dr. Allard was no longer so fast as he had been—she sat in a trance of rapture, right on the edge of the overhanging drop, her feet dangling gaily into several hundred feet of blue air, eating her lunch and gazing at the view. Dr. Allard's hopes rose ; it really seemed as if his expedient had succeeded beyond expectation. If only they could keep it up—not return to Zermatt at all, perhaps, but go on to Zinal or Arolla, letting their luggage follow them. He set off for the descent in spirits almost as high as Phyllis's own.

The descent from the Rothhorn to the Mountet hut is at no time such a simple matter as the ascent from the Trift. Three large towers of rock, known to climbers as gendarmes, block the ridge and must be carefully negotiated. The third and largest of these is rather a teaser: a steep and very exposed wall of rock, straddling the narrow ridge below it ; cracks in the surface of the slabs afford the only hand- and foot-hold. It is a place needing care and a good head even when the conditions are good, and on this occasion they were not good. The party were now on the north side of the mountain, and whereas on the southern side the rocks had been warm and dry, here on the northern ridge snow and even ice still lingered in all the interstices—the cracks on the great gendarme were plastered with them, making the negotiation of the steep face a matter of extreme difficulty. They

had to unrope, and using one of the ropes, looped round a
point of rock, as an extra handhold, go down one at
a time, after old Franz, with much swearing and scuffling,
had been lowered and cleared the cracks as well as he could.
All this delayed them considerably, and it was 3 p.m., four
hours after they had left the summit, before they were all re-
assembled on the ridge at the foot of the gendarme. By this
time the weather was becoming a source of anxiety. The
threat of that warm wind at daybreak, that rosy flush at
sunrise, seemed about to be fulfilled—clouds were gathering
to the south, behind them, and puffs of grey vapour were
beginning to boil through the wide gap in the ridge between
the Rothhorn and the Weisshorn. The guides, as usual
when bad weather threatens, became nervous and fidgety, and
wanted to hurry on down; but Dr. Allard, to whom Phyllis's
health was an over-riding consideration, insisted on a pause
and a little food as soon as they should reach a suitable
place.

They took it, perched as and where they could find room
on both sides of the ridge; it so happened that Dr. Allard
and Franz alone were on the west side—the other three guides
and the two children were on the opposite side, looking out
towards the Weisshorn. The valley in which the Mountet
hut stands still lay in sunshine, a vast expanse of dazzling
snow, narrowing on the north where the Durand glacier,
hidden by the slope of the Besso, swept round the corner to
flow down the Val d'Anniviers; Dr. Allard could see the hut
at the foot of this slope, just above the moraine. Studying the
surface of the glaciers with the automatic care of the
mountaineer, the doctor's eye was caught by something—some
tracks in the snow below them, leading in the direction of
the hut. There was nothing unusual in this—the ordinary
route off the ridge down to the Mountet would strike the
glacier about where the tracks were visible, but he could not
see quite where they came from. He took his field-glasses out
of his rucksack, focused them, and began to examine the
tracks.

What he saw made him start so violently that the leather
case of the glasses, which he had carelessly laid on his knee
instead of slinging it round his neck by the strap, fell, and
went clattering down the rocks to the glacier below. The
footprints were indeed going towards the hut, well out on

the open snow, clear of the rocks and in plain sight—but
*no other tracks led from the foot of the rocks towards
them*! As those others on the Bies-glacier had done, they
began, impossibly, out on the open glacier, coming from
nowhere.

For a moment Dr. Allard felt almost physically sick when
he saw that ominous sight through his glasses. But he pulled
himself together at once, and took a hurried decision on the
next thing to be done. As luck would have it, seated on the
farther side of the ridge, Phyllis and Roger had not seen
the tracks, and at all costs they must, if possible, be prevented
from seeing them. The loss of the case created a certain
amount of fuss, of which the doctor made the most; it also
furnished him with an excellent excuse for changing the
route of their descent, leaving the ridge earlier than usual, so
that they would strike the glacier at a considerable distance
from the unaccountable start of those beastly footprints. He
did not much like the idea of crossing them, as they would
have to do to reach the hut, but there was nothing else to
be done; there was no other shelter within reach, and even
as they re-roped and started down the rocks, snow began
to fall.

They climbed down easily enough, retrieved the case, and
set out across the glacier. But even as Dr. Allard feared,
Phyllis's mood suddenly changed; she crossed the tracks
themselves without comment, but she grew first listless, then
uneasy—was silent even when addressed, and occasionally
glanced behind her. These signs knocked cold on the
doctor's heart. He treated them as fatigue; on reaching
the hut, in snow now falling thickly, he gave her a hot brandy
before supper, and sent her off to bed immediately afterwards. But her symptoms of distress increased, and with
them the doctor's despair—oh God, what *could* he do?

What he could do, he did. The Mountet hut has two stories,
the upper reached by a sort of ladder-like stair. Here he put
Phyllis and Roger to sleep; he took occasion to remind the
boy not to leave her alone, and gave Phyllis an even stronger
sleeping-draught than the night before. Then he went downstairs. On the straw-filled bunks the guides lay, snoring
already; Dr. Allard stoked up the stove, drew a chair close to
it, and once more settled down to keep watch. Outside, when

he took a last look from the door, the snow was still falling, thickly and silently.

But Dr. Allard had had a long, stiff day's climbing, and this was his second night of watching. The warmth of the stove was soothing; he nodded drowsily. Time after time he jerked himself upright, only to nod again; and at last, overcome, he fell asleep.

He was awakened by a feeling of cold, and a sense of light near him. He started up, looking confusedly round. No wonder it was cold—the door stood wide open; outside the snow had ceased, and bright moonlight was pouring, with the keen night air, into the hut.

v

Dr. Allard glanced at his watch. It was half past two. He went to the door and looked out. Footprints—smallish footprints—led away from it in the smooth newly fallen snow, down over the rough slope towards the glacier. Full of foreboding, he turned back into the hut and climbed the ladder to the upper room. It was as he feared—the straw-filled sleeping-shelf was empty, the dark fusty blankets flung aside in two tumbled heaps. The children were gone.

Cursing himself for his wretched drowsiness, his unpardonable lack of self-control, Dr. Allard bundled down the ladder again. Hurriedly he roused the four guides; with muttered grunts, of which the doctor caught more of the sense than the guides realised, the men tumbled up, pulled on their boots, their jackets; collected the ropes and the ice-axes, and fitted new candles into the lanterns. Lacing up his own boots, his back aching with stiffness, Dr. Allard listened to them. Those tracks yesterday had not escaped the notice of the Kaufmatters anyhow, and whatever form their discomfort took, they had managed to communicate it to Franz and Peter. The Kaufmatters were Grindel-walders and Lutherans, but the Catholic Franz crossed himself as he stepped over the threshold and into the cold bright moonlight outside.

The tracks led down to the edge of the glacier and out across it in a southerly direction. In the clear moonlight there was no difficulty about following them in the freshly fallen snow, and the five men moved forward at a brisk pace. Dr. Allard's mind was moving even faster than his legs. How on earth the pair could have managed to climb down the ladder, put on their boots, open the door, and leave without rousing anyone, was a mystery—though he reflected presently that none of the guides had heard him go up and down the ladder; they were fast asleep when he roused them up. And what impulse had led the children to leave the hut? Was it flight, or some strong enticement? And where were they making for? Anxiety filled him—farther up the glacier, under the Gabelhorn and the Rudihorn, crevasses might be expected, and they appeared to have taken no rope. Clear as the moonlight was for things near at hand, it was deceptive for distances; peer as he would, he could see no sign of any living thing on the white reaches ahead. And how long a start they had, he had no idea.

Suddenly Christian Kaufmatter, who was leading, stopped dead with a prodigious and startled oath. The rest, coming up to him, halted too. So far there had been just the one set of tracks, with an occasional longer or shorter step showing that two people, not one, had passed that way— but when Dr. Allard came up to where Christian and the rest had halted, he saw that two more sets of footprints had appeared suddenly, one on each side of those which they had been following. The fresh prints did not approach the track —they just began there, suddenly. For a moment the group of men stood staring—then Franz crossed himself again, and suddenly young Hans Kaufmatter began to whisper. For some reason the horror of that moment was complete. With an effort the doctor roused himself—" *Vorwärts! Schnell!*" At first the guides were so demoralised that he actually had some difficulty in forcing them to go on along that unholy triple track; they walked well to one side of it, and in spite of all his urgings, not quite so quickly as before.

Presently the moon went down, and behind them dawn began to break. As the light grew stronger Christian, who was now going second, immediately behind Dr. Allard, gave another exclamation. Dr. Allard stopped. Christian came up to him and pointed towards the slopes of the Rudihorn ahead of them. On a snowy ridge two small black figures were visible, moving swiftly upwards. Dr. Allard took out his Zeiss glasses. Yes, sure enough, it was Phyllis and Roger, climbing unroped. But through the glasses the doctor could see something which filled him with fresh dismay. The pair were climbing terribly fast, and though there was no one else in sight, they constantly looked back over their shoulders, as if pursued, and then hurried on faster than before. The ridge of the Rudihorn was no place for such reckless speed; even where the children were climbing, it called for care, with the rocks smothered as they were in new snow; higher up it steepened considerably, till eventually the angle became altogether impracticable. And what would they do then in their desperate flight? For that it was a flight from some unseen pursuit the doctor was now certain.

But the sight of the children themselves seemed to have driven away the guides' fear. They shouted and whistled to them; there was no reply, and they then set off in pursuit, crossing the glacier at prodigious speed. The Kaufmatters and Peter soon forged ahead—Franz and Dr. Allard could not keep pace with them, but followed as fast as they could. No words were needed; it was clear that the Kaufmatters were determined to catch up their truant patrons. Soon they, followed by Dr. Allard and Franz, were close in under the lower slopes of the Rudihorn; the children at the same time began to move more slowly, the steepness of the going hindering their progress. Now, suddenly, the pair left the ridge, and still with those terrible backward glances, scrambled helter-skelter down into a snow-couloir or gully, crossed it, and traversed out on to a snow-slope on the farther side. Up this they began to race again. But owing to this change of direction, their visible pursuers, the guides, had gained on them; and though high up, they were now not far away, in level distance, from where Franz and Dr. Allard stood. The two older men shouted to them till the rocks echoed, but it was as if they had no ears; they paid not the smallest attention, but kept on their desperate course. And how desperate that course was, Dr. Allard could now see clearly. The snow-slope up which they were moving abutted at the top against a blue wall of ice, and on the right sank with appalling steepness into the upper part of the couloir which they had just crossed lower down; on the left it ended abruptly in a cornice—that curious formation, curved out over space like the crest of a wave, into which the wind often moulds the snow. When they reached the top of the slope they would find themselves completely cut off. And in their state of panic, what would they do then?

But the Kaufmatters had evidently grasped the situation too. Cutting left-handed across the glacier, so as to lessen the distance, they took to the rocks below the snow-slope and started directly up them, with the obvious intention of trying to intercept the pair before they reached either the cornice or the ice-wall. They were climbing at terrific speed, and unroped, to increase their freedom of movement—even in that moment of desperate anxiety Dr. Allard noted their superb skill; Christian Kaufmatter, moving fast on difficult rocks, was a beautiful sight. Franz and the doctor now halted —there was nothing they could do, and Dr. Allard was pretty well exhausted as it was by crossing the glacier at such speed in the deep soft snow. They stood where they were, watching that horrible race. The guides' speed was astonishing, but the children were going up the slope as if their feet were winged. Now, instead of only looking back, Dr. Allard saw through his glasses that they were looking ahead too, and must have noticed the ice-wall above them, cutting off their escape, for they checked for a moment, and glanced wildly to right and left. They chose the left, and started off diagonally across the slope towards the cornice. This sudden move lessened the guides' chances of intercepting them in time; as the seconds passed, Dr. Allard saw, with sickened certainty, that with all Christian's matchless skill he must be too late. And now, despairingly, the doctor shouted at them: "Phyllis! Roger! Stop!" . . . shouted till he was hoarse, calling their names, calling on Heaven, calling their names again. Once old Franz heard him cry the name "Rose!" in tones of agony and desperation.

But it was all of no use. Swiftly as Christian climbed—he was close behind them now—the two terrified creatures went faster still. Now, if they had only looked back, they might have seen a familiar face and found safety; but they went on. They reached the cornice and started to go up it, several feet from the edge, but unaware—if they had wits left to be aware of anything—that the solid-seeming snow under their feet overhung empty space. And still, though almost voice-lessly now, the doctor cried to them. There was suddenly a curious cracking sound, as a great piece of the cornice gave way under the small extra weight, the vibration of those light hurrying feet—and then a moment of utter silence before the huge mass of falling ice and snow plunged on to the rocks below, to come roaring and thundering down, a white river of leaping blocks and foam-like snow-dust, almost to the doctor's very feet.

It was evening before they got them dug out, with the help of relief parties from Zinal; but the doctor would not leave the scene of operations for a moment till the two stretchers were on their way down the glacier, the centre of a silent and weary procession. They took them right on to Zinal, the last part of the way by lantern-light, and lodged them in the church; nor would the doctor take food or rest till he had arranged with the old priest that the latter should watch with them all through the night.

Dr. Allard's fellow-climbers speculated a good deal, both at the time and afterwards, as to why he should have been so insistent with the Strangways family that the two victims of that odd accident on the Rudihorn should not be buried either in Zinal or Zermatt; and actually insisted on bearing the whole cost of having the two coffins taken back to England, to lie in the quiet Sussex churchyard, under the yews and looking towards the Downs. They could not know, of course, how often he saw a sleepy childish face smile up at him from a coarse pillow, trustfully, and heard his own voice saying: "Sleep well, child; I'll take care of you." The guides did not know that either. But they did not speculate about his reasons. They knew.

NOT ON THE PASSENGER-LIST

Barry Pain

I had not slept. It may have been the noise which prevented me. The entire ship groaned, creaked, screamed, and sobbed. In the staterooms near mine the flooring was being torn up, and somebody was busy with a very blunt saw just over my head—at least it sounded like that. The motion, too, was not favourable for sleep. There was nothing but strong personal magnetism to keep me in my bunk. If I had relaxed it for a moment, I should have fallen out.

Then the big trunk under my berth began to be busy, and I switched on the light to look at it. In a slow and portly way it began to lollop across the floor towards the door. It was trying to get out of the ship, and I never blamed it. But before it could reach the door, a suitcase dashed out from under the couch and kicked it in the stomach. I switched off the light again, and let them fight it out in the dark.

I recalled that an elderly pessimist in the smoking-room the night before had expressed his belief that we were overloaded and that if the ship met any heavy weather she'd break in two for sure. And then I was playing chess with a fat Negress who said she was only black when she was playing the black pieces ; but in the middle of it somebody knocked and said that my bath was ready.

The last part turned out to be true. My bath was even more than ready, it was impatient ; as I entered the bathroom the water jumped out to meet me and did so. Then, when the bath and I had finished with each other, my steward came slanting down the passage, at an angle of thirty degrees to the floor, without spilling my morning tea, and said that the weather was improving.

There were very few early risers at breakfast that morning, but I was not the first. Mrs. Derrison was coming out as I entered the saloon. I thought she looked ill, but it was not particularly surprising. We said good morning, and then she hesitated for a moment.

" I want to speak to you," she said. " Do you mind? Not now. Come up on deck when you've finished breakfast."

She was not an experienced traveller, and had already consulted me about various small matters. I supposed she wanted to know what was the right tip for a stewardess or something of that kind. Accordingly, after breakfast I went up, and found her wrapped in furs—very expensive furs—in her deck-chair. I could see now that she was not in the least sea-sick, but she said she had not slept all night. I moved her chair into a better position, and chatted as I wrapped the rug round her. I confessed that with the exception of an hour's nightmare about a fat Negress I also had not slept. As a rule, she would have smiled at this, for she smiled easily and readily. But now she stared out over the sea as if she had heard the words without understanding them. She was a woman of thirty-four or thirty-five, I should think and had what is generally called an interesting face. You noticed her eyes particularly.

"Well," I said, "the wind's dropping and we shall all sleep better to-night. Look, there's the sun coming out at last. And now, what's the trouble? What can I do for you?"

"I don't think that even you can help," she said drearily, "though you've done lots of kind things for me. Still I've got to tell somebody. I simply can't stand it alone. Oh, if I were only the captain of this ship!"

"I don't think you'd like it! Why, what would you do?"

"Turn round and go back to New York."

"It couldn't be done. The ship doesn't carry enough coal. And we shall be at Liverpool the morning after next. But why? What's the matter?"

She held out one hand in the sunlight. It looked very small and transparent. It shook.

"The matter is that I'm frightened. I'm simply frightened out of my life."

I looked hard at her. There was no doubt about it. She was a badly-frightened woman. I resisted an impulse to pat her on the shoulder.

"But really, Mrs. Derrison, if you'll forgive me for saying so, this is absolute nonsense. The boat's slower than she ought to be, and I'll admit that she rolls pretty badly, but she's as safe as a church all the same."

"Yes, I know. In any case, that is not the kind of thing that would frighten me. This is something quite different.

And when I have told you it, you will probably think that
I am insane."

"No," I said, "I shall not think that."

"Very well. I told you that I was a widow. I wear no
mourning, and I did not tell you that Alec, my husband,
died only three months ago. Nor did I tell you, which is
also the truth, that I am going to England in order to marry
another man."

"I understand all that. Go on."

"Alec died three months ago. But he is on this boat. I saw
him last night. I think he has come for me."

She made that amazing statement quietly and without
excitement. But you cannot tell a ghost-story convincingly
to a man who is sitting in the sun at half past nine in the
morning. I neither doubted her sincerity nor her sanity. I
merely wondered how the illusion had been produced.

"Well," I said, "you know that's quite impossible, don't
you?"

"Yesterday, I should have said so."

"So you will to-morrow. Tell me how it happened, and I
will tell you the explanation."

"I went to my room at eleven last night. The door was
a little way open—fixed by that hook arrangement—the
way I generally leave it. I switched on the light and went in.
He was sitting on the berth with his legs dangling, his profile
towards me. The light shone on the bald patch on his head.
He wore blue pyjamas and red slippers—the kind that he
always wore. The pocket of the coat was weighed down, and
I remembered what he had told me—that when he was
travelling he put his watch, money, and keys there at night. He
turned his head towards me. It came round very slowly, as
if with an effort. That was strange, because, so far, I had
been startled and surprised, but not frightened. When the
head turned round, I became really frightened. You see, it was
Alec—and yet it was not."

"I don't think I understand. How do you mean?"

"Well, it was like him—a roundish face, clean-shaven,
heavily lined—he was fifteen years older than I was—with his
very heavy eyebrows and his ridiculously small mouth.
His mouth was really abnormal. But the whole thing looked
as if it had been modelled out of wax and painted. And,
then, when a head turns towards you, you expect the eyes

to look at you. These did not. They remained with the lids half down—very much as I remembered him after the doctors had gone. Oh, I was frightened! I fumbled with one hand behind me, trying to find the bell-push. And yet I could not help speaking out loud. I said: 'What does this mean, Alec?' Just then I got my finger on the bell-push. He knew I had rung—I could see that. His lips kept opening and shutting as if he were trying hard to speak. When the voice came at last, it was only a whisper. He said: 'I want you!' Then the stewardess tapped at the door, and I did not see him any more."

" Did you tell the stewardess?"

" Oh, no! I did not mean to tell anybody then. I pretended to be nervous about the ship rolling too much, and managed to keep her with me for a long time. She offered to fetch the doctor for me, so that I could ask him for a sleeping-draught, but I wouldn't have that."

" Why not?"

" I was afraid to go to sleep. I wanted to be ready in case —in case it happened again. You see, I knew why it was."

" I don't think you did, Mrs. Derrison. But I will tell you why it was, if you like. The explanation is very simple and also very prosaic."

" What is it?"

" The cause of the illusion was merely sea-sickness."

" But I've not felt ill at all."

" Very likely not. If you had been ill in the ordinary way, the way in which it has taken a good many of our friends, you would never have had the illusion. Brain and stomach act and react on one another. The motion of the boat, too, is particularly trying to the optic nerves. In some cases, not very common perhaps, but quite well-known and recognised—it is the brain and not the other organ which is temporarily affected."

I do not know anything about it really, and had merely invented the sea-sickness theory on the spur of the moment. It was necessary to think of something plausible and very commonplace. Mrs. Derrison was suffering a good deal, and I had to stop it.

" If I could only think that," she said, " what a comfort it would be!"

" Whether you believe it or not, it's the truth," I said. " I've known a similar case. It won't happen to you again, because the weather's getting better, and so you won't be ill."

She wanted to know all about the "similar case," and I made up a convincing little story about it. Gradually, she began to be reassured.

"I wish I had known about it before," she said. "All last night I sat in my room, with the light turned on, getting more and more frightened. I don't think there's anything hurts one so much as fear. I can understand people being driven mad by it. You see, I had a special reason to be afraid, because Alec was jealous, very jealous. He had even, I suppose, some grounds for jealousy."

She began to tell me her story. She had married Alec Derrison nine years before. She liked him at that time, but she did not love him, and she told him so. He said that it did not matter, and that in time she would come to love him. I dare say a good many marriages that begin in that way turn out happily, but this marriage was a mistake.

He took her to his house in New York, and there they lived for a year without actual disaster. He was very kind to her, and she was touched by his kindness. She had been quite poor, and she now had plenty of money to spend, and liked it. But it became clear to her in that year not only that she did not love her husband, but that she never would love him. And she was, I could believe, a rather romantic and temperamental kind of woman by whom many men were greatly attracted. Alec Derrison began to be very jealous —at that time quite absurdly and without reason.

At the end of the year Derrison took her to Europe for a holiday. And there, in England, in her father's country rectory, she met the man whom she ought to have married —an artist of the same age as herself. The two fell desperately in love with one another. The man wanted to take her away with him and ultimately to marry her. She refused.

There is a curious mixture of conscience and temperament which is sometimes mistaken for cowardice, and is often accompanied by extraordinary courage. She went to her husband and, so to speak, put her cards down on the table. "I love another man," she said. "I love him in the way in which I wished to love you but cannot. I did not want this and I did not look for it, but it has happened to me. I am sorry it has happened, but I do not ask you to forgive me, for you have nothing to forgive. I want to know what you mean to do."

His answer was to take her straight back to New York. There for eight years before he died he treated her with kindness and gave her every luxury, but all the time he had her watched. Traps were laid for her, but in vain. He had for business reasons to go to England every year, but he never took her with him. When he was away, two of his sisters came to the house and watched for him.

And yet, because in some things a woman is cleverer than a man, and also because the feminine conscience always has its limitations, during the whole of those eight years she corresponded regularly with the other man without being found out. They never met, but she had his letters. And now she was going back to marry him.

It was, perhaps, a little curious that she should tell all this to a man whom she had known only for a few days. But intimacies grow quickly on board ship, and besides she wanted to explain her terror.

"You see how it was," she said. "If a dead man could come back again, then certainly he would come back. And when one begins to be frightened the fear grows and grows. One thinks of things. For instance, he crossed more than once in this very boat—I thought of that."

"Well, Mrs. Derrison," I said, "the dead cannot and do not come back. But a disordered interior does sometimes produce an optical illusion. That's all there is to it. However, if you like, I'll go to the purser and get your room changed for another; I can manage that all right."

It was not a very wise suggestion, and she refused it. She said that it would be like admitting that there was something in it beyond sea-sickness.

"Good!" I said. "I think you're quite right. I thought it might ease your mind not to see again the room where you were frightened, but it is much better to be firm about it. In fact, you had better take a cup of soup and then go back to your room now, and get an hour's sleep before lunch."

"I wonder if I could."

"Of course you can. You're getting your colour back, and there's much less motion on the boat. You won't have another attack. You've had a sort of suppressed form of sea-sickness, that's all. And I can quite understand that it scared you at the time, when you didn't know; but there's no reason why it should scare you now when you do know."

She took my advice. A woman will generally take advice from any man except her husband—because he's the only man she really knows. She was disproportionately grateful. Gratitude is rare but, when found, it is in very large streaks. She had also decided to believe that I knew everything, could do everything, and had other admirable qualities. When a woman decides to believe, facts do not hamper her.

She was much better at lunch and afterwards. Next day she was apparently normal, and was taking part in the usual deck-games. I began to think that my sea-sickness theory might have been a lucky shot. I consulted the ship's doctor about it, without giving him names or details, but he was very non-committal. He was a general practitioner, of course, and I was taking him into the specialist regions. Besides, naturally enough, a doctor does not care to talk his own shop with a layman. He gave me an impression that any conclusions to which I came would necessarily be wrong. But it did not worry me much. I did not see a great deal of Mrs. Derrison, but it was quite obvious that she had recovered her normal health and spirits. I believed that the trouble was over.

But it was not.

On the night before we arrived, after the smoking-room had been closed, old Bartlett asked me to come to his rooms for a chat and a whisky-and-soda. The old man slept badly, and was inclined to a late sitting. We discussed various subjects, and amongst them memory for faces.

" I've got that memory," he said. " Names bother me, but not faces. For instance, I remember the faces of the seventy or eighty in the first-class here."

" I thought we were more than that."

" No. People don't cross the Atlantic for fun in February. It's a pretty light list. It's a funny thing, too—we've got one man on board who's never showed up at all. I saw him for the first time this morning—to be accurate, yesterday morning—coming from the bath, and I've not seen him since.

        st have been hiding in his state-room all the time."

    probably."

" No, not ill. I asked the doctor. I suppose he don't enjoy the society of his fellow-men for some reason or other."

" Well, now," I said, " let's test your memory. What was he like?"

" You've given me an easy one as it happens, for he was rather a curious chap to look at, and easy to remember in consequence. A man in the fifties, I should say ; medium height; wore blue pyjamas with a gold watch-chain trickling out of the pocket, and those red slippers that you buy in Cairo. But his face what what I noticed particularly. He's got a one-inch mouth—smallest mouth I ever saw on a man. But the whole look on his face was queer, just as if it had been painted and then varnished.

" He was bald, round-faced, wrinkled, and clean-shaven. He walked very slowly, and he looked as if he were worried out of his life. There's the portrait, and you can check it when we get off the boat—you're bound to see him then."

" Yes, you've a good memory. If I had just passed a man in a passage, I shouldn't have remembered a thing about him ten minutes afterwards. By the way, have you spoken about the hermit passenger to anybody else?"

" No. Oh, yes, I did mention it to some of the ladies after dinner! Why?"

" I wondered if anybody besides yourself had seen him."

" Well, they didn't say they had. Bless you, I've known men like that. It's a sort of sulkiness. They'd sooner be alone."

A few minutes later I said good night and left him. It was between one and two in the morning. His story had made a strong impression upon me. My theory of sea-sickness had to go, and I was scared. Quite frankly, I was afraid of meeting something in blue pyjamas. But I was more afraid about Mrs. Derrison. There were very few ladies on board, and it was almost certain she was in the group to whom Bartlett had told his story. If that were so, anything might have happened. I decided to go past her state-room, listening as I did so.

But before I reached her room the door opened, and she swung out in her nightdress. She had got her mouth open and one hand at her throat. With the other hand she clutched the handle of the door, as if she were trying to hold it shut against somebody. I hurried towards her, and she turned and saw me. In an instant she was in my arms, clinging to me in sheer mad, helpless terror.

She was hysterical, of course, but fortunately she did not make much noise. She kept saying: " I've got to go back to him—into the sea! "

It seemed a long time before I could get her calm enough to listen to me.

" You've had a bad dream, and it has frightened you, poor child."

" No, no. Not a dream! "

" It didn't seem like one to you, but that's what it was. You're all right now. I'm going to take care of you."

" Don't let go of me for a moment. He wants me. He's in there."

" Oh, no! I'll show you that he's not there."

I opened the door. Within all was darkness. I still kept one arm round her, or she would have fallen.

" I left the light on," she whispered.

" Yes," I said, " but your sleeve caught the switch as you came out. I saw it." It was a lie, of course, but one had to lie.

I switched the light on again. The room was empty. There were the tumbled bedclothes on the berth, and a pillow had fallen to the floor. On the table some toilet things gleamed brightly. There was a pile of feminine garments on the couch. I drew her in and closed the door.

" I'll put you back into bed again," I said, " if you don't mind."

" If you'll promise not to go."

" Oh, I won't go! "

I picked her up and laid her on the berth, and drew the clothes over her. I put the pillow back under her head. With both her hands she clutched one of mine.

" Now, then," I said, " do you happen to have any brandy here? "

" In a flask in my dressing-bag. It's been there for years. I don't know if it's any good still."

She seemed reluctant to let go my hand, and clutched it again eagerly when I brought the brandy. She was quite docile, and drank as I told her. I have not put down half of what she said. She was muttering the whole time. The phrase " into the sea " occurred frequently. All ordinary notions of the relationship of a man and a woman had vanished. I was simply a big brother who was looking after her. That was felt by both of us. We called each other " dear " that night frequently, but there was not a trace of sex-sentimentality between us.

Gradually she became more quiet, and I was no longer afraid that she would faint. Still holding my hand, she said:

" Shall I tell you what it was?"

" Yes, dear, if you like. But you needn't. It was only a dream, you know."

" I don't think it was a dream. I went to sleep, which I had never expected to do after the thing that Mr. Bartlett told us. I couldn't have done it, only I argued that you must be right and the rest must be just a coincidence. Then I was awakened by the sound of somebody breathing close by my ear. It got farther away, and I switched on the light quickly. He was standing just there—exactly as I described him to you—and he had picked up a pair of nail-scissors. He was opening and shutting them. Then he put them down again, and shook his head. (Look, they're open now, and I always close them.) And suddenly he lurched over, almost falling, and clutched the wooden edge of the berth. His red hands —they were terribly red, far redder than they used to be —came on to the wood with a slap. ' Go into the sea, Sheila,' he whispered. ' I'm waiting. I want you.' And after that I don't know what happened, but suddenly I was hanging on to you, dear. How long was it ago? Was it an hour? It doesn't matter. I'm safe while you're here."

I released her hands gently. Suddenly the paroxysm of terror returned.

" You're not going?" she cried, aghast.

" Of course not." I sat down on the couch opposite her. " But what makes you think you're safe while I'm here?"

" You're stronger than he is," she said.

She said it as if it were a self-evident fact which did not admit of argument. Certainly, though no doubt unreasonably, it gave me confidence. I felt somehow that he and I were fighting for the woman's life and soul, and I had got him down. I knew in some mysterious way I was the stronger.

" Well," I said, " the dream that one is awake is a fairly common dream. But what was the thing that Bartlett told you?"

"He saw him—in blue pyjamas and red slippers. He mentioned the mouth, too."

"I'm glad you told me that," I said, and began a few useful inventions. "The man that Bartlett saw was Curwen. We've just been talking about it."

"Who's Curwen?"

"Not a bad chap—an electrical engineer, I believe. As soon as Bartlett mentioned the mole on the cheek and the little black moustache I spotted that it was Curwen."

"But he said he had never seen him before."

"Nor had he. Curwen's a bad sailor and has kept to his state-room—in fact, that was his first public appearance. But I saw Curwen when he came on board and had a talk with him. As soon as Bartlett mentioned the mole, I knew who it was."

"Then the colour of the slippers and . . ."

"They were merely a coincidence, and a mighty unlucky one for you."

"I see," she said. Her muscles relaxed. She gave a little sigh of relief and sank back on the pillow. I was glad I had invented Curwen and the mole.

I changed the subject now, and began to talk about Liverpool—not so many miles away now. I asked her if she had changed her American money yet. I spoke about the customs, and confessed to some successful smuggling that I had once done. In fact, I talked about anything that might take her mind away from her panic. Then I said:

"If you will give me about ten seconds start now, so that I can get back to my own room, you might ring for your stewardess to come and take care of you. It will mean an extra tip for her, and she won't mind."

"Yes," she said, "I ought not to keep you any longer. Indeed, it is very kind of you to have helped me and to have stayed so long. I'll never forget it. But even now I daren't be alone for a moment. Will you wait until she's actually here?"

I was not ready for that.

"Well," I said hesitatingly.

"Of course," she said. "I hadn't thought of it. I can't keep you. You've had no sleep at all. And yet if you go, he'll . . . Oh, what am I to do? What am I to do?"

I was afraid she would begin to cry.

" That's all right," I said. " I can stay for another hour or two easily enough."

She was full of gratitude. She told me to throw the things off the end of the couch so that I could lie at full length. I dozed for a while, but I do not think she slept at all. She was wide awake when I opened my eyes. I talked to her for a little, and found her much reassured and calmed. People were beginning to move about. It was necessary for me to go immediately if I was not to be seen.

She agreed at once. When I shook hands with her, and told her to try for an hour's sleep, she kissed my hand fervently in a childish sort of way. Frightened people behave rather like children.

I was not seen as I came from her room. The luck was with me. It is just possible that on the other side of the ship a steward saw me enter my own room in evening clothes at a little after five. If he did, it did not matter.

I have had the most grateful and kindly letters from her and from her new husband—the cheery and handsome man who met her at Liverpool. In her letters she speaks of her " awful nightmare, that even now seems sometimes as if it must have been real." She has sent me a cigarette-case that I am afraid I cannot use publicly. A gold cigarette-case with a diamond push-button would give a wrong impression of my income, and the inscription inside might easily be misunderstood. But I like to have it.

Thanks to my innocent mendacity, she has a theory which covers the whole ground. But I myself have no theory at all. I know this—that I might travel to New York by that same boat to-morrow, and that I am waiting three days for another.

I have suppressed the name of the boat, and I think I have said nothing by which she could be identified. I do not want to spoil business. Besides, it may be funk and superstition that convinces me that on every trip she carries a passenger whose name is not on the list. But, for all that, I *am* quite convinced.

THE SPHINX WITHOUT A SECRET

Oscar Wilde

One afternoon I was sitting outside the Café de la Paix, watching the splendour and shabbiness of Parisian life, and wondering over my vermouth at the strange panorama of pride and poverty that was passing before me, when I heard someone call my name. I turned round, and saw Lord Murchison. We had not met since we had been at college together, nearly ten years before, so I was delighted to come across him again, and we shook hands warmly. At Oxford we had been great friends. I had liked him immensely, he was so handsome, so high-spirited, and so honourable. We used to say of him that he would be the best of fellows, if he did not always speak the truth, but I think we really admired him all the more for his frankness. I found him a good deal changed. He looked anxious and puzzled, and seemed to be in doubt about something. I felt it could not be modern scepticism, for Murchison was the stoutest of Tories, and believed in the Pentateuch as firmly as he believed in the House of Peers; so I concluded that it was a woman, and asked him if he was married yet.

" I don't understand women well enough," he answered.

" My dear Gerald," I said, " women are meant to be loved, not to be understood."

" I cannot love where I cannot trust," he replied.

" I believe you have a mystery in your life, Gerald," I exclaimed ; " tell me about it."

" Let us go for a drive," he answered, " it is too crowded here. No, not a yellow carriage, any other colour—there, that dark green one will do " ; and in a few moments we were trotting down the boulevard in the direction of the Madeleine.

" Where shall we go to?" I said.

" Oh, anywhere you like!" he answered—" to the restaurant in the Bois ; we will dine there, and you shall tell me all about yourself."

" I want to hear about you first," I said. " Tell me your mystery."

He took from his pocket a little silver-clasped morocco case, and handed it to me. I opened it. Inside there was the photograph of a woman. She was tall and slight, and strangely picturesque with her large vague eyes and loosened hair. She looked like a clairvoyante, and was wrapped in rich furs.

"What do you think of that face?" he said; "is it truthful?"

I examined it carefully. It seemed to me the face of someone who had a secret, but whether that secret was good or evil I could not say. Its beauty was a beauty moulded out of many mysteries—the beauty, in fact, which is psychological, not plastic—and the faint smile that just played across the lips was far too subtle to be really sweet.

"Well," he cried impatiently, "what do you say?"

"She is the Gioconda in sables," I answered. "Let me know all about her."

"Not now," he said; "after dinner," and began to talk of other things.

When the waiter brought us our coffee and cigarettes I reminded Gerald of his promise. He rose from his seat, walked two or three times up and down the room, and, sinking into an arm-chair, told me the following story:—

"One evening," he said, "I was walking down Bond Street about five o'clock. There was a terrific crush of carriages, and the traffic was almost stopped. Close to the pavement was standing a little yellow brougham, which, for some reason or other, attracted my attention. As I passed by there looked out from it the face I showed you this afternoon. It fascinated me immediately. All that night I kept thinking of it, and all the next day. I wandered up and down that wretched Row, peering into every carriage, and waiting for the yellow brougham; but I could not find *ma belle inconnue*, and at last I began to think she was merely a dream. About a week afterwards I was dining with Madame de Rastail. Dinner was for eight o'clock; but at half past eight we were still waiting in the drawing-room. Finally the servant threw open the door, and announced Lady Alroy. It was the woman I had been looking for. She came in very slowly, looking like a moonbeam in grey lace, and, to my intense delight, I was asked to take her into dinner. After we had sat down, I remarked quite innocently, 'I think I caught sight of you in Bond Street some time ago, Lady Alroy.' She grew very pale, and said to me in a low voice, ' Pray do not talk so loud ; you may be overheard.' I felt miserable at having made such a bad beginning, and plunged recklessly into the subject of the French plays. She spoke very little, always in the same low musical voice, and seemed as if she was afraid of someone listening. I fell passionately, stupidly in love, and the indefinable atmosphere of mystery that surrounded her excited my most ardent curiosity. When she was going away, which she did very soon after dinner, I asked her if I might call and see her. She hesitated for a moment, glanced round to see if anyone was near us, and then said, ' Yes ; to-morrow at a quarter to five.' I begged Madame de Rastail to tell me about her ; but all that I could learn was that she was a widow with a beautiful house in Park Lane, and as some scientific bore began a dissertation on widows, as exemplifying the survival of the matrimonially fittest, I left and went home.

" The next day I arrived at Park Lane punctual to the moment, but was told by the butler that Lady Alroy had just gone out. I went down to the club quite unhappy and very much puzzled, and after long consideration wrote her a letter, asking if I might be allowed to try my chance some other afternoon. I had no answer for several days, but at last I got a little note saying she would be at home on Sunday at four and with this extraordinary postcript: ' Please do not write to me here again ; I will explain when I see you.' On Sunday she received me, and was perfectly charming ; but when I was going away she begged of me, if I ever had occasion to write to her again, to address my letter to ' Mrs. Knox, care of Whittaker's Library, Green Street.' ' There are reasons,' she said, ' why I cannot receive letters in my own house.'

" All through the season I saw a great deal of her, and the atmosphere of mystery never left her. Sometimes I thought that she was in the power of some man, but she looked so unapproachable that I could not believe it. It was really very difficult for me to come to any conclusion, for she was like one of those strange crystals that one sees in museums, which are at one moment clear, and at another clouded. At last I determined to ask her to be my wife: I was sick and tired of the incessant secrecy that she imposed on all my visits, and on the few letters I sent her. I wrote to her at the library to ask her if she could see me the following Monday at six. She answered yes, and I was in the seventh heaven of delight. I was infatuated with her: in spite of the mystery, I thought then—in consequence of it, I see now. No; it was the woman herself I loved. The mystery troubled me, maddened me. Why did chance put me in its track?"

" You discovered it, then?" I cried.

" I fear so," he answered. " You can judge for yourself."

"When Monday came round I went to lunch with my uncle, and about four o'clock found myself in the Marylebone Road. My uncle, you know, lives in Regent's Park. I wanted to get to Piccadilly, and took a short cut through a lot of shabby little streets. Suddenly I saw in front of me Lady Alroy, deeply veiled and walking very fast. On coming to the last house in the street, she went up the steps, took out a latch-key, and let herself in. ' Here is the mystery,' I said to myself ; and I hurried on and examined the house. It seemed a sort of place for letting lodgings. On the doorstep lay her handkerchief, which she had dropped. I picked it up and put it in my pocket. Then I began to consider what I should do. I came to the conclusion that I had no right to spy on her, and I drove to the club. At six I called to see her. She was lying on a sofa, in a tea-gown of silver tissue looped up by some strange moonstones that she always wore. She was looking quite lovely. ' I am so glad to see you,' she said ; ' I have not been out all day.' I stared at her in amazement, and pulling the handkerchief out of my pocket, handed it to her. ' You dropped this in Cumnor Street this afternoon, Lady Alroy,' I said very calmly. She looked at me in terror, but made no attempt to take the handkerchief. ' What were you doing there?' I asked. ' What right have you to question me?' she answered. ' The right of a man who loves you,' I replied ; ' I came here to ask you to be my wife.' She hid her face in her hands, and burst into floods of tears. ' You must tell me,' I continued. She stood up, and, looking me straight in the face, said, ' Lord Murchison, there is nothing to tell you.' . . . ' You went to meet some-one,' I cried ; ' this is your mystery.' She grew dreadfully white, and said, ' I went to meet no one.' . . . ' Can't you tell the truth?' I exclaimed. ' I have told it,' she replied. I was mad, frantic ; I don't know what I said, but I said terrible things to her. Finally I rushed out of the house. She wrote me a letter the next day; I sent it back unopened, and started for Norway with Alan Colville. After a month I came back, and the first thing I saw in the *Morning Post* was the death of Lady Alroy. She had caught a chill at the Opera, and had died in five days of congestion of the lungs. I shut myself up and saw no one. I had loved her so much, I had loved her so madly. Good God! how I had loved that woman!"

"You went to the street, to the house in it?" I said.

"Yes," he answered.

"One day I went to Cumnor Street. I could not help it; I was tortured with doubt. I knocked at the door, and a respectable-looking woman opened it to me. I asked her if she had any rooms to let. 'Well, sir,' she replied, 'the drawing-rooms are supposed to be let; but I have not seen the lady for three months, and as rent is owing on them, you can have them.' . . . 'Is this the lady?' I said, showing the photograph. 'That's her, sure enough,' she exclaimed; 'and when is she coming back, sir?' . . . 'The lady is dead,' I replied. 'Oh, sir, I hope not!' said the woman; 'she was my best lodger. She paid me three guineas a week merely to sit in my drawing-room now and then.' . . . 'She met someone here?' I said; but the woman assured me that it was not so, that she always came alone, and saw no one. 'What on earth did she do here?' I cried. 'She simply sat in the drawing-room, sir, reading books, and sometimes had tea,' the woman answered. I did not know what to say, so I gave her a sovereign and went away. Now, what do you think it all meant? You don't believe the woman was telling the truth?"

"I do."

"Then why did Lady Alroy go there?"

"My dear Gerald," I answered, "Lady Alroy was simply a woman with a mania for mystery. She took these rooms for the pleasure of going there with her veil down, and imagining she was a heroine. She had a passion for secrecy, but she herself was merely a Sphinx without a secret."

"Do you really think so?"

"I am sure of it," I replied.

He took out the morocco case, opened it, and looked at the photograph. "I wonder?" he said at last.

WHEN I WAS DEAD

Vincent O'Sullivan

" And yet my heart
Will not confess he owes the malady
That doth my life besiege."

All's Well that Ends Well.

That was the worst of Ravenel Hall. The passages were long and gloomy, the rooms were musty and dull, even the pictures were sombre and their subjects dire. On an autumn evening, when the wind soughed and wailed through the trees in the park, and the dead leaves whistled and chattered, while the rain clamoured at the windows, small wonder that folk with gentle nerves went a-straying in their wits! An acute nervous system is a grievous burthen on the deck of a yacht under sunlit skies: at Ravenel the chain of nerves was prone to clash and jangle a funeral march. Nerves must be pampered in a tea-drinking community; and the ghost that your grandfather, with a skinful of port, could face and never tremble, sets you, in your sobriety, sweating and shivering; or, becoming scared (poor ghost!) of your bulged eyes and dropped jaw, he quenches expectation by not appearing at all. So I am left to conclude that it was tea which made my acquaintance afraid to stay at Ravenel. Even Wilvern gave over; and as he is in the Guards, and a polo player, his nerves ought to be strong enough. On the night before he went I was explaining to him my theory, that if you place some drops of human blood near you, and then concentrate your thoughts, you will after a while see before you a man or a woman who will stay with you during long hours of the night, and even meet you at unexpected places during the day. I was explaining this theory, I repeat, when he interrupted me with words, senseless enough, which sent me fencing and parrying strangers—on my guard.

"I say, Alistair, my dear chap!" he began, " you ought to get out of this place, and go up to town and knock about a bit—you really ought, you know."

"Yes," I replied, "and get poisoned at the hotels by bad food, and at the clubs by bad talk, I suppose. No, thank you: and let me say that your care for my health enervates me."

"Well, you can do as you like," says he, rapping with his feet on the floor; "I'm hanged if I stay here after to-morrow —I'll be staring mad if I do!"

He was my last visitor. Some weeks after his departure I was sitting in the library with my drops of blood by me. I had got my theory nearly perfect by this time; but there was one difficulty.

The figure which I had ever before me was a figure of an old woman with her hair divided in the middle; and her hair fell to her shoulders, white on one side and black on the other. She was a very complete old woman; but, alas! she was eyeless, and when I tried to construct the eyes she would shrivel and rot in my sight. But to-night I was thinking, thinking, as I had never thought before, and the eyes were just creeping into the head, when I heard a terrible crash outside as if some heavy substance had fallen. Of a sudden the door was flung open, and two maid-servants entered. They glanced at the rug under my chair, and at that they turned a sick white, cried on God, and huddled out.

"How dare you enter the library in this manner?" I demanded, sternly. No answer came back from them, so I started in pursuit. I found all the servants of the house gathered in a knot at the end of the passage.

"Mrs. Pebble," I said smartly, to the housekeeper, "I want those two women discharged to-morrow. It's an outrage! You ought to be more careful."

But she was not attending to me. Her face was distorted with terror.

"Ah dear, ah dear!" she went. "We had better all go to the library together," says she to the others.

"Am I still master of my own house, Mrs. Pebble?" I inquired, bringing my knuckles down with a bang on a table.

None of them seemed to see me or hear me: I might as well have been shrieking in a desert. I followed them down the passage, and forbade them with strong words to enter the library. But they trooped past me, and stood with a clutter round the hearth-rug. Then three or four of them began dragging and lifting, as if they were lifting a helpless ʋody, and stumbled with their imaginary burthen over to a sofa. Old Soames, the butler, stood near.

"Poor young gentleman!" he said, with a sob; "I've knowed him since he was a baby. And to think of him being dead like this—and so young too!"

I crossed the room. "What's all this, Soames?" I cried, shaking him roughly by the shoulders. "I'm not dead, I'm here—here!" As he did not stir, I got a little scared. "Soames, old friend," I called, "don't you know me? Don't you know the little boy you used to play with? Say I'm not dead, Soames, please, Soames!"

He stooped down and kissed the sofa. "I think one of the men ought to ride over to the village for the doctor, Mr. Soames," says Mrs. Pebble, and he shuffled out to give the order.

Now, this doctor was an ignorant dog, whom I had been forced to exclude from the house, because he went about proclaiming his belief in a saving God, at the same time that he proclaimed himself a man of science. He, I was resolved, should never cross my threshold, and I followed Mrs. Pebble through the house, screaming out prohibition. But I did not catch even a groan from her, not a nod of the head nor cast of the eye, to shew that she had heard.

. I met the doctor at the door of the library. "Well!" I sneered, throwing my hand in his face, "have you come to teach me some new prayers?"

He brushed by me as if he had not felt the blow, and knelt down by the sofa.

"Rupture of a vessel on the brain, I think," he says to Soames and Mrs. Pebble after a moment. "He has been dead some hours. Poor fellow! You had better telegraph for his sister, and I will send up the undertaker to arrange the body."

"You liar!" I yelled. "You whining liar! How have you the insolence to tell my servants that I am dead, when you see me here face to face?"

He was far in the passage, with Soames and Mrs. Pebble at his heels, ere I had ended, and not one of the three turned round.

All that night I sat in the library. Strangely enough, I had no wish to sleep, nor, during the time that followed, had I any craving to eat. In the morning the men came, and although I ordered them out, they proceeded to minister about something I could not see. So all day I stayed in the library or wandered about the house, and at night the men came again, bringing with them a coffin. Then, in my humour, thinking it shame that so fine a coffin should be empty, I lay the night in it, and slept a soft, dreamless sleep—the softest sleep I have ever slept. And when the men came the next day, I rested still, and the undertaker shaved me. A strange valet!

On the evening after that, I was coming down stairs, when I noted some luggage in the hall, and so learned that my sister had arrived. I had not seen this woman since her marriage, and I loathed her more than I loathed any creature in this ill-organised world. She was very beautiful I think —tall, and dark, and straight as a ramrod—and she had an unruly passion for scandal and dress. I suppose the reason I disliked her so intensely was, that she had a habit of making one aware of her presence when she was several yards off. At half past nine o'clock my sister came down to the library in a very charming wrap, and I soon found that she was as insensible to my presence as the others. I trembled with rage to see her kneel down by the coffin—my coffin ; but when she bent over to kiss the pillow I threw away control.

A knife which had been used to cut string was lying on a table: I seized it and drove it into her neck. She fled from the room screaming.

" Come, come ! " she cried, her voice quivering with anguish, " the corpse is bleeding from the nose."

Then I cursed her.

On the morning of the third day there was a heavy fall of snow. About eleven o'clock I observed that the house was filled with blacks, and mutes, and folk of the county, who came for the obsequies. I went into the library and sat still, and waited. Soon came the men, and they closed the lid of the coffin and bore it out on their shoulders. And yet I sat, feeling rather sadly that something of mine had been taken away: I could not quite think what. For half an hour perhaps—dreaming—dreaming ; and then I glided to the hall door. There was no trace of the funeral ; but after a while I sighted a black thread winding slowly across the white plain.

" I'm not dead," I moaned, and rubbed my face in the pure snow and tossed it on my neck and hair. " Sweet God, I am not dead."

THE QUEEN OF SPADES

*Translated by T. Keane from the Russian of
Alexander Pushkin*

There was a card party at the rooms of Naroumoff of the
Horse Guards. The long winter night passed away imper-
ceptibly, and it was five o'clock in the morning before
the company sat down to supper. Those who had won ate
with a good appetite; the others sat staring absently at their
empty plates. When the champagne appeared, however,
the conversation became more animated, and all took a part in
it.

" And how did you fare, Sourin?" asked the host.

" Oh, I lost as usual. I must confess that I am unlucky: I
play mirandole, I always keep cool, I never allow anything
to put me out, and yet I always lose!"

" And you did not once allow yourself to be tempted to
back the red? ... Your firmness astonishes me."

" But what do you think of Hermann?" said one of the
guests, pointing to a young Engineer; " he has never had a
card in his hand in his life, he has never in his life laid a wager,
and yet he sits here till five o'clock in the morning watching
our play."

" Play interests me very much," said Hermann; " but I am
not in the position to sacrifice the necessary in the hope of
winning the superfluous."

" Hermann is a German: he is economical—that is all!"
observed Tomsky. " But if there is one person that I cannot
understand, it is my grandmother, the Countess Anna
Fedorovna."

" How so?" inquired the guests.

" I cannot understand," continued Tomsky, " how it is that
my grandmother does not punt."

" What is there remarkable about an old lady of eighty not
punting?" said Naroumoff.

" Then you do not know the reason why?"

" No, really; haven't the faintest idea."

" Oh! then listen. You must know that, about sixty

years ago, my grandmother went to Paris, where she created quite a sensation. People used to run after her to catch a glimpse of the ' Muscovite Venus.' Richelieu made love to her, and my grandmother maintains that he almost blew out his brains in consequence of her cruelty. At that time ladies used to play at faro. On one occasion at the Court, she lost a very considerable sum to the Duke of Orleans. On returning home, my grandmother removed the patches from her face, took off her hoops, informed my grandfather of her loss at the gaming-table and ordered him to pay the money. My deceased grandfather, as far as I remember, was a sort of house-steward to my grandmother. He dreaded her like fire ; but on hearing of such a heavy loss, he almost went out of his mind ; he calculated the various sums she had lost, and pointed out to her that in six months she had spent half a million francs, that neither their Moscow nor Saratoff estates were in Paris, and finally refused point blank to pay the debt. My grandmother gave him a box on the ear and slept by herself as a sign of her displeasure. The next day she sent for her husband, hoping that this domestic punishment had produced an effect upon him, but she found him inflexible. For the first time in her life, she entered into reasonings and explanations with him, thinking to be able to convince him by pointing out to him that there are debts and debts, and that there is a great difference between a prince and a coach-maker. But it was all in vain, my grandfather still remained obdurate. But the matter did not rest there. My grandmother did not know what to do. She had shortly before become acquainted with a very remarkable man. You have heard of Count St. Germain, about whom so many marvellous stories are told. You know that he represented himself as the Wandering Jew, as the discoverer of the elixir of life, of the philosopher's stone, and so forth. Some laughed at him as a charlatan ; but Casanova, in his memoirs, says that he was a spy. But be that as it may, St. Germain, in spite of the mystery surrounding him, was a very fascinating person, and was much sought after in the best circles of society. Even to this day my grandmother retains an affectionate recollection of him, and becomes quite angry if anyone speaks disrespectfully of him. My grandmother knew that St. Germain had large sums of money at his disposal. She resolved to have recourse to him, and she wrote a letter to him asking him to come to her without delay. The queer old man immediately waited upon her and found her overwhelmed with grief. She described to him in the blackest colours the barbarity of her husband, and ended by declaring that her whole hope depended upon his friendship and amiability.

" St. Germain reflected.

" ' I could advance you the sum you want,' said he; ' but I know that you would not rest easy until you had paid me back, and I should not like to bring fresh troubles upon you. But there is another way of getting out of your difficulty; you can win back your money."

" ' But, my dear Count,' replied my grandmother, ' I tell you that I haven't any money left.'

" ' Money is not necessary,' replied St. Germain; ' be pleased to listen to me.'

" Then he revealed to her a secret, for which each of us would give a good deal. . . ."

The young officers listened with increased attention. Tomsky lit his pipe, puffed away for a moment, and then continued:

" That same evening my grandmother went to Versailles to the *jeu de la reine*. The Duke of Orleans kept the bank; my grandmother excused herself in an off-handed manner for not having yet paid her debt, by inventing some little story, and then began to play against him. She chose three cards and played them one after the other: all three won *sonika*,* and my grandmother recovered every farthing that she had lost."

" Mere chance!" said one of the guests.

" A tale!" observed Hermann.

" Perhaps they were marked cards!" said a third.

" I do not think so," replied Tomsky gravely.

" What!" said Naroumoff, " you have a grandmother who knows how to hit upon three lucky cards in succession, and you have never yet succeeded in getting the secret of it out of her?"

" That's the deuce of it!" replied Tomsky; " she had four sons, one of whom was my father; all four were determined gamblers, and yet not to one of them did she ever

---

* Said of a card when it wins or loses in the quickest possible time.

reveal her secret, although it would not have been a bad thing either for them or for me. But this is what I heard from my uncle, Count Ivan Ilitch, and he assured me, on his honour, that it was true. The late Chaplitsky—the same who died in poverty after having squandered millions—once lost, in his youth, about three hundred thousand roubles—to Zoritch, if I remember rightly. He was in despair. My grandmother, who was always very severe upon the extravagance of young men, took pity, however, upon Chaplitsky. She gave him three cards, telling him to play them one after the other, at the same time exacting from him a solemn promise that he would never play at cards again as long as he lived. Chaplitsky then went to his victorious opponent, and they began a fresh game. On the first card he staked fifty thousand roubles and won *sonika*; he doubled the stake and won again, till at last, by pursuing the same tactics, he won back more than he had lost ...

" But it is time to go to bed: it is a quarter to six already."

And indeed, it was already beginning to dawn: the young men emptied their glasses and then took leave of each other.

The old Countess A—— was seated in her dressing-gown in front of her looking-glass. Three waiting-maids stood around her. One held a small pot of rouge, another a box of hairpins, and the third a tall cap with bright red ribbons. The Countess had no longer the slightest pretensions to beauty, but she still preserved the habits of her youth, dressed in strict accordance with the fashion of seventy years before, and made as long and as careful a toilette as she would have done sixty years previous. Near the window, at an embroidery frame, sat a young lady, her ward.

" Good morning, Grandmamma," said a young officer, entering the room. " *Bonjour*, Mademoiselle Lise. Grandmamma, I want to ask you something."

" What is it, Paul?"

" I want you to let me introduce one of my friends to you, and to allow me to bring him to the ball on Friday."

" Bring him direct to the ball and introduce him to me there. Were you at B——'s yesterday?"

" Yes ; everything went off very pleasantly, and dancing was kept up until five o'clock. How charming Eletskaia was!"

" But, my dear, what is there charming about her? Isn't she like her grandmother, the Princess Daria Petrovna? By the way, she must be very old, the Princess Daria Petrovna."

" How do you mean, old?" cried Tomsky thoughtlessly; " she died seven years ago."

The young lady raised her head and made a sign to the young officer. He then remembered that the old Countess was never to be informed of the death of any of her contemporaries, and he bit his lips. But the old Countess heard the news with the greatest indifference.

" Dead!" said she; " and I did not know it. We were appointed maids of honour at the same time, and when we were presented to the Empress . . ."

And the Countess for the hundredth time related to her grandson one of her anecdotes.

" Come, Paul," said she, when she had finished her story, help me to get up. Lizanka, where is my snuff-box?"

And the Countess with her three maids went behind a screen to finish her toilette. Tomsky was left alone with the young lady.

" Who is the gentleman you wish to introduce to the Countess?" asked Lizaveta Ivanovna in a whisper.

" Naroumoff. Do you know him?"

" No. Is he a soldier or a civilian?"

" A soldier."

" Is he in the Engineers?"

" No, in the Cavalry. What made you think that he was in the Engineers?"

The young lady smiled, but made no reply.

" Paul," cried the Countess from behind the screen, " send me some new novel, only pray don't let it be one of the present day style."

" What do you mean, Grandmother?"

" That is, a novel, in which the hero strangles neither his father nor his mother, and in which there are no drowned bodies. I have a great horror of drowned persons."

" There are no such novels nowadays. Would you like a Russian one?"

" Are there any Russian novels? Send me one, my dear, pray send me one!"

" Good-bye, Grandmother; I am in a hurry . . . Good-bye, Lizaveta Ivanovna. What made you think that Naroumoff was in the Engineers?"

And Tomsky left the boudoir.

Lizaveta Ivanovna was left alone: she laid aside her work and began to look out of the window. A few moments afterwards, at a corner house on the other side of the street, a young officer appeared. A deep blush covered her cheeks; she took up her work again and bent her head down over the frame. At the same moment the Countess returned completely dressed.

" Order the carriage, Lizaveta," said she; " we will go out for a drive."

Lizaveta arose from the frame and began to arrange her work.

" What is the matter with you, my child, are you deaf?" cried the Countess. " Order the carriage to be got ready at once."

" I will do so this moment," replied the young lady, hastening into the ante-room.

A servant entered and gave the Countess some books from Prince Paul Alexandrovitch.

" Tell him that I am much obliged to him," said the Countess. " Lizaveta! Lizaveta! where are you running to?"

" I am going to dress."

" There is plenty of time, my dear. Sit down here. Open the first volume and read to me aloud."

Her companion took the book and read a few lines.

" Louder," said the Countess. " What is the matter with you, my child? Have you lost your voice? Wait—give me that footstool—a little nearer—that will do!"

Lizaveta read two more pages. The Countess yawned.

" Put the book down," said she; " what a lot of nonsense! Send it back to Prince Paul with my thanks . . . But where is the carriage?"

" The carriage is ready," said Lizaveta, looking out into the street.

" How is it that you are not dressed?" said the Countess. " I must always wait for you. It is intolerable, my dear!"

Liza hastened to her room. She had not been there two minutes, before the Countess began to ring with all her might. The three waiting-maids came running in at one door and the valet at another.

" How is it that you cannot hear me when I ring for you?" said the Countess. " Tell Lizaveta Ivanovna that I am waiting for her."

Lizaveta returned with her hat and cloak on.

" At last you are here!" said the Countess. " But why such an elaborate toilette? Whom do you intend to captivate? What sort of weather is it? It seems rather windy."

" No, your ladyship, it is very calm," replied the valet.

" You never think of what you are talking about. Open the window. So it is; windy and bitterly cold. Unharness the horses. Lizaveta, we won't go out—there was no need for you to deck yourself like that."

" What a life is mine!" thought Lizaveta Ivanovna.

And, in truth, Lizaveta Ivanovna was a very unfortunate creature. " The bread of the stranger is bitter," says Dante, " and his staircase hard to climb." But who can know what the bitterness of dependence is so well as the poor companion of an old lady of quality? The Countess A—— had by no means a bad heart, but she was capricious, like a woman who had been spoilt by the world, as well as being avaricious and egotistical, like all old people who have seen their best days, and whose thoughts are with the past and not the present. She participated in all the vanities of the great world, went to balls, where she sat in a corner, painted and dressed in old-fashioned style, like a deformed but indispensable ornament of the ball-room; all the guests on entering approached her and made a profound bow, as if in accordance with a set ceremony, but after that nobody took any further notice of her. She received the whole town at her house, and observed the strictest etiquette, although she could no longer recognise the faces of people. Her numerous domestics, growing fat and old in her ante-chamber and servants' hall, did just as they liked, and vied with each other in robbing the aged Countess in the most bare-faced manner. Lizaveta Ivanovna was the martyr of the household. She made tea, and was reproached with using too much sugar; she read novels aloud to the Countess, and the faults of the author were visited upon her head; she accompanied the Countess in her walks, and was held answerable for the weather or the state of the pavement. A salary was attached to the post, but she very rarely received it, although she was expected to dress like everybody else, that is to say, like very few indeed. In society, she played the most pitiable role. Everybody knew her, and nobody paid her any attention. At balls she danced only when a partner was wanted, and ladies would only take hold of her arm when it was necessary to lead her out of the room to attend to their dresses. She was very self-conscious, and felt her position keenly, and she looked about her with impatience for a deliverer to come to her rescue ; but the young men, calculating in their giddiness, honoured her with but very little attention, although Lizaveta Ivanovna was a hundred times prettier than the bare-faced and cold-hearted marriageable girls around whom they hovered. Many a time did she quietly slink away from the glittering but wearisome drawing-room to go and cry in her own poor little room, in which stood a screen, a chest of drawers, a looking-glass, and a painted bedstead, and where a tallow candle burnt feebly in a copper candle-stick.

One morning—this was about two days after the evening party described at the beginning of this story, and a week previous to the scene at which we have just assisted —Lizaveta Ivanovna was seated near the window at her embroidery frame, when, happening to look out into the street, she caught sight of a young Engineer officer, standing motionless with his eyes fixed upon her window. She lowered her head and went on again with her work. About five minutes afterwards she looked out again—the young officer was still standing in the same place. Not being in the habit of coquetting with passing officers, she did not continue to gaze out into the street, but went on sewing for a couple of hours, without raising her head. Dinner was announced. She rose up and began to put her embroidery away but, glancing casually out of the window, she perceived the officer again. This seemed to her very strange. After dinner she went to the window with a certain feeling of uneasiness, but the officer was no longer there—and she thought no more about him.

A couple of days afterwards, just as she was stepping into the carriage with the Countess, she saw him again. He was standing close behind the door, with his face half-concealed by his fur collar, but his dark eyes sparkled beneath his cap.

Lizaveta felt alarmed, though she knew not why, and she trembled as she seated herself in the carriage.

On returning home, she hastened to the window—the officer was standing in his accustomed place, with his eyes fixed upon her. She drew back, a prey to curiosity and agitated by a feeling which was quite new to her.

From that time forward not a day passed without the young officer making his appearance under the window at the customary hour, and between him and her there was established a sort of mute acquaintance. Sitting in her place at work, she used to feel his approach; and, raising her head, she would look at him longer and longer each day. The young man seemed to be very grateful to her; she saw with the sharp eye of youth, how a sudden flush covered his pale cheeks each time their glances met. After about a week she commenced to smile at him. . . .

When Tomsky asked permission of his grandmother, the Countess, to present one of his friends to her, the young girl's heart beat violently. But hearing that Naroumoff was not an Engineer, she regretted that, by her thoughtless question, she had betrayed her secret to the volatile Tomsky.

Hermann was the son of a German who had become a naturalised Russian, and from whom he had inherited a small capital. Being firmly convinced of the necessity of preserving his independence, Hermann did not touch his private income, but lived on his pay, without allowing himself the slightest luxury. Moreover, he was reserved and ambitious, and his companions rarely had an opportunity of making merry at the expense of his extreme parsimony. He had strong passions and an ardent imagination, but his firmness of disposition preserved him from the ordinary errors of young men. Thus, though a gamester at heart, he never touched a card, for he considered his position did not allow him—as he said—" to risk the necessary in the hope of winning the superfluous," yet he would sit for nights together at the card table and follow with feverish anxiety the different turns of the game.

The story of the three cards had produced a powerful impression upon his imagination, and all night long he could think of nothing else. " If," he thought to himself the following evening, as he walked along the streets of St. Petersburg, " if the old Countess would but reveal her secret to me! if she would only tell me the names of the three winning cards. Why should I not try my fortune? I must get introduced to her and win her favour—become her lover . . . But all that will take time, and she is eighty-seven years old: she might be dead in a week, in a couple of days even! . . . But the story itself: can it really be true? . . . No! Economy, temperance, and industry: those are my three winning cards; by means of them I shall be able to double my capital—increase it sevenfold, and procure for myself ease and independence."

Musing in this manner, he walked on until he found himself in one of the principal streets of St. Petersburg, in front of a house of antiquated architecture. The street was blocked with equipages; carriages one after the other drew up in front of the brilliantly illuminated doorway. At one moment there stepped out on to the pavement the well-shaped little foot of some young beauty, at another the heavy boot of a cavalry officer, and then the silk stockings and shoes of a member of the diplomatic world. Furs and cloaks passed in rapid succession before the gigantic porter at the entrance.

Hermann stopped. "Whose house is this?" he asked of the watchman at the corner.

"The Countess A——'s," replied the watchman.

Hermann started. The strange story of the three cards again presented itself to his imagination. He began walking up and down before the house, thinking of its owner and her strange secret. Returning late to his modest lodging, he could not go to sleep for a long time, and when at last he did doze off, he could dream of nothing but cards, green tables, piles of banknotes, and heaps of ducats. He played one card after the other, winning uninterruptedly, and then he gathered up the gold and filled his pockets with the notes. When he woke up late the next morning, he sighed over the loss of his imaginary wealth, and then, sallying out into the town, he found himself once more in front of the Countess's residence. Some unknown power seemed to have attracted him thither. He stopped and looked up at the windows. At one of these he saw a head with luxuriant black hair, which was bent down probably over some book or an embroidery frame. The head was raised. Hermann saw a fresh complexion and a pair of dark eyes. That moment decided his fate.

Lizaveta Ivanovna had scarcely taken off her hat and cloak, when the Countess sent for her and again ordered her to get the carriage ready. The vehicle drew up before the door, and they prepared to take their seats. Just at the moment when the two footmen were assisting the old lady to enter the carriage, Lizaveta saw her Engineer standing close beside the wheel; he grasped her hand; alarm caused her to lose her presence of mind, and the young man disappeared—but not before he had left a letter between her fingers. She concealed it in her glove, and during the whole of the drive she neither saw nor heard anything. It was the custom of the Countess, when out for an airing in her carriage, to be constantly asking such questions as: "Who was that person that met us just now? What is the name of this bridge? What is written on that signboard?" On this occasion, however, Lizaveta returned such vague and absurd answers, that the Countess became angry with her.

"What is the matter with you, my dear?" she exclaimed. "Have you taken leave of your senses, or what is it? Do you not hear me or understand what I say? . . .Heaven be thanked, I am still in my right mind and speak plainly enough!"

Lizaveta Ivanovna did not hear her. On returning home she ran to her room, and drew the letter out of her glove: it was not sealed. Lizaveta read it. The letter contained a declaration of love; it was tender, respectful, and copied word for word from a German novel. But Lizaveta did not know anything of the German language, and she was quite delighted.

For all that, the letter caused her to feel exceedingly uneasy. For the first time in her life she was entering into secret and confidential relations with a young man. His boldness alarmed her. She reproached herself for her imprudent behaviour, and knew not what to do. Should she cease to sit at the window and, by assuming an appearance of in-difference towards him, put a check upon the young officer's desire for further acquaintance with her? Should she send his letter back to him, or should she answer him in a cold and decided manner? There was nobody to whom she could turn in her perplexity, for she had neither female friend nor adviser. . . . At length she resolved to reply to him.

She sat down at her little writing-table, took pen and paper, and began to think. Several times she began her letter, and then tore it up: the way she had expressed herself seemed to her either too inviting or too cold and decisive. At last she succeeded in writing a few lines with which she felt satisfied.

"I am convinced," she wrote, "that your intentions are honourable, and that you do not wish to offend me by any imprudent behaviour, but our acquaintance must not begin in such a manner. I return you your letter, and I hope that I shall never have any cause to complain of this undeserved slight."

The next day, as soon as Hermann made his appearance, Lizaveta rose from her embroidery, went into the drawing-room, opened the ventilator and threw the letter into the street, trusting that the young officer would have the perception to pick it up.

Hermann hastened forward, picked it up and then repaired to a confectioner's shop. Breaking the seal of the envelope he found inside it his own letter and Lizaveta's reply. He had expected this, and he returned home, his mind deeply occupied with his intrigue.

Three days afterwards, a bright-eyed young girl from a milliner's establishment brought Lizaveta a letter. Lizaveta opened it with great uneasiness, fearing that it was a demand for money, when suddenly she recognised Hermann's handwriting.

"You have made a mistake, my dear," said she; "this letter is not for me."

"Oh, yes, it is for you," replied the girl, smiling very knowingly. "Have the goodness to read it."

Lizaveta glanced at the letter. Hermann requested an interview.

"It cannot be," she cried, alarmed at the audacious request, and the manner in which it was made. "This letter is certainly not for me."

And she tore it into fragments.

"If the letter was not for you, why have you torn it up?" said the girl. "I should have given it back to the person who sent it."

"Be good enough, my dear," said Lizaveta, disconcerted by this remark, "not to bring me any more letters for the future, and tell the person who sent you that he ought to be ashamed . . ."

But Hermann was not the man to be thus put off. Every day Lizaveta received from him a letter, sent now in this way, now in that. They were no longer translated from the German. Hermann wrote them under the inspiration of passion, and spoke in his own language, and they bore full testimony to the inflexibility of his desire and the disordered condition of his uncontrollable imagination. Lizaveta no longer thought of sending them back to him: she became intoxicated with them and began to reply to them, and little by little her answers became longer and more affectionate. At last she threw out of the window to him the following letter:

"This evening there is going to be a ball at the Embassy. The Countess will be there. We shall remain until two o'clock. You have now an opportunity of seeing me alone. As soon as the Countess is gone, the servants will very probably go out, and there will be nobody left but the Swiss, but he usually goes to sleep in his lodge. Come about half past eleven. Walk straight upstairs. If you meet anybody in the ante-room, ask if the Countess is at home. You will be told 'No,' in which case there will be nothing left for you to do but to go away again. But it is most probable that you will meet nobody. The maidservants will all be together in one room. On leaving the ante-room, turn to the left, and walk straight on until you reach the Countess's bedroom. In the bedroom, behind a screen, you will find two doors: the one on the right leads to a cabinet, which the Countess never enters; the one on the left leads to a corridor, at the end of which is a little winding staircase; this leads to my room."

Hermann trembled like a tiger, as he waited for the appointed time to arrive. At ten o'clock in the evening he was already in front of the Countess's house. The weather was terrible; the wind blew with great violence; the sleety snow fell in large flakes; the lamps emitted a feeble light, the streets were deserted; from time to time a sledge, drawn by a sorry-looking hack, passed by, on the look out for a belated passenger. Hermann was enveloped in a thick overcoat and felt neither wind nor snow.

At last the Countess's carriage drew up. Hermann saw two footmen carry out in their arms the bent form of the old lady, wrapped in sable fur, and immediately behind her, clad in a warm mantle, and with her head ornamented with a wreath of fresh flowers, followed Lizaveta. The door was closed. The carriage rolled away heavily through the yielding snow. The porter shut the street-door; the windows became dark.

Hermann began walking up and down near the deserted house; at length he stopped under a lamp, and glanced at his watch: it was twenty minutes past eleven. He remained standing under the lamp, his eyes fixed upon the watch, impatiently waiting for the remaining minutes to pass. At half past eleven precisely, Hermann ascended the steps of the house, and made his way into the brightly-illuminated vestibule. The porter was not there. Hermann hastily ascended the staircase, opened the door of the ante-room, and saw a footman sitting asleep in an antique chair by the side of a lamp. With a light firm step Hermann passed by him. The drawing-room and dining-room were in darkness, but a feeble reflection penetrated thither from the lamp in the ante-room.

Hermann reached the Countess's bedroom. Before a shrine, which was full of old images, a golden lamp was burning. Faded stuffed chairs and divans with soft cushions stood in melancholy symmetry around the room, the walls of which were hung with China silk. On one side of the room hung two portraits painted in Paris by Madame Lebrun. One of these represented a stout, red-faced man of about forty years of age in a bright-green uniform and with a star upon his breast; the other—a beautiful young woman, with an aquiline nose, forehead curls, and a rose in her powdered hair. In the corners stood porcelain shepherds and shepherdesses, dining-room clocks from the workshop of the celebrated Lefroy, bandboxes, roulettes, fans and the various playthings for the amusement of ladies that were in vogue at the end of the last century, when Montgolfier's balloons and Mesmer's magnetism were the rage. Hermann stepped behind the screen. At the back of it stood a little iron bedstead; on the right was the door which led to the cabinet; on the left—the other which led to the corridor. He opened the latter, and saw a little winding staircase which led to the room of the poor companion . . . But he retraced his steps and entered the dark cabinet.

The time passed slowly. All was still. The clock in the drawing-room struck twelve; the strokes echoed through the room one after the other, and everything was quiet again. Hermann stood leaning against the cold stove. He was calm; his heart beat regularly, like that of a man resolved upon a dangerous but inevitable undertaking. One o'clock in the morning struck; then two; and he heard the distant noise of carriage-wheels. An involuntary agitation took possession of him. The carriage drew near and stopped. He heard the sound of the carriage-steps being let down. All was bustle within the house. The servants were running hither and thither, there was a confusion of voices, and the rooms were lit up. Three antiquated chamber-maids entered the bedroom, and they were shortly afterwards followed by the Countess who, more dead than alive, sank into a Voltaire arm-chair. Hermann peeped through a chink. Lizaveta Ivanovna passed close by him, and he heard her hurried steps as she hastened up the little spiral staircase. For a moment his heart was assailed by something like a pricking of conscience, but the emotion was only transitory, and his heart became petrified as before.

The Countess began to undress before her looking-glass. Her rose-bedecked cap was taken off, and then her powdered wig was removed from off her white and closely-cut hair. Hairpins fell in showers around her. Her yellow satin dress, brocaded with silver, fell down at her swollen feet.

Hermann was a witness of the repugnant mysteries of her toilette; at last the Countess was in her nightcap and dressing-gown, and in this costume, more suitable to her age, she appeared less hideous and deformed.

Like all old people in general, the Countess suffered from sleeplessness. Having undressed, she seated herself at the window in a Voltaire arm-chair and dismissed her maids. The candles were taken away, and once more the room was left with only one lamp burning in it. The Countess sat there looking quite yellow, mumbling with her flaccid lips and swaying to and fro. Her dull eyes expressed complete vacancy of mind, and, looking at her, one would have thought that the rocking of her body was not a voluntary action of her own, but was produced by the action of some concealed galvanic mechanism.

Suddenly the death-like face assumed an inexplicable expression. The lips ceased to tremble, the eyes became animated: before the Countess stood an unknown man.

"Do not be alarmed, for Heaven's sake, do not be alarmed!" said he in a low but distinct voice. "I have no intention of doing you any harm, I have only come to ask a favour of you."

The old woman looked at him in silence, as if she had not heard what he had said. Hermann thought that she was deaf, and, bending down towards her ear, he repeated what he had said. The aged Countess remained silent as before.

"You can insure the happiness of my life," continued Hermann, "and it will cost you nothing. I know that you can name three cards in order——"

Hermann stopped. The Countess appeared now to understand what he wanted; she seemed as if seeking for words to reply.

"It was a joke," she replied at last: "I assure you it was only a joke."

"There is no joking about the matter," replied Hermann angrily. "Remember Chaplitsky, whom you helped to win."

The Countess became visibly uneasy. Her features expressed strong emotion, but they quickly resumed their former immobility.

"Can you not name me these three winning cards?" continued Hermann.

The Countess remained silent; Hermann continued:

"For whom are you preserving your secret? For your grandsons? They are rich enough without it; they do not know the worth of money. Your cards would be of no use to a spendthrift. He who cannot preserve his parental inheritance will die in want, even though he had a demon at his service. I am not a man of that sort; I know the value of money. Your three cards will not be thrown away upon me. Come! ..."

He paused and tremblingly awaited her reply. The Countess remained silent; Hermann fell upon his knees.

"If your heart has ever known the feeling of love," said he, "if you remember its rapture, if you have ever smiled at the cry of your new-born child, if any human feeling has ever entered into your breast, I entreat you by the feelings of a wife, a lover, a mother, by all that is most sacred in life, not to reject my prayer. Reveal to me your secret. Of what use is it to you? . . . Maybe it is connected with some terrible sin, with the loss of eternal salvation, with some bargain with the devil . . . Reflect, you are old; you have not long to live—I am ready to take your sins upon my soul. Only reveal to me your secret. Remember that the happiness of a man is in your hands, that not only I, but my children, and grandchildren will bless your memory and reverence you as a saint . . ."

The old Countess answered not a word.

Hermann rose to his feet.

"You old hag!" he exclaimed, grinding his teeth, "then I will make you answer!"

With these words he drew a pistol from his pocket.

At the sight of the pistol, the Countess for the second time exhibited strong emotion. She shook her head and raised her hands as if to protect herself from the shot . . . then she fell backwards and remained motionless.

"Come, an end to this childish nonsense!" said Hermann, taking hold of her hand. "I ask you for the last time; will you tell me the names of your three cards, or will you not?"

The Countess made no reply. Hermann perceived that she was dead.

Lizaveta Ivánovna was sitting in her room, still in her ball dress, lost in deep thought. On returning home, she had hastily dismissed the chambermaid who very reluctantly came forward to assist her, saying that she would undress herself, and with a trembling heart had gone up to her own room, expecting to find Hermann there, but yet hoping not to find him. At the first glance she convinced herself that he was not there, and she thanked her fate for having prevented him keeping the appointment. She sat down without undressing, and began to recall to mind all the circumstances which in so short a time had carried her so far.

It was not three weeks since the time when she first saw the young officer from the window—and yet she was already in correspondence with him, and he had succeeded in inducing her to grant him a nocturnal interview! She knew his name only through his having written it at the bottom of some of his letters; she had never spoken to him, had never heard his voice, and had never heard him spoken of until that evening. But strange to say, that very evening at the ball, Tomsky, being piqued with the young Princess Pauline N——, who, contrary to her usual custom, did not flirt with him, wished to revenge himself by assuming an air of indifference: he therefore engaged Lizaveta Ivanovna and danced an endless mazurka with her. During the whole of the time he kept teasing her about her partiality for Engineer officers; he assured her that he knew far more than she imagined, and some of his jests were so happily aimed, that Lizaveta thought several times that her secret was known to him.

"From whom have you learnt all this?" she asked, smiling.

"From a friend of a person very well known to you," replied Tomsky, "from a very distinguished man."

"And who is this distinguished man?"

"His name is Hermann."

Lizaveta made no reply; but her hands and feet lost all sense of feeling.

"This Hermann," continued Tomsky, "is a man of romantic personality. He has the profile of a Napoleon and the soul of a Mephistopheles. I believe that he has at least three crimes upon his conscience . . . How pale you have become!"

"I have a headache . . . But what did this Hermann—or whatever his name is—tell you?"

"Hermann is very much dissatisfied with his friend: he says that in his place he would act very differently . . . I even think that Hermann himself has designs upon you; at least, he listens very attentively to all that his friend has to say about you."

"And where has he seen me?"

"In church, perhaps; or on the parade—God alone knows where. It may have been in your room, while you were asleep, for there is nothing that he——"

Three ladies approaching him with the question: "*Oubli*

où regret?" interrupted the conversation, which had become so tantalisingly interesting to Lizaveta.

The lady chosen by Tomsky was the Princess Pauline herself. She succeeded in effecting a reconciliation with him during the numerous turns of the dance, after which he conducted her to her chair. On returning to his place, Tomsky thought no more either of Hermann or Lizaveta. She longed to renew the interrupted conversation, but the mazurka came to an end, and shortly afterwards the old Countess took her departure.

Tomsky's words were nothing more than the customary small talk of the dance, but they sank deep into the soul of the young dreamer. The portrait, sketched by Tomsky, coincided with the picture she had formed within her own mind, and thanks to the latest romances, the ordinary countenance of her admirer became invested with attributes capable of alarming her and fascinating her imagination at the same time. She was now sitting with her bare arms crossed and with her head, still adorned with flowers, sunk upon her uncovered bosom. Suddenly the door opened and Hermann entered. She shuddered.

" Where were you?" she asked in a terrified whisper.

" In the old Countess's bedroom," replied Hermann ; " I have just left her. The Countess is dead."

" My God! What do you say?"

" And I am afraid," added Hermann, " that I am the cause of her death."

Lizaveta looked at him, and Tomsky's words found an echo in her soul: " This man has at least three crimes upon his conscience!" Hermann sat down by the window near her, and related all that had happened.

Lizaveta listened to him in terror. So all those passionate letters, those ardent desires, this bold obstinate pursuit—all this was not love! Money—that was what his soul yearned for! She could not satisfy his desire and make him happy! The poor girl had been nothing but the blind tool of a robber, of the murderer of her aged benefactress! . . . She wept bitter tears of agonised repentance. Hermann gazed at her in silence: his heart, too, was a prey to violent emotion, but neither the tears of the poor girl nor the wonderful charm of her beauty, enhanced by her grief, could produce any impression upon his hardened soul. He felt no pricking of conscience at the thought of the dead old woman. One thing only grieved him: the irreparable loss of the secret from which he had expected to obtain great wealth.

" You are a monster!" said Lizaveta at last.

" I did not wish for her death," replied Hermann: " my pistol was not loaded."

Both remained silent.

The day began to dawn. Lizaveta extinguished her candle: a pale light illumined her room. She wiped her tear-stained eyes and raised them towards Hermann: he was sitting near the window, with his arms crossed and with a fierce frown on his forehead. In this attitude he bore a striking resemblance to the portrait of Napoleon. This resemblance struck Lizaveta even.

" How shall I get you out of the house?" she said at last. " I thought of conducting you down the secret staircase, but in that case it would be necessary to go through the Countess's bedroom, and I am afraid."

" Tell me how to find this secret staircase—I will go alone."

Lizaveta arose, took from her drawer a key, handed it to Hermann and gave him the necessary instructions. Hermann pressed her cold, powerless hand, kissed her bowed head, and left the room.

He descended the winding staircase, and once more entered the Countess's bedroom. The dead old lady sat as if petrified; her face expressed profound tranquillity. Hermann stopped before her, and gazed long and earnestly at her, as if he wished to convince himself of the terrible reality; at last he entered the cabinet, felt behind the tapestry for the door, and then began to descend the dark staircase, filled with strange emotions. " Down this very staircase," thought he, " perhaps coming from the very same room, and at this very same hour sixty years ago, there may have glided, in an embroidered coat, with his hair dressed à l'oiseau royal and pressing to his heart his three-cornered hat, some young gallant who has long been mouldering in the grave, but the heart of his aged mistress has only to-day ceased to beat. . . ."

At the bottom of the staircase Hermann found a door which he opened with a key, and then traversed a corridor which conducted him into the street.

Three days after the fatal night, at nine o'clock in the

morning, Hermann repaired to the Convent of ——, where the last honours were to be paid to the mortal remains of the old Countess. Although feeling no remorse, he could not altogether stifle the voice of conscience, which said to him: " You are the murderer of the old woman!" In spite of his entertaining very little religious belief, he was exceedingly superstitious ; and, believing that the dead Countess might exercise an evil influence on his life, he resolved to be present at her obsequies in order to implore her pardon.

The church was full. It was with difficulty that Hermann made his way through the crowd of people. The coffin was placed upon a rich catafalque beneath a velvet baldachin. The deceased Countess lay within it, with her hands crossed upon her breast, with a lace cap upon her head and dressed in a white satin robe. Around the catafalque stood the members of her household: the servants in black caftans, with armorial ribbons upon their shoulders, and candles in their hands ; the relatives—children, grandchildren, and great-grandchildren—in deep mourning.

Nobody wept; tears would have been *une affectation*. The Countess was so old, that her death could have surprised nobody, and her relatives had long looked upon her as being out of the world. A famous preacher pronounced the funeral sermon. In simple and touching words he described the peaceful passing away of the righteous, who had passed long years in calm preparation for a Christian end. "The angel of death found her," said the orator, " engaged in pious meditation and waiting for the midnight bridegroom."

The service concluded amidst profound silence. The relatives went forward first to take farewell of the corpse. Then followed the numerous guests, who had come to render the last homage to her who for so many years had been a participator in their frivolous amusements. After these followed the members of the Countess's household. The last of these was an old woman of the same age as the deceased. Two young women led her forward by the hand. She had not strength enough to bow down to the ground—she merely shed a few tears and kissed the cold hand of her mistress.

Hermann now resolved to approach the coffin. He knelt down upon the cold stones and remained in that position for some minutes; at last he arose, as pale as the deceased Countess herself; he ascended the steps of the catafalque and bent over the corpse. . . . At that moment it seemed to him that the dead woman darted a mocking look at him and winked with one eye. Hermann started back, took a false step and fell to the ground. Several persons hurried forward and raised him up. At the same moment Lizaveta Ivanovna was borne fainting into the porch of the church. This episode disturbed for some minutes the solemnity of the gloomy ceremony. Among the congregation rose a deep murmur, and a tall thin chamberlain, a near relative of the deceased, whispered in the ear of an Englishman who was standing near him, that the young officer was a natural son of the Countess, to which the Englishman coldly replied: "Oh!"

During the whole of that day, Hermann was strangely excited. Repairing to an out-of-the-way restaurant to dine, he drank a great deal of wine, contrary to his usual custom, in the hope of deadening his inward agitation. But the wine only served to excite his imagination still more. On returning home, he threw himself upon his bed without undressing, and fell into a deep sleep.

When he woke up it was already night, and the moon was shining into the room. He looked at his watch: it was a quarter to three. Sleep had left him; he sat down upon his bed and thought of the funeral of the old Countess.

At that moment somebody in the street looked in at his window and immediately passed on again. Hermann paid no attention to this incident. A few moments afterwards he heard the door of his ante-room open. Hermann thought that it was his orderly, drunk as usual, returning from some nocturnal expedition, but presently he heard footsteps that were unknown to him: somebody was walking softly over the floor in slippers. The door opened, and a woman dressed in white entered the room. Hermann mistook her for his old nurse, and wondered what could bring her there at that hour of the night. But the white woman glided rapidly across the room and stood before him—Hermann recognised the Countess!

"I have come to you against my wish," she said in a firm voice; "but I have been ordered to grant your request. Three, seven, ace, will win for you if played in succession, but only on these conditions: that you do not play more than one card in twenty-four hours, and that you never play again during the rest of your life. I forgive you my death, on condition that you marry my companion, Lizaveta Ivanovna."

With these words she turned round very quietly, walked with a shuffling gait towards the door and disappeared. Hermann heard the street-door open and shut, and again he saw someone look in at him through the window.

For a long time Hermann could not recover himself. He then rose up and entered the next room. His orderly was lying asleep on the floor, and he had much difficulty in waking him. The orderly was drunk as usual, and no information could be obtained from him. The street-door was locked. Hermann returned to his room, lit his candle, and wrote down all the details of his vision.

Two fixed ideas can no more exist together in the moral world than two bodies can occupy one and the same place in the physical world. " Three, seven, ace," soon drove out of Hermann's mind the thought of the dead Countess. " Three, seven, ace," were perpetually running through his head and continually being repeated by his lips. If he saw a young girl, he would say: " How slender she is! quite like the three of hearts." If anybody asked: " What is the time?" he would reply: " Five minutes to seven." Every stout man that he saw reminded him of the ace. " Three, seven, ace " haunted him in his sleep and assumed all possible shapes. The threes bloomed before him in the forms of magnificent flowers, the sevens were represented by Gothic portals, and the aces became transformed into gigantic spiders. One thought alone occupied his whole mind—to make a profitable use of the secret which he had purchased so dearly. He wanted to go to Paris and tempt fortune in some of the public gambling-houses that abounded there. Chance spared him all this trouble.

There was in Moscow a society of rich gamesters, presided over by the celebrated Chekalinsky, who had passed all his life at the card-table and had amassed millions, accepting bills of exchange for his winnings and paying his losses in ready money. His long experience secured for him the confidence of his companions, and his open house, his famous cook, and his agreeable and fascinating manners gained for him the respect of the public. He came to St. Petersburg. The young men of the capital flocked to his rooms, forgetting balls for cards, and preferring the emotions of faro to the seductions of flirting. Naroumoff conducted Hermann to Chekalinsky's residence.

They passed through a suite of magnificent rooms, filled with attentive domestics. The place was crowded. Generals and Privy Counsellors were playing at whist; young men were lolling carelessly upon the velvet-covered sofas, eating ices and smoking pipes. In the drawing-room, at the head of a long table, around which were assembled about a score of players, sat the master of the house keeping the bank. He was a man of about sixty years of age, of a very dignified appearance; his head was covered wtih silvery-white hair; his full, florid countenance expressed good nature, and his eyes twinkled with a perpetual smile. Naroumoff introduced Hermann to him. Chekalinsky shook him by the hand in a friendly manner, requested him not to stand on ceremony, and then went on dealing.

The game occupied some time. On the table lay more than thirty cards. Chekalinsky paused after each throw, in order to give the players time to arrange their cards and note down their losses, listened politely to their requests, and, more politely still, put straight the corners of cards that some player's hand had chanced to bend. At last the game was finished. Chekalinsky shuffled the cards and prepared to deal again.

"Will you allow me to take a card?" said Hermann, stretching out his hand from behind a stout gentleman who was punting.

Chekalinsky smiled and bowed silently, as a sign of acquiescence. Naroumoff laughingly congratulated Hermann on adjuration of that abstention from cards which he had practised for so long a period, and wished him a lucky beginning.

"Stake!" said Hermann, writing some figures with chalk on the back of his card.

"How much?" asked the banker, contracting the muscles of his eyes; "excuse me, I cannot see quite clearly."

"Forty-seven thousand roubles," replied Hermann.

At these words every head in the room turned suddenly round, and all eyes were fixed upon Hermann.

" He has taken leave of his senses!" thought Naroumoff.

" Allow me to inform you," said Chekalinsky, with his eternal smile, " that you are playing very high; nobody here has ever staked more than two hundred and seventy-five roubles at once."

" Very well," replied Hermann; " but do you accept my card or not?"

Chekalinsky bowed in token of consent.

" I only wish to observe," said he, " that although I have the greatest confidence in my friends, I can only play against ready money. For my own part, I am quite convinced that your word is sufficient, but for the sake of the order of the game, and to facilitate the reckoning up, I must ask you to put the money on your card."

Hermann drew from his pocket a bank-note and handed it to Chekalinsky, who, after examining it in a cursory manner, placed it on Hermann's card.

He began to deal. On the right a nine turned up, and on the left a three.

" I have won!" said Hermann, showing his card.

A murmur of astonishment arose among the players. Chekalinsky frowned, but the smile quickly returned to his face.

" Do you wish me to settle with you?" he said to Hermann.

" If you please," replied the latter.

Chekalinsky drew from his pocket a number of bank-notes and paid at once. Hermann took up his money and left the table. Naroumoff could not recover from his astonishment. Hermann drank a glass of lemonade and returned home.

The next evening he again repaired to Chekalinsky's. The host was dealing. Hermann walked up to the table; the punters immediately made room for him. Chekalinsky greeted him with a gracious bow.

Hermann waited for the next deal, took a card and placed upon it his forty-seven thousand roubles, together with his winnings of the previous evening.

Chekalinsky began to deal. A knave turned up on the right, a seven on the left.

Hermann showed his seven.

There was a general exclamation. Chekalinsky was evidently ill-at-ease, but he counted out the ninety-four thousand roubles and handed them over to Hermann, who pocketed them in the coolest manner possible and immediately left the house.

The next evening Hermann appeared again at the table. Everyone was expecting him. The generals and Privy Counsellors left their whist in order to watch such extraordinary play. The young officers quitted their sofas and even the servants crowded into the room. All pressed round Hermann. The other players left off punting, impatient to see how it would end. Hermann stood at the table and prepared to play alone against the pale, but still smiling Chekalinsky. Each opened a pack of cards. Chekalinsky shuffled. Hermann took a card and covered it with a pile of bank-notes. It was like a duel. Deep silence reigned around.

Chekalinsky began to deal; his hands trembled. On the right a queen turned up, and on the left an ace.

" Ace has won!" cried Hermann, showing his card.

" Your queen has lost," said Chekalinsky, politely.

Hermann started; instead of an ace, there lay before him the queen of spades; He could not believe his eyes, nor could he understand how he had made such a mistake.

At that moment it seemed to him that the queen of spades smiled ironically and winked her eye at him. He was struck by her remarkable resemblance . . .

" The old Countess!" he exclaimed, seized with terror.

Chekalinsky gathered up his winnings. For some time, Hermann remained perfectly motionless. When at last he left the table, there was a general commotion in the room.

" Splendidly punted!" said the players. Chekalinsky shuffled the cards afresh, and the game went on as usual.

Hermann went out of his mind, and is now confined in Room Number 17 of the Oboukhoff Hospital. He never answers any questions, but he constantly mutters with unusual rapidity: " Three, seven, ace! Three, seven, queen!"

Lizaveta Ivanovna has married a very amiable young man, a son of the former steward of the old Countess. He is in the service of the State somewhere, and is in receipt of a good income. Lizaveta is also supporting a poor relative.

Tomsky has been promoted to the rank of captain, and has become the husband of the Princess Pauline.

PARGITON AND HARBY

Desmond MacCarthy

Robert Harby and Thomas Pargiton had known each other well in youth; indeed, they had once been devoted to each other; then, for more than twenty years, their friendship had lapsed. On going down from Cambridge together they had shared lodgings in London. Both had had to make their way in the world, but while Harby dreaded the prospect and would have preferred a safe civil service or academic career, Pargiton had looked forward avidly to competitive adventure. At Cambridge Harby had envied his friend his ambitious temperament, but he soon began to deplore it. The tough-mindedness he used to admire at the university showed up in London as unscrupulousness; and some of the transactions in the city in which Pargiton had become involved struck Harby as certainly mean if not positively illegal. He had not been sorry when, one morning, Pargiton abruptly informed him that he could no longer afford to live at such "a bad address," and moved to an ostentatious flat in a fashionable part of London. After that Harby had seen less and less of Pargiton. At last he only heard of him now and then; once he saw his name in the papers in connection with a commercial case which hinted blackmail.

Meanwhile, Robert Harby had gone quickly along the path which opportunity had first opened to him. He had been employed by a firm of map-publishers which, thanks to the demand for new maps after the war, had prospered, and in course of time he had been taken into partnership. The firm had recently been putting on the market a series of guide books, and this enterprise, which had proved lucrative, was in his particular charge. It necessitated frequent journeys abroad, and it was on one of these expeditions, which combined business and pleasure in proportions agreeable to his temperament, that, after twenty years, he had met Pargiton again.

Harby had just arrived at Dieppe one wet February afternoon, when, looking out of his bedroom window, which faced the cobbled market-place, he noticed a tall man in a brown coat buying sweets at one of the stalls below. His figure struck him as familiar, but when the man moved away to distribute what he had just bought among a group of children, Harby thought he must have been mistaken. The man in the brown coat walked with a heavy limp. He appeared now to be making for Harby's hotel. It was—no, was it?—Pargiton! The largess of sweets Harby had just witnessed was not at all like Pargiton, nor was it like him to be staying at a commercial hotel rather than at one of the glittering palaces on the sea-front, and Pargiton was not lame. Still, in spite of that, in spite, too, of that painful, hitching gait, Harby felt sure that this was none other than his old friend; but it was curiosity rather than eagerness which the next moment made him descend the corkscrew stairs to meet him. Although he could not see the face of the man who had just entered, for the hall of the hotel was a mere passage and only lit by the open door, he went straight up to him and addressed him by name. It was Pargiton; and Pargiton was glad to see him—pathetically glad, so Harby reflected late that night while he undressed.

After meeting they had repaired at once to one of the cafés under the arches which face Dieppe harbour. There they sat and talked over apéritifs, dinner, and cognacs, watching, through the plate glass, craft of all sorts gently rocking on the dark water, and now and then a train draw up, jangling and panting, on the quay. Harby was starting early next morning for Caen; meanwhile, for the sake of his company, Pargiton contentedly allowed the Newhaven boat to depart without him into the night.

Reviewing their conversation in the train next day, Harby was surprised to discover how little, after all, Pargiton had told him about the last twenty years. By tacit consent they had gone back to their pre-London memories, and Pargiton had touched him a little by saying, " I have always associated you with my better self," adding, " Now I have found you again, I don't mean to let you go." His career had apparently been chequered, till he inherited, about two years ago, his elder brother's fortune and tea-broking business. Harby had also gathered that Pargiton's brother had been engaged to a widow at the time of his death, and that the widow's son was now being educated at Oxford at Pargiton's expense, and that it was his intention soon to hand over the business to him.

He had not spoken of his brother directly, but Harby gathered that it was not compulsion, but loyalty, which was actuating him in these matters. This rather astonished Harby, for it came back to him that the brothers had been very indifferent in old days; " My ass of a brother," was a phrase which he remembered had often been on Pargiton's lips. Harby would have supposed that he was probably in love with the widow, had not a question elicited the fact that he had never seen her. As for his lameness (one leg was decidedly shorter than the other), about that, too, Pargiton had been decidedly laconic: he had had a fall on the ice and smashed his thigh near the hip joint. What was past was, thank heaven, past; he had suffered incessant and awful pain for nine months; now his leg only troubled him sometimes. He was living in a little house at Greenwich to save money, as he would soon have to give up the business to the boy. Harby must come to see him often, very often. He was lonely and hated new friends, but old friends were different. It was at this point in their talk that Pargiton had touched him by saying, with an almost frightened earnestness, " I have always associated you with my better self." He was certainly changed, very much changed.

Harby's tour in France lasted some months, during which he had several letters from Pargiton. Near the end of the time a telegram announced that Pargiton would join him at once, but it was followed next day by another, " All well. No need to bother you now. Look forward to your return." Harby had no idea that Pargiton had ever had any " need " of him. Perhaps he had missed a letter while on the move? Two days later he received one which, though it mystified him still more, at least cleared up that point:

Dear Robert,

I am afraid you must have thought from my last letter (so there had been another letter) either that I was making an absurd fuss about nothing or that I was going off my head. I wrote in great agitation. The fact is, I have experienced symptoms of the same kind before, but never so late in the year. January is my bad month, and I thought it was well over, when I suddenly discovered that someone had been marking my books, an annoyance which preceded last time that feeling of never being alone which I told you in my last letter I dreaded. I happened to take down Newman's *Apologia*. (He has changed! thought Harby.) You remember, perhaps, the passage in which he tells how on one of his solitary walks the Provost of Oriel quoted as he bowed and passed, " *Nunquam minus solus, quam cum solus.*" Well, *in my copy these words were underlined in a brownish, deep-red ink.* You will say I must have done it myself and forgotten. But I never mark my books, and I have never had red ink in the house. " Never less alone than when alone!" You can imagine how these words alarmed me. I hurriedly pulled out another book. (I must tell you that on occasions I believe my hand is strangely guided.) There was nothing marked in it. I turned over every page. In the third and fourth I examined I also found nothing, but in my Wordsworth, opposite the line, " That inward eye which is the bliss of solitude," was written—in my own hand—the word, " Bliss!" with an ironical exclamation mark after it. You will say that the fact that the writing was exactly like my own proves that I must have done it myself—perhaps in my sleep or in some strange state of unconsciousness. Of course, I gave that explanation full weight, but listen. It was Saturday afternoon ; I felt I could not stay in the house. I wired to my chief clerk, who is a good fellow, saying that I was unwell and asking him to come down to Westgate with me for two nights. While we were there, I was burgled. The loss was trifling, a suit-case, a suit of clothes, a shirt or two, sponge, pyjamas, in fact—except that I had taken my brushes with me—the things one usually packs for a week-end. But that's not all. I must tell you first that I purposely tested my condition while at Westgate. I took a longish walk by myself and I felt all right. The sea-air did me good. I had intended to keep the door between Sparling's room and mine open at night, but it was not necessary. I felt perfectly secure, and slept well. The next day I sent my second wire to you. I returned to London on Monday with Sparling, but I begged him to come back to Greenwich with me for the night, as I was not yet absolutely certain that I should be easy in my own home. The maids met us with the story of the sense-less theft. They had found the drawers in my bedroom pulled

out on Sunday morning, and they had reported the matter
to the police. The policeman on duty that night was a new
man on the beat; he said he had seen a man come out of
the house with a suitcase about 10 p.m., but had thought
nothing of it. Now comes the extraordinary and disconcerting
thing. The same constable came to see me to ask the
necessary questions, and the moment he entered the room
I saw him give a start of surprise. He recovered himself
quickly and grinned in rather an insolent way. When I
asked him point-blank what he meant by his behaviour, he
put on a knowing air and said, " I expect *you* can clear
this little matter up. It don't seem a case for the police." I
again asked him to explain himself, and went to the
sideboard to mix him a whisky-and-soda. It had the usual
propritiatory effect, for he then said, rather apologetically,
" Well, sir, the person I see coming out of that front door
Saturday night was a gentleman as didn't walk quite easily."
At this, my glass shook in my hand so that I had to put
it down. I managed, however, to assert pretty emphatically
that *I* was at Westgate with a friend that night. He noticed
my agitation, and smiling with a cocksure benevolence
terrible to me, he replied, " Gentlemen does sometimes find
it handy to be in two places at once. Good evening, sir." I
know I dropped into a chair like one stunned. How long
I sat there I don't know. I cannot tell you now all the
thoughts which rose in my mind in connection with what
had happened. Had I better stay where I was, or fly? You
will see from the address at the top of this letter that I
decided to return to Westgate. I have not been followed.
The bad moments I endure are those when I first come
into the hotel from a walk. Among the luggage of new
arrivals I am always terrified of seeing my lost suitcase. But
I am afraid of becoming afraid again.

Robert, after our long estrangement, I cannot ask you to
leave your work and join me, but if old days still mean
anything to you, as, thank God, they seemed to when we
met, do not desert me. It is not in the name of affection I
ask you to hasten your return and come to me—I have
no right to anyone's affection, let alone yours—but take pity
on me, help me. Come. Wire that you will come. With you
I am my better self, my *old* self; I feel it. Then I am safe.

I must tell you that I took a Shakespeare to Westgate. This morning I picked it up, thinking it might distract my mind. On the page I opened I found these lines marked:

It will be short: the interim is mine;
And a man's life is no more than to say, one.

I have not dared to look at any more.

Below the signature of the letter was scrawled this P.S.: "I have not told you all."

On first reading this letter, Harby concluded that Pargiton was going off his head, but on second thoughts he was inclined to suspend judgment. He would, in any case, be returning shortly to England, so he decided to wire that he would join him at Westgate. He left for England the next day.

On the journey his thoughts were naturally much concerned with Pargiton, and he re-read his letter several times in the train. It was clear that he imagined himself to be the victim of some kind of supernatural persecution. Of course, the most plausible explanation of the facts was that he was suffering from incipient persecution mania, which had been intensified by the odd coincidence of his house having been broken into by a man who was also as lame as himself. The marking of the books was certainly an odd feature of the case, but it was probably self-justificatory evidence forged by the unhappy man himself to account for terrors peculiar to his state of mind.

When Harby stepped off the steamer at Dover, almost the first person he noticed in the crowd was Pargiton, who raised his hand in a kind of solemn, Roman gesture of greeting. He wanted to return straight to London.

All attempts on the journey to talk of things in general broke down, and the presence of other people in the carriage prevented confidences. They dined in London, and Pargiton's spirits seemed slightly to revive, but he was not communicative. They drooped again on reaching Greenwich.

His house was, as he had said, a small one; a semi-detached villa standing back from a road shaded by tall old trees.

A short paved path led from the little gate to its pillared but modest portico. Pargiton's sitting-room on the ground-floor struck Harby as a delightful room. It was lined with books, and a large square mirror over the mantelpiece reflected prettily the green trees outside. Pargiton threw himself into a chair with something like a sigh of relief.

"You're thinking I ought to be happy here. Well, I am —as long as you are with me. I wish, old fellow, we could live together as we used to in old days. Anyhow," he added, "don't leave me yet awhile."

"About your letter," Harby began . . . but Pargiton seemed reluctant to discuss that and proposed a game of chess. "Just like old times," he said, setting the men; "it is the best dope in the world," and for half an hour he appeared to find it so. Then he suddenly jumped up before the game was finished and said he must have a breath of fresh air before going to bed.

As soon as the small iron wicket had clicked behind them, and they found themselves in the road, Pargiton, taking his friend's arm, said, "You noticed my postscript? I think now I can tell you everything. I have what I want—now, yet it hàs come to me in a way which has robbed me of all power to enjoy it. You remember I was very set on getting on? I was reckless, unscrupulous; I was also a failure. Do you remember my brother? No, of course you don't, but you must remember my talking about him. It was his death that saved me. I never cared about him, but I wish he hadn't died." He stopped speaking, and for some time they walked on in silence up the road towards the open heights of Blackheath. "My trouble—my trouble, which I wrote to you about, is, I'm certain . . . and yet I am not . . . My brother was drowned. Did you see anything about it in the papers? —skating on the lake at his place in the country. I was with him at the time. It was terrible."

They had now emerged from the avenue into the open moonlight and the road lay white before them. Harby's eyes had been for some time fixed on the ground, for he had been filled with that uneasy feeling which possesses us when a companion is endeavouring to speak openly and yet is obviously unable to do so. He could not meet Pargiton's eye, who was continually turning his head towards him, as though he hoped to see that he was conveying more than he had actually succeeded in saying. "It was terrible," he began again. "The ice broke whenever he tried to hoist himself on to it." But Harby, though he heard the words, hardly took in their meaning; his eyes were fixed on what was in front of him. He stopped in amazement: their united shadows had unmistakably three heads. "It was my fault, too," Pargiton went on, still trying to read his face, "I challenged him to a race. If I had not fallen myself and broken my thigh, I should have been done for, too." Part of the composite shadow slowly elongated itself, and a pair of shoulders appeared beneath the extra head. Harby felt a grip on his arm; Pargiton had jerked him round. "Don't you understand?" he said, in a voice of extraordinary tension; "it was partly my fault, *my fault*. My God, man, what's the matter with you? Listen, you must listen; it seems to me now that it is possible that—I am tortured by the suspicion that I believe I *knew* the ice near the other side of the lake was unsound." Harby again turned his eyes from the agitated man beside him to the road. He was about to point to the shadow, when a cloud covered the moon. Perhaps it had been fancy. Yet, at the back of his mind he still thought he had seen what he had seen. Anyhow, the cat was out of the bag; Pargiton had made his confession, or as complete a one as he could bring himself to make. They presently turned back and descended the avenue together.

It was not abhorrence that Harby felt for his companion; or, if it was, it was so mixed with pity that it amounted only to a neutral feeling of indifference; but the sensation of Pargiton's arm in his had become unpleasant, and he could hardly listen to what he was saying: Pargiton was talking volubly about his past life. He did not mention his brother again, but he began to pour out an account of all he had done and regretted in the past. The past was the past—that was the refrain. A man could make a fresh start, couldn't he? He, Pargiton, was certainly now a different man. Hadn't Harby himself noticed that? A man might be too hard on himself, mightn't he? Might fancy he had been baser than he had been, especially if there was really a lot of good in him? By the time they reached the house, Pargiton had talked himself into a sort of wild gaiety. When they parted on saying good night, he wrung Harby's hand with an earnest squeeze, which made him more anxious than ever to leave the next morning.

Pargiton was still standing in the hall. To feel those imploring eyes upon his back as he ascended the stairs was bad enough, to return their gaze impossible. He passed the landing corner without looking back. How—in what words —should he tell Pargiton in the morning that he could have nothing more to do with him, that he must leave him to his fate? Was it horror at his crime, he asked himself (Harby was quite certain he was guilty), or fear of having to share some horrible experience with him that lay behind his resolve to g   In his mind's eye he saw again that third shadow detach itself from their combined shadows upon the white road. Was it, then, merely fear? In that case, ought he to yield? Did he care for Pargiton? No: that was over long ago. Yet he had undoubtedly begun a kind of friendship with him again—at any rate, he had roused in the wretched man some hope that he would not be in the future left utterly alone. What was the decent thing to do? Of course he could make work an excuse to-morrow, and the easiest way would be to say he must go up to London, then wire that he was detained. But Pargiton would guess; he would insist on coming with him. To be followed about by a haunted murderer was unbearable. Yet he could not blame Pargiton for clutching on to him. What *ought* he to do?

He remained awake for hours, so it seemed, his thoughts revolving round and round the same problem, only sometimes interrupting them to strain his ears to catch some tiny noise or other in the dark. Once or twice, when his thoughts were busiest about his own predicament, he had been nearly certain that he had heard, not the dreaded creak of Pargiton's footsteps on the stairs, but a strange, low, ringing sound, and twice he had switched on the light; but when he concentrated upon listening he could hear absolutely nothing.

At last, without knowing it, he must have fallen asleep. For he found himself standing on the edge of a sheet of black ice. The moon was up, yet daylight had not quite left the sky, and a white mist lay knee-high round the shores of a long lake. Someone was waiting there in a creeping agony of excitement, but Harby could not tell whether it was he himself or another who was experiencing this horrible sense of expectation, for he seemed to be both the man he saw and a disembodied percipient. Again his listening attention caught faint, faint at first, that low, sweet, ringing sound. It was coming nearer now, growing louder, and mingled with it he could distinctly hear the hiss of skates. Presently, he too was moving, travelling with effortless rapidity over a hard slightly yielding surface. He felt the wind of his own speed against his face; he heard the bubbles run chirruping under the sweep of his strokes and tinkle against the frozen edges of the lake; he felt the ice elastic beneath him, and his chest oppressed by a difficulty in breathing which was also somehow indistinguishable from a glow of triumph. Suddenly from the mist in front of him, he heard a crash, a cry. The echo seemed to be still in the room, when with flying heart and shaking hand he touched the switch of his lamp.

His door had been thrown violently open, and in the doorway stood Pargiton.

He was still fully dressed, but Harby only noticed his face. The stricken man stood with his mouth a little open, swaying slightly. Harby went up to him, took him by the hand, led him to the bed, and made him lie down, but neither spoke, till Harby tried to disengage his hand and said, " I'll go and fetch a doctor."

Pargiton, who was lying motionless with open mouth, staring at the ceiling, rocked his head twice upon the pillow, and without moving his lips, breathed out the words: " No use."

" What's your maid's name? I'll call her."

Harby felt the grasp upon his hand tighten: " I mean I'll shout for her," he added, " and tell her to fetch some brandy from downstairs."

" She musn't go into that room," Pargiton breathed again.

" All right, but what's her name?"

"·Bertha."

Without changing his position by the bed, Harby began to shout her name. It required a considerable effort of courage to raise his voice, but presently two startled women with outdoor coats over their nightgowns appeared. Harby took the situation in hand.

" I want you both to dress at once and go together to the nearest doctor. Your master has been taken ill. And tell him it's a heart case. No; tell him the patient is in bad pain. Tell him anything, to come prepared for anything—restoratives, sedatives. Quick."

A few minutes later the closing of the front door sent a shiver through Pargiton, and the next half-hour was the most painful vigil in Harby's life. For some time the sick man

lay still; then he raised the forefinger of his disengaged hand
as though he were listening, or bidding his companion listen,
while his face became festered with terror. Presently he
sat bolt upright, staring into the passage. Harby wrenched
away his hand and jumped up to shut the door. As he
crossed the room the thought leapt at him that it might not
shut—not quite; so vividly had those staring eyes imprinted,
even for him, upon the framed oblong darkness, the sense of
something on the threshold. Terrified himself, he flung his
shoulder at the door and slammed it with a crash that shook
the house. Pargiton sank back in a state of collapse upon
the pillow; he seemed to have lost consciousness, and
Harby made no attempt to rouse him from that happy
state. A little later the sound of the doctor's footsteps on
the stairs, however, did so only too effectively; all four of
them found themselves engaged in a struggle with a wildly
delirious man. At last they succeeded in holding him
down while a strong morphia injection brought at last relief.
The doctor remained until a trained nurse arrived, and the
dusk of early morning had already begun to brighten into
day when he left. The same day Pargiton was removed
by two trained attendants to a home for mental cases.

It was an inexpressible relief to Harby to find himself again
in his own rooms. He went straight to bed, utterly exhausted,
and awoke from a short sleep with steadied nerves, though
with a strong reluctance either to think over what he had
been through or to be alone. He decided to wire to ask an
old friend, who was married to a particularly sensible and
cheerful wife and surrounded by children of all ages, to
receive him for a few days. The suggestion was warmly
accepted, and Harby caught a late train. His hosts were
puzzled by his looks and the suddenness of his visit, but they
were kind enough to ask no questions, and a few days in
their company did much to restore his equanimity. The
first report he received of Pargiton (he had left directions
that he should be kept informed) told him little beyond the
fact that the condition of the patient was considered grave; the
second, that he had had no more violent attacks, but that his
despondent condition required the constant presence of an
attendant. His physical state was also alarmingly low. The
third report enclosed a letter from Pargiton himself; it ran
as follows:

My Dear Harby,

I have enjoyed to-day and yesterday a peace of
mind such as I have not experienced for a long time. I know
what is the matter with me, and you know, but those who
are looking after me do not. I know, too, that my release is
near, and I have an inward confidence that it will not
come in too cruel a way. I have paid my awful debt—my
death is but the small item which still remains due. The
worst is over ; but I should like at least one other human
being to know how bad it has been, and, especially, that you,
my old friend, should know what I have had to endure. It
may help you to think more mercifully of one whom you have
reason to number among the basest of men. Verbally incomplete as my confession was on our walk at Greenwich, you
grasped the whole truth. I was aware of it, as I watched
you go upstairs to bed that night; and when you did not
turn to look back at me, I knew that I had lost even the
little claim I had upon your sympathy.

I find some difficulty in describing my state of mind at that
moment. My confession, shirking, halting—for it concealed
from you my certainty of my own guilt—lying as it was, had
brought me extraordinary relief, and my courage had been
artificially heightened by the whisky I had just drunk. I saw
that I was repulsive to you, but depression at that was
quickly succeeded by hope. I went into my room and drank
another whisky and sat down in that big chair which faces
the looking-glass over the fireplace. My thoughts were
busy with all I intended to do to atone, with my plans for
that boy and his mother—the woman my brother intended to
marry—and for you. I have no doubt I was maudlin ; but
you cannot imagine how sweet it was, even for awhile,
to feel that I was not a scoundrel. The persecution I have
suffered has not come from my poor brother, I am certain.
The very nature of it had from the start pointed to a very
different origin, even if the revelation I am about to describe
had not occurred. Had I been pursued by his revengeful
spirit, believe me, I should not have suffered so much, for I
am capable of feeling enough genuine remorse to have bowed
my head with recognition of its justice. No : my persecutor
has been a being so intimately identified with myself that
escape from him, or it, has been impossible, and propitiation

a contradiction in terms. I have been pursued and tortured by a being who has as good a claim to be myself as the Pargiton you know, but who is now utterly repellent to me, and to whom every attempt on my part to dissociate myself from him—can you imagine the horror of this to one who longs, as I do, to have done with the past?—gives an intensified power of independent action. After every attempt I made to make amends I have felt his power grow stronger. It was not until I first tried to help mother and son that I was conscious of him at all. I think now that it was because in your company I was a better man that he came so close to me after we parted. What followed my confession to you, which was the greatest effort I ever made to reconquer self-respect, you shall hear.

How long I had been sitting in my chair planning how I should give up my ill-gotten wealth and lead the life of service, pure devoted service, which seemed miraculously open to me, I do not know. Perhaps I fell asleep; my sleep has been very poor and thin for a long time, hardly filming over a riot of thoughts and consciously created images. My future life was unrolling before me in comforting colours when, suddenly, the series of pictures was shattered by the clash of the iron wicket in the front of the house. I did not start, my new-found happiness was too strong upon me, though the thought occurred to me that the hour was singularly late for anyone—and who could it be?—to come to see me. It was the next sound which set my heart thumping; someone was approaching up the stone path to the porch. Now a lame man learns to know well the rhythm of his own footfalls, especially if he walks alone as often as I do. A heavy step, the click of a stick, a scraping, light step and then a heavy one again—Harby, those approaching steps were my own! I heard the grate of my latch-key in the lock and the heavy breathing of a cripple pausing on the mat. Two lurching steps would bring him, I knew well, within reach of the handle of the study door and from it I could not take my eyes; I tried to cover them, but I could not move my hands. I heard a stumble, a fumble; the brass knob turned and the door began to open slowly—nothing came in!

There are moments of terror so dreadful that nature in man cries out, " This can't be true," and I pray for all men

that our death may not be such a moment ; but there is, believe
me, a terror beyond that, one which carries with it a sensation
of absolute certainty against which the brain can raise no
protest of frantic disbelief. I spun round in the agony of
one who, not finding his assailant in front, looks behind, and
I saw a face, an awful face. It was mine. Oh! sweet relief, I
knew in an instant it was my own reflection in the glass ;
that wild white face was mine, those glaring eyes were mine.
I was still alone.

But the profound relief of that moment of recognition
did not last. While I was still staring at myself, holding
myself at arms' length from the mantelpiece, I thought the
lips of my reflection smiled. When I put one hand to my
mouth to feel if I too were smiling, the gesture was not
repeated by the figure in front of me! The next moment that
ultimate terror was on me with the spring of a tiger; though
both my hands were clutching the mantelpiece and I could
swear to the chill of the stone beneath them, the hands in
the mirror were slowly stretching out to reach me. I heard
a crash ; I must have fallen ; I don't remember picking myself
up. When consciousness returned I was standing at your
bedroom door. You know the rest.

I have only one more thing to tell you. Lying here in this
place, where everyone is kind and no one understands, I have
been thinking things out. Those hopes of a new life were
all false dreams ; I could never live such a life. I see what
I must do: I understand now that to go on defying my
Past Self, though every act of defiance intensifies his power
to destroy me, *is* my proper expiation, and when I think of
him in that light I am no longer afraid. What is death without
terror? Nothing—an event that isn't part of life. Even my
weakling's confession to you almost enabled him to get his
hands upon my throat. I have written to my brother's wife
—for so I always think of her—telling her how and why the
idea entered my head of luring my brother on to ice I had
tested and knew did not bear. I have not spared myself. I
have of course left everything I possess to her and her boy.
My end therefore is now certain. If you care to see me
again, come, but don't think that I am asking for or depending
upon support.

When Harby read this letter he wired to say that he would

be with him that afternoon, but a telegram, which crossed with his, informed him that Pargiton had died in his sleep the night before. What had been, Harby wondered, his last dream? In his coffin he looked stern and peaceful, but the faces of the dead tell us nothing.

THE SNOW

Hugh Walpole

The second Mrs. Ryder was a young woman not easily frightened, but now she stood in the dusk of the passage leaning back against the wall, her hand on her heart, looking at the grey-faced window beyond which the snow was steadily falling against the lamp-light.

The passage where she was, led from the study to the dining-room, and the window looked out on to the little paved path that ran at the edge of the Cathedral green. As she stared down the passage she couldn't be sure whether the woman were there or no. How absurd of her! She knew the woman was not there. But if the woman was not, how was it that she could discern so clearly the old-fashioned grey cloak, the untidy grey hair, and the sharp outline of the pale cheek and pointed chin? Yes, and more than that, the long sweep of the grey dress, falling in folds to the ground, the flash of a gold ring on the white hand. No. No. No. This was madness. There was no one and nothing there. Hallucination . . .

Very faintly a voice seemed to come to her: "I warned you. This is for the last time. . . ."

The nonsense! How far now was her imagination to carry her? Tiny sounds about the house, the running of a tap somewhere, a faint voice from the kitchen, these and something more had translated themselves into an imagined voice. "The last time . . ."

But her terror was real. She was not normally frightened by anything. She was young and healthy and bold, fond of sport, hunting, shooting, taking any risk. Now she was truly *stiffened* with terror—she could not move, could not advance down the passage as she wanted to and find light, warmth, safety in the dining-room. All the time the snow fell steadily, stealthily, with its own secret purpose, maliciously beyond the window in the pale glow of the lamplight.

Then, unexpectedly, there was noise from the hall, opening of doors, a rush of feet, a pause, and then in clear, beautiful

oices the well-known strains of " Good King Wenceslas." It
vas the Cathedral choir-boys on their regular Christmas
ound. This was Christmas Eve. They always came just at
his hour on Christmas Eve.

With an intense, almost incredible relief she turned back
nto the hall. At the same moment her husband came out of
he study. They stood together, smiling at the little group
f muffiered, be-coated boys who were singing, heart and
oul in the job, so that the old house simply rang with their
nelody.

Reassured by the warmth and human company, she lost her
error. It had been her imagination. Of late she had been
one too well. That was why she had been so irritable.
)ld Dr. Bernard was no good: he d¹dn't understand her
ase at all. After Christmas she would go to London and
ave the very best advice. . . .

Had she been well she could not, half an hour ago, have
hown such miserable temper over nothing. She knew that
t was over nothing, and yet that knowledge did not make
t any easier for her to restrain herself. After every bout of
emper she told herself that there should never be another
—and then Herbert said something irritating, one of his
illy, muddle-headed stupid¹ties, and she was off again!

She could see now as she stood beside him at the bottom of
he staircase that he was still feeling it. She had certainly
alf an hour ago said some abominably rude personal things
—things that she had not meant at all—and he had taken them
n his meek, quiet way. Were he not so meek and qu¹et,
id he only pay her back in her own coin, she would never
ose her temper. Of that she was sure.

But who wouldn't be irritated by that meekness and by the
nly reproachful thing that he ever said to her: " Elinor
nderstood me better, my dear "? To throw the first wife up
gainst the second! Wasn't that the most tactless thing that
man could possibly do? And Elinor, that worn, elderly
oman, the very opposite of her own gay, bright, amusing
elf? That was why Herbert had loved her, because she was
ay and bright and young. It was true that Elinor had been
evoted, that she had been so utterly wrapped up in Herbert
hat she lived only for him. People were always recalling her
evotion, which was sufficiently rude and tactless of them.

Well, she could not give anyone that kind of old-fashioned

sugary devotion ; it wasn't in her, and Herbert knew it by thi
time.

Nevertheless, she loved Herbert in her own way, as h
must know, know it so well that he ought to pay no attention
to the bursts of temper. She wasn't well. She would se
a doctor in London. . . .

The little boys finished their carols, were properly re
warded, and tumbled like feathery birds out into the snov
again. They went into the study, the two of them, and
stood beside the big open log-fire. She put her hand up and
stroked his thin, beautiful cheek.

" I'm so sorry to have been cross just now, Bertie. I didn'
mean half I said, you know."

But he didn't, as he usually did, kiss her and tell her tha
it didn't matter. Looking straight in front of him, h
answered :

" Well, Alice, I do wish you wouldn't. It hurts, horribly. I
upsets me more than you think. And it's growing on you
You make me miserable. I don't know what to do abou
it. And it's all about nothing."

Irritated at not receiving the usual commendation for he
sweetness in making it up again, she withdrew a little an
answered :

" Oh, all right. I've said I'm sorry. I can't do any more."

" But tell me," he insisted, " I want to know. What make
you so angry, so suddenly—and about nothing at all?"

She was about to let her anger rise, her anger at hi
obtuseness, obstinacy, when some fear checked her, a strang
unanalysed fear, as though someone had whispered to he
" Look you! This is the last time!"

" It's not altogether my own fault," she answered, an
left the room.

She stood in the cold hall, wondering where to go. Sh
could feel the snow falling outside the house and shivered
She hated the snow, she hated the winter, this beastly col
dark English winter, that went on and on, only at last t
change into a damp, soggy English spring.

When she urged Herbert to winter abroad—which he coul
quite easily do—he answered her impatiently ; he had th
strongest affection for this poky dead-and-alive Cathedra
town. The Cathedral seemed to be precious to him ; h
wasn't happy if he didn't go and see it every day! Sh

wouldn't wonder if he didn't think more of the Cathedral than he did of herself. Elinor had been the same; she had even written a little book about the Cathedral, about the Black Bishop's Tomb and the stained glass and the rest. . . .

What was the Cathedral after all? Only a building!

She was standing in the drawing-room looking out over the dusky ghostly snow to the great hulk of the Cathedral that Herbert said was like a flying ship, but to herself was more like a crouching beast licking its lips over the miserable sinners that it was for ever devouring.

As she looked and shivered, feeling that in spite of herself her temper and misery were rising so that they threatened to choke her, it seemed to her that her bright and cheerful firelit drawing-room was suddenly open to the snow. It was exactly as though cracks had appeared everywhere, in the ceiling, the walls, the windows, and that through these cracks the snow was filtering, dribbling in little tracks of wet down the walls, already perhaps making pools of water on the carpet.

This was, of course, imagination, but it was a fact that the room was most dreadfully cold, although a great fire was burning and it was the cosiest room in the house.

Then, turning, she saw the figure standing by the door. This time there could be no mistake. It was a grey shadow, and yet a shadow with form and outline—the untidy grey hair, the pale face like a moonlit leaf, the long grey clothes, and something obstinate, vindictive, terribly menacing in its pose.

She moved and the figure was gone; there was nothing there and the room was warm again, quite hot, in fact. But young Mrs. Ryder, who had never feared anything in all her life, save the vanishing of her youth, was trembling so that she had to sit down, and even then her trembling did not cease. Her hand shook on the arm of her chair.

She had created this thing out of her imagination of Elinor's hatred of her and her own hatred of Elinor.

It was true that they had never met, but who knew but that the spiritualists were right, and Elinor's spirit, jealous of Herbert's love for her, had been there driving them apart, forcing her to lose her temper and then hating her for losing it? Such things might be! But she had not much time for speculation. She was preoccupied with her fear. It was a definite, positive fear, the kind of fear that one has just before one goes under an operation. Someone or something was threatening her. She clung to her chair as though to leave it were to plunge into disaster.

She longed for Herbert to come and protect her. She felt most kindly to him. She would never lose her temper with him again—and at that same moment some cold voice seemed to whisper in her ear: "You had better not. It will be for the last time."

At length she found courage to rise, cross the room and go up to dress for dinner. In her bedroom courage came to her once more. It was certainly cold, and the snow, as she could see when she looked between her curtains, was falling more heavily than ever, but she had a warm bath, sat in front of her fire and was sensible again.

For many months this odd sense that she was watched and accompanied by someone hostile to her had been growing. It was stronger perhaps because of the things that Herbert told her about Elinor; she was the kind of woman, he said, who, once she loved anyone, would never relinquish her grasp; she was utterly faithful. He implied that her tenacious fidelity had been at times a little difficult.

"She always said," he added once, "that she would watch over me until I rejoined her in the next world. Poor Elinor!" he sighed. "She had a fine religious faith, stronger than mine, I fear."

It was always after one of her tantrums that young Mrs. Ryder had been most conscious of this hallucination, this dreadful discomfort of feeling that someone was near you who hated you—but it was only during the last week that she began to fancy that she actually saw anyone, and with every day her sense of this figure had grown stronger.

It was, of course, only nerves, but it was one of those nervous afflictions that became tiresome indeed if you did not rid yourself of it. Mrs. Ryder, secure now in the warmth and intimacy of her bedroom, determined that henceforth everything should be sweetness and light. No more tempers! Those were the things that did her harm.

Even though Herbert were a little trying, was not that the case with every husband in the world? And was it not Christmas time? Peace and Good Will to men! Peace and Good Will to Herbert!

They sat down opposite to one another in the pretty little

lining-room hung with Chinese woodcuts, the table gleaming nd the amber curtains richly dark in the firelight.

But Herbert was not himself. He was still brooding, she upposed, over their quarrel of the afternoon. Weren't men hildren? Incredible the children that they were!

ɔ when the maid was out of the room she went over to im, bent down and kissed his forehead.

" Darling . . . you're still cross. I can see you are . You ustn't be. Really, you mustn't. It's Christmas time, and f I forgive you, you must forgive me."

" You forgive me?" he asked, looking at her in his most ggravating way. " What have you to forgive me for?"

Well, that was really too much. When she had taken all the teps, humbled her pride.

She went back to her seat, but for a while could not answer im because the maid was there. When they were alone gain, she said, summoning all her patience:

" Bertie, dear, do you really think that there's anything to e gained by sulking like this? It isn't worthy of you. It n't, really."

He answered her quietly:

" Sulking? No, that's not the right word. But I've got to eep quiet. If I don't I shall say something I'm sorry for." hen, after a pause, in a low voice, as though to himself: These constant rows are awful."

Her temper was rising again, another self that had nothing ɔ do with her real self, a stranger to her and yet a very ld familiar friend.

" Don't be so self-righteous," she answered, her voice embling a little. " These quarrels are entirely my own ault, aren't they?"

" Elinor and I never quarrelled," he said, so softly that she carcely heard him.

" No! Because Elinor thought you perfect. She adored ou. You've often told me. I don't think you perfect. I'm ot perfect either. But we've both got faults. I'm not the nly one to blame."

" We'd better separate," he said suddenly, looking up. We don't get on now. We used to. I don't know what's hanged everything. But, as things are, we'd better separate."

She looked at him and knew that she loved him more than

ever, but because she loved him so much she wanted to
hurt him, and because he had said that he thought he could
get on without her she was so angry that she forgot all caution.
Her love and her anger helped one another. The more
angry she became the more she loved him.

"I know why you want to separate," she said. "It's
because you're in love with someone else. ('How funny'
something inside her said. 'You don't mean a word of this.')
You've treated me as you have, and then you leave me."

"I'm not in love with anyone else," he answered her
steadily, "and you know it. But we are so unhappy together
that it's silly to go on ... silly. The whole thing has failed."

There was so much unhappiness, so much bitterness, in his
voice that she realised that at last she had truly gone too far.
She had lost him. She had not meant this. She was frightened,
and her fear made her so angry that she went across to him.

"Very well, then ... I'll tell everyone ... what you've
been. How you've treated me."

"Not another scene," he answered wearily. "I can't
stand any more. Let's wait. To-morrow is Christmas
Day ..."

He was so unhappy that her anger with herself maddened
her. She couldn't bear his sad, hopeless disappointment with
herself, their life together, everything.

In a fury of blind temper she struck him ; it was as though
she were striking herself. He got up and without a word
left the room. There was a pause, and then she heard
the hall door close. He had left the house.

She stood there, slowly coming to her control again. When
she lost her temper it was as though she sank under water.
When it was all over she came once more to the surface of
life, wondering where she'd been and what she had been
doing. Now she stood there, bewildered, and then at once she
was aware of two things, one that the room was bitterly
cold and the other that someone was in the room with her.

This time she did not need to look around her. She did not
turn at all, but only stared straight at the curtained window,
seeing them very carefully, as though she were summing them
up for some future analysis, with their thick amber folds, gold
rod, white lines—and beyond them the snow was falling.

She did not need to turn, but, with a shiver of terror, she
was aware that that grey figure who had, all these last

weeks, been approaching ever more closely, was almost at her very elbow. She heard quite clearly: " I warned you. That was the last time."

At the same moment Onslow the butler came in. Onslow was broad, fat, and rubicund—a good faithful butler with a passion for church music.

He was undisturbed, his ceremonial complacency clothed him securely.

" Mr. Ryder has gone out," she said firmly. Oh, surely he must see something, feel something.

" Yes, madam!" Then smiling rather grandly: " It's snowing hard. Never seen it harder here. Shall I build up the fire in the drawing-room, madam?"

" No, thank you. But Mr. Ryder's study . . ."

" Yes, madam. I only thought that as this room was so warm you might find it chilly in the drawing-room."

This room warm, when she was shivering from head to foot; but holding herself lest he should see . . . She longed to keep him there, to implore him to remain; but in a moment he was gone, softly closing the door behind him.

Then a mad longing for flight seized her, and she could not move. She was rooted there to the floor, and even as, wildly trying to cry, to scream, to shriek the house down, she found that only a little whisper would come, she felt the cold touch of a hand on hers.

She did not turn her head: her whole personality, all her past life, her poor little courage, her miserable fortitude were summoned to meet this sense of approaching death, which was as unmistakable as a certain smell, or the familiar ringing of a gong. She had dreamt in nightmares of approaching death, and it had always been like this, a fearful constriction of the heart, a paralysis of the limbs, a choking sense of disaster like an anaesthetic.

" You were warned," something said to her again.

She knew that if she turned she would see Elinor's face, set, white, remorseless. The woman had always hated her, been vilely jealous of her, protecting her wretched Herbert.

A certain vindictiveness seemed to release her. She found that she could move, her limbs were free.

She passed to the door, ran down the passage into the hall. Where would she be safe? She thought of the Cathedral, where to-night there was a carol service. She opened the hall door and, just as she was, meeting the thick, involving, muffling snow, she ran out.

She started across the green towards the Cathedral door. Her thin black slippers sank in the snow. Snow was everywhere—in her hair, her eyes, her nostrils, her mouth, on her bare neck between her breasts.

"Help! Help! Help!" she wanted to cry, but the snow choked her. Lights whirled about her. The Cathedral rose like a huge black eagle and flew towards her.

She fell forward, and even as she fell, a hand, far colder than the snow, caught her neck. She lay struggling in the snow, and as she struggled there two hands of an icy fleshless chill closed about her throat.

Her last knowledge was of the hard outline of a ring pressing into her neck. Then she lay still, her face in the snow, and the flakes eagerly, savagely covered her.

CARLTON'S FATHER

Eric Ambrose

My friendship with John Carlton was never bound by very strong ties. He was about twelve when we first met, and I, although two years his senior, always lagged far behind him in class.

Yet, until he came, I automatically headed the lists and I suppose really I should have been jealous of him, but he was physically weak and my feeling of superiority led me to protect him from the bullying of others whom I disliked, so that he came to be looked upon as my protégé. He was likeable enough, did my prep when I felt lazy—which was pretty often after I'd been made a prefect—and during those last few months, when I was beginning to realise that play days were drawing to a close, extraordinarily interesting.

He told me once, on one of those rare occasions when he unburdened his inner thoughts—the result of some particular cruelty on the part of a master—that his father was a scientist. I think it was the extraordinary way in which his face lit up as he spoke of his father which aroused my curiosity, and not so much the subject, which seemed to suggest that if his father was a genius he was also a crank. He never talked to me about him again after that.

It is no exaggeration to say that young Carlton, at the age of sixteen, possessed a knowledge of physics and chemistry far in advance of any of his teachers. If a master or demonstrator was temporarily at a loss for a word Carlton could, and did, supply it, usually to his own detriment.

He was not popular with the staff. There were occasions when he would argue with them about established beliefs and, whether he was right or wrong, his powers of argument were superior to theirs, so that they sought means of arresting those powers and, being schoolmasters, they did not have far to seek.

Personally, I liked to listen to him because he was always so convincing, however outrageous the premises of his

argument might be, and always as I listened to him I thought
of the father whom he worshipped as a demi-God. That was
why I asked him to stay with me during my last summer
holidays, expecting in return a similar invitation to his home
when I should meet his father. The invitation was not forth-
coming, and I felt slighted. It wasn't that the fellow couldn't
afford to entertain—he was always amply supplied with funds
—nor did he ever pretend to excuse the omission.

I remember just before the last Founder's Day I asked him
whether his father was coming. He was definitely uncomfortable then and said that his father was a busy man and could
not leave his work. Then I tried a shot in the dark. "Well,
why don't the other members of your family come—your
sister or your mother?"

Of course, only an important schoolboy would have asked
a question like that, and I could see that he was hurt. "I
haven't a sister," he said, but he didn't mention his mother and
and I thought it must have been as I suspected, that she was
dead.

When I left school I went to London, into my father's
office. Then the war came and I was fortunate enough to
come through unscathed. Afterwards I got a County Surveyor's
job and went to live at Spelford. Of course I had forgotten
all about Carlton by that time—in fact when I did see his
name I never connected it with the precocious schoolboy I
had known.

We, that is, my department, had condemned a group of
farmhouses, for structural reasons, and it appeared that the
group was Carlton's property. I had not seen the places
myself, but judging from my assistant's report, they were
pretty bad.

He recognised me as soon as he came into the room, and I
thought he looked mightily relieved. For my part, I resolved
to give him the benefit of my experience, but to keep
rigidly to my duty—I had given the fellow too much in
the past without his appreciating the fact.

Our conversation was cordial enough. We chatted about
old times and those whom we had seen and those whom we
had not, those who had succeeded and those who had
failed. He himself, he told me, had become a physicist and,
although he had published little, one day he would startle the

world, and that day was not far off . . . and so on and so forth.

Frankly, I was disappointed when I heard him talking like that because I felt that he was a greater failure than all those others we had discussed, because his potentialities which had seemed so great were now proved to be merely the reflection of precocious eccentricity.

But at last he came to the subject of his call. He wanted me to realise that the premises were old, almost of historic interest, and even if my assistant had reported an overhang of four inches on some walls, they were in no way dangerous. Oh yes, he understood all about the "middle third" and although he had not calculated it in this case, he knew quite definitely that the structure hadn't moved within the last twenty years. However dry the summer had been, it was absurd to suggest that there had been a settlement, because it would have shown itself on the inside; wouldn't it?

I had always possessed a great respect for his oratorical powers and his ability to start from a fallacy and then argue logically, to prove you finally and utterly wrong. Experience had taught me that to take up the trend and answer him was fatal. Besides, tucked away in the back of my mind was the memory that years before I had wanted to see this place of his and now, strange irony, I was to be almost the sole arbiter as to whether or not its structure should be razed to the ground.

"I'll come and lunch with you to-morrow," I said, "and we'll examine the parts which you say are unaffected."

"You mean, you'll want to see inside," he said.

"Yes, if it's convenient."

He hesitated ever so slightly, "I suppose it will be necessary?"

"I don't know about it being necessary, it may be quite useless," I said bluntly.

He hesitated again, as though not quite sure whether to leave matters as they were or take me into his confidence. "You see, MacIre," he said, "it's not myself I'm worrying about—but my father is engaged on some very delicate experiments, and I don't want him worried."

"Your father still alive!" I said, and apologised. "You see I never imagined"—and my voice trailed off in embarrassment.

"Yes, he is still alive, with my elder brother "—then he bit his lip—very noticeably, because he was angry at what he imagined to be an indiscretion.

But now there was a guard upon my tongue. I did not want to offend him, and it was obvious that he was hurt. I remembered at school he had never answered my query about his mother. "To-morrow," I said, "at lunch."

The next day I arrived punctually at Carlton's place. I had brought more instruments than I needed, but he had always overawed me by his use of scientific apparatus and this was where I was going to get my own back.

A glance at the building showed that I had a good case. If only the ass had made some attempt to tie in the bulges he might have had grounds on which to base his protest. But once *inside* the building, my sympathies veered round a little towards him. The interior certainly was worth while preserving.

There was a man to serve at table, and a girl who brought in the food. After all, I felt, if the man could afford to live in some sort of syle, he could afford to rebuild a few bulging walls, even if it did cost a little more to preserve the character of the place.

Only the two of us sat down to eat. "Your father isn't here?" I asked, and I think he must have detected the note of disappointment in my voice. At least *one* of the reasons for my presence there had been the hope of meeting his father.

He answered my question casually—except that he did not look at me—rather like an actor saying his lines to his dresser before a first-night—" No, they don't eat here. As a matter of fact they live in their own house—over there," and he pointed through the open window to a large, gabled, barn-like affair.

The meal was good enough, and the wine execrable. I complimented him on both, took his proffered cigar and came straight to the point. "Let's see that wall, Carlton."

So two of his men held the ladder and I plumbed the wall. I made a mental note to speak pretty sharply to Barter, my assistant. One part bulged five and three-eighths inches!

I was quite blunt with Carlton—there was no hope of saving the front—he'd have to pull the whole lot down, provide new foundations if he wanted to rebuild it, and that went for part of the flank also.

He took it quite differently from what I had expected. " If it's got to be done, MacIre, then it will be done. I'd like to leave the whole thing in your hands if it's permissible."

I told him it was, and gave him the name of a fairly honest builder.

" What will it cost?" he asked. It was the first time I had ever heard him mention money.

" About £350."

" Very good," he replied.

" But that's not all." He looked up at me—I had always been a good three inches taller than he—" Not all?" and now his face was a pale sickly colour.

" No, there's the other place where your father lives."

I knew he thought that he himself had drawn my attention to the place during dinner.

He did not answer, but just stood looking at me as though trying to make out what I was thinking—what my attitude towards him was.

" I'll have to plumb it," I said. I was feeling uncomfortable beneath his gaze. His eyes never left me as I had the ladder adjusted and got one of the men to hold the plumb aloft. I measured the overhang.

" It's five inches," I told him.

He said nothing.

" I can't pass it, you know."

He opened his mouth and seemed to have difficulty in speaking. " It's a historic building."

" Then you'd better protect it by rebuilding this front and the corner-returns. You can re-use the old bricks."

There was dead silence. He looked a picture of misery.

" Is it a question of money?" I asked, knowing perfectly well that it wasn't.

" Tell me, MacIre," he said after a long pause, " why do you have to condemn a building?"

" Because it is a danger to those people living in it, or likely to pass by it."

" And to which class does this belong?"

" Both."

" The walls are bulged, they can only fall outwards."

" That is probable."

" I will build piers against them."

" You couldn't make a proper job of it—the bulge is too big and there are several nasty cracks."

" I would build a continuous buttress."

That knocked me off my stride for a bit. It was absurd. " There would be a weakness over the windows."

" I would build the buttress over the windows."

I laughed. " Don't be an idiot, Carlton."

" But listen, MacIre, it shows no defect inside."

" Impossible," I said. " With a five-inch bulge! Still I'll have a look at it, then you won't be able to say I wasn't reasonable."

He just stared at me again—that look half of misery, half of interrogation. " Look here, MacIre, that wall won't fall. I'll deposit any sum in the bank you like to name, to cover you. I'll insure you against dismissal, or a claim for negligence."

" I'm sorry, Carlton," I said. " I would if I could—but you're being very childish. Why save that wall (how I wanted to know!) when you can build a new home for your father and brother with the greatest of ease?"

Then his attitude changed. He blustered, he took the strong-man attitude, he tried to do to *me*, what I had prevented others from doing to *him*. It was pitiful because he over-acted.

" I shall appeal to the court," he raved. " I shall bring the finest opinions money can buy. I will make you look a fool."

I could have been dignified then and walked off, but I knew what I wanted. " In that case, Carlton, I shall *have* to examine the inside of the house," I lied. I chuckled inwardly at my astuteness. Would to God that I had not been so clever!

" You cannot come in," he said.

" I have a right of entry," I reminded him, " at any reasonable time."

I felt that it was fully on the cards for him to call the two labourers who had helped with the ladders and order them to throw me off the farm. My position would have been a particularly unpleasant one then, but one never knew just how Carlton would act.

" We'd better go in," he said.

I followed him to the front door of the place, not without a certain trepidation. He took a bunch of keys from his pocket and used two of them before the heavy oak door swung inwards on its hinges. I followed him in.

He switched on the light and shut the door behind us. We were in a completely closed lobby. On one of the side walls two wheels were fixed. He crossed and turned the nearer one, and for a moment or two, I did not realise what was happening. Then I saw that a wall was rising behind us, through the floor, to shut off the oaken door.

It seems strange to me now, that I just watched him and did nothing, but that is what did happen. Then he moved to the second wheel and turned that. Silently the wall in front of us began to drop, revealing a door. I felt as though I were leaving a submarine by means of a flooded chamber.

He unlocked the door, again using two keys, and we passed through.

I do not know which was the greatest surprise—the fact that the hall in which I found myself was brilliantly lit with electric candelabra in the middle of the day ; or the fact that there was no sign of a door or window in the bare smooth walls ; or the two people who were in the hall.

One of the figures rose as we entered and came towards us. That was another surprise. You see, I had understood Carlton to refer to his *elder* brother, but this person was a mere youth of eleven or twelve, except that the eyes possessed a shrewdness one would not ordinarily associate with a child.

The boy caught sight of me, took a step backwards, and his mouth dropped open. He turned to Carlton, and I could see that there was anger in those shrewd eyes, but he did not speak.

Carlton advanced into the centre of the room and I followed him. I could see a second figure with its back towards us, reading.

At the sound of our footsteps, the seated figure rose and turned towards us.

That was another surprise. You see I had expected to see Carlton's father—a venerable old man with a long beard but he was a young man, tall and slim, no older than thirty.

And then I really did become afraid. It was he, Carlton, who had lied to me, and lured me into this place and not vice versa. I had been tricked. His whole attitude that afternoon had hardly been that of a normal, sane man, and I shivered as I thought what it might mean.

But however vague my fear had been, it took definite shape when Carlton addressed the young man. I was then certain beyond any doubt that I was dealing with a maniac.

"Father," he said, "this is the surveyor who has come to see our outer structure. I had to ask him in—because the law is on his side and it was the last hope."

The young man looked at me, and his look was not unkindly, but his words in answer to Carlton turned the fear that was upon me into something akin to terror.

"The law," he said, "well, well, well. But to which law does he refer?"

Nobody moved. "But there isn't anything wrong with the structure, is there, John—how can there be, eh, son?" and he laughed.

I could think of only one thing. No one knew where I was, I had not troubled to tell even Barter, and here I was with a group of people, one of whom wanted to support a brick wall with a continuous pier running over the windows and another who believed he was the father of a man at least ten years his senior. If there hadn't been the thought of those secret surrounding walls, I think my sense of humour might have come to the rescue.

I jumped as my sleeve was jerked. "My father is talking to you," said Carlton. I apologised. It was essential that I should humour these people.

"The walls are perfectly sound, you can see that. They have to be, or else the insulation would be useless. You *must* see that . . ."

Carlton interrupted him. "I have told him nothing father."

The "father" looked surprised. "Cannot you trust him?"

"I thought he was my friend. We were at school together —you remember E. B. MacIre?"

The young man smiled and looked at me. "Of course I do. There was a MacIre who was very good to you . . . invited you to his home during the holidays and protected you from the bullies. You wanted to bring him home, here . . . remember, but that was impossible after we died."

I fell on my knees. I had always imagined myself a courageous man, but now before these people I was a craven.

"Let me go," I implored, "only let me go, I will not touch your farm."

"Get off your knees," said Carlton. "This isn't the MacIre I knew, the MacIre who was slightly contemptuous of fear and physical weakness."

But I could not rise. I just remained there, sweating, incapable of movement except for the chattering of my teeth, and the trembling in my palsied body. They helped me to rise and put me in a chair.

"Listen to me," said Carlton. "You have promised to spare the farm, but I am sorry, I do not believe you. The first thing you would do would be to communicate with the medical officer of health and try to put us all in an asylum. Oh yes, you would, even though you may not intend to at the moment. But you would not succeed. You see this *is* my father and this *is* my brother, and they *are* both dead, dead, do you understand? My mother, too, is dead, but she is not here . . . she . . . she is dead, too . . . but she is not here."

No one spoke. We all watched Carlton—the boy with his lips tightly drawn, the "father" smiling slightly.

"You heard my father say this room is insulated. It *is* insulated, insulated against something that is not material, not even spiritual. It is insulated against a dimension . . . against Time itself. For those who are in this room the wheel of Time does not turn, there is duration but no Time. I cannot expect you to understand that."

Then something within me broke the spell. "You cannot insulate against Time," I cried, "not in a stationary system. You would have to travel with the speed of light and that is impossible, because the Lorentz transformation formula shows . . ." and I jabbered on to prove to him that he was raving.

Carlton waited till I was finished. "You are wrong as usual, MacIre. This room is outside the ordinary four dimensions of space and time. My father constructed this room when he was a young man. He was ready to give his secret to the world when the accident, the tragedy occurred . . ." He paused for a moment.

"They were riding in a car, in the early days of motoring.

I was only eleven years old, but I had spent much time in this room with my father and people called me precocious.

"They brought back my father and brother. They brought back my mother, too. I ordered the servants to take them to this place. They obeyed me because they thought I was soon to be the head of the household.

"The doctor who came said he could do nothing. I watched him, silently, noting his surprise when he saw that my brother and my father did not die. My mother, you see, was already dead. . . .

"Then, I said to the doctor, ' please operate.' I know he thought it was hopeless, but because the bodies grew no older, no germs multiplied, and no poison spread, he operated and they lived. For them, the time in this room has remained February 17th, 1907. If they go from here, it is death, death as you understand it, and they will be unable to return to this dimension, the fifth dimension of a space—time—universe — in the second dimension of Time. That is why you must not disturb the fabric of this barn, lest you injure the insulation within."

"I understand," I said.

"I thought you would," said Carlton.

I got up from the chair. "Now that I understand, I will see that you are not molested." Once more I saw a way of escaping from these lunatics. "I think I had better be going."

I saw him look at the others and I did not like the look.

"I shall come and visit you, perhaps, in a few weeks' time."

Still there was silence. "Will you please open the door?"

"You cannot go," said Carlton.

I took up a menacing attitude. My courage seemed to have returned. "Why not?"

"Because if you go outside, you will die."

I laughed uneasily. "I'll take the risk."

"But I won't," said Carlton. "You see they might hang me for murder. Tell me honestly, did you enjoy the wine at lunch?"

"It was horrible," I said, smiling at his delightfully inconsequential remark.

"That was because I poisoned it. You see, whilst time

oes not exist in this room time rolls on outside. Actually
ou died about seven minutes ago, according to my calcula-
ons."

I laughed, roared with laughter, genuine, hysterical laughter.
o mad were they that I had almost become convinced
y their talk.

"You will write a letter to Barter, your assistant, and
ell him he is not to worry about the walls here."

"Certainly," I said. So I wrote: "You need not trouble
bout the wall here as it is only four and a half inches out of
lumb." I signed it. I knew that as soon as Barter got that
ote he would suspect either that I was crazy, and search for
ne here, or foul play.

According to Carlton that was "three weeks" ago. It is a
trange thing that I do not want to escape from this place
ny more, but many strange things have happened. My
vatch ticks but does not "go." They allowed me to shave on
vhat seemed to be the second day, but my beard has not
rown since. I have eaten nothing since I have been here.
'hey say that it is because there is no Time, only duration
ere. I spend my duration either in reading or listening
o Carlton's father. They cannot have given Barter the note
et or he would have come here. They tell me I am dead, so
suppose it doesn't matter much, what happens.

                                        E. B. MacIre.

he above document was sent to me by a gentleman who
ound it between the leaves of a volume of *Encyclopaedia
ritannica* which he purchased in a second-hand book shop.
: is without doubt in the handwriting of Esor B. MacIre, who
·as my superior until his disappearance in 1934.

I found it very interesting reading, but hardly what I would
ave expected from the very sober County Surveyor. However,
: serves one purpose—it strengthens the theory that I gave to
ne police, when MacIre disappeared, that he had overworked
nd was still living in the district. He probably saw the
ccount in the local paper of the three male skeletons we
iscovered when we pulled down Carlton's Barn. Carlton
imself was never found, he probably murdered the three. It
·as a strange place, that barn.

There is one point, however, which still worries me. The

Encyclopaedia Britannica, in which the document was found
bore the name " Harold Carlton," written in faded ink.

I must admit that it seems strange that MacIre, who was
probably unbalanced, should have taken the trouble to attend
to such a small detail. Still, the ways of a madman, and I am
convinced that MacIre was such, are strange and beyond
understanding.

A SCHOOL STORY

M. R. James

Two men in a smoking-room were talking of their private-school days. "At *our* school," said A., "we had a ghost's foot-mark on the staircase. What was it like? Oh, very unconvincing. Just the shape of a shoe, with a square toe, if I remember right. The staircase was a stone one. I never heard any story about the thing. That seems odd, when you come to think of it. Why didn't somebody invent one, I wonder?"

"You can never tell with little boys. They have a mythology of their own. There's a subject for you, by the way—'The Folklore of Private Schools'."

"Yes; the crop is rather scanty, though. I imagine, if you were to investigate the cycle of ghost stories, for instance, which the boys at private schools tell each other, they would all turn out to be highly compressed versions of stories out of books."

"Nowadays, the fiction magazines would be extensively drawn upon."

"No doubt; they weren't born or thought of in *my* time. Let's see. I wonder if I can remember the staple ones that I was told. First, there was the house with a room in which a series of people insisted on passing a night; and each of them in the morning was found kneeling in a corner, and had just time to say, 'I've seen it,' and died."

"Wasn't that the house in Berkeley Square?"

"I dare say it was. Then there was the man who heard a noise in the passage at night, opened his door, and saw someone crawling towards him on all fours with his eye hanging out on his cheek. There was besides, let me think —yes! the room where a man was found dead in bed with a horseshoe mark on his forehead, and the floor under the bed was covered with marks of horseshoes also; I don't know why. Also there was the lady who, on locking her bedroom door in a strange house heard a thin voice among the bed-curtains say, 'Now we're shut in for the night.' None of

those had any explanation or sequel. I wonder if they go on
still, those stories."

"Oh, likely enough—with additions from the magazines, as
I said. You never heard, did you, of a real ghost at a
private school? I thought not; nobody has that ever I came
across."

"From the way in which you said that, I gather that
you have."

"I really don't know; but this is what was in my mind.
It happened at my private school thirty odd years ago, and I
haven't any explanation of it.

"The school I mean was near London. It was established
in a large and fairly old house—a great white building with
very fine grounds about it; there were large cedars in the
garden, as there are in so many of the older gardens in
the Thames valley, and ancient elms in the three or four
fields which we used for our games. I think probably it was
quite an attractive place, but boys seldom allow that their
schools possess any tolerable features.

"I came to the school in a September, soon after the
year 1870; and among the boys who arrived on the same
day was one whom I took to: a Highland boy, whom I
will call McLeod. I needn't spend time in describing him: the
main thing is that I got to know him very well. He was not
an exceptional boy in any way—not particularly good at books
or games—but he suited me.

"The school was a large one: there must have been from a
hundred and twenty to a hundred and thirty boys there as
a rule, and so a considerable staff of masters was required
and there were rather frequent changes among them.

"One term—perhaps it was my third or fourth—a new
master made his appearance. His name was Sampson. He
was a tallish, stoutish, pale, black-bearded man. I think we
liked him: he had travelled a good deal, and had stories
which amused us on our school walks, so that there was
some competition among us to get within earshot of him.
remember, too—dear me, I have hardly thought of it since
then!—that he had a charm on his watch-chain that attracted
my attention one day, and he let me examine it. It was,
now suppose, a gold Byzantine coin; there was an effigy of
some absurd emperor on one side; the other side had been

worn practically smooth, and he had cut on it—rather barbarously—his own initials, G.W.S., and a date, July 24, 1865. Yes, I can see it now: he told me he had picked it up in Constantinople: it was about the size of a florin, perhaps rather smaller.

"Well, the first odd thing that happened was this. Sampson was doing Latin grammar with us. One of his favourite methods—perhaps it is good one—was to make us construct sentences out of our own heads to illustrate the rules he was trying to make us learn. Of course, that is a thing which gives a silly boy a chance of being impertinent: there are lots of school stories in which that happens—or, anyhow, there might be. But Sampson was too good a disciplinarian for us to think of trying that on with him. Now, on this occasion he was telling us how to express *remembering* in Latin: and he ordered us each to make a sentence bringing in the verb *memini*, 'I remember.' Well, most of us made up some ordinary sentence such as, 'I remember my father,' or 'He remembers his book,' or something equally uninteresting: and I dare say a good many put down *memino librum meum*, and so forth: but the boy I mentioned—McLeod —was evidently thinking of something more elaborate than that. The rest of us wanted to have our sentences passed, and get on to something else, so some kicked him under the desk, and I, who was next to him, poked him and whispered to him to look sharp. But he didn't seem to attend. I looked at his paper and saw he had put down nothing at all. So I jogged him again harder than before and upbraided him sharply for keeping us all waiting. That did have some effect. He started and seemed to wake up, and then very quickly scribbled about a couple of lines on his paper, and showed it up with the rest.

"As it was the last, or nearly the last, to come in, and as Sampson had a good deal to say to the boys who had written *meminiscimus patri meo* and the rest of it, it turned out that the clock struck twelve before he got to McLeod, and McLeod had to wait afterwards to have his sentence corrected. There was nothing much going on outside when I got out, so I waited for him to come. He came very slowly when he did arrive, and I guessed there had been some sort of trouble. 'Well,' I said, 'what did you get?' 'Oh, I don't know,' said McLeod, 'nothing much: but I think Sampson's rather sick with me.' 'Why, did you show him up some rot?' 'No fear,' he said. 'It was all right as far as I could see; it was like this: *Memento*—that's right enough for remember, and it takes a genitive—*memento putei inter quatuor taxos.*' 'What silly rot! What made you shove that down? What does it mean?' 'That's the funny part,' said McLeod. 'I'm not quite sure what it does mean. All I know is it just came into my head and I corked it down. I know what I *think* it means, because just before I wrote it down I had a sort of picture of it in my head; I believe it means "Remember the well among the four"—what are those dark sort of trees that have red berries on them?' 'Mountain ashes, I s'pose you mean.' 'I never heard of them,' said McLeod; 'no—*I'll tell you*—yews.' 'Well, and what did Sampson say?' 'Why, he was jolly odd about it. When he read it he got up and went to the mantelpiece and stopped quite a long time without saying anything, with his back to me. And then he said, without turning round, and rather quietly, 'What do you suppose that means?' I told him what I thought; only I couldn't remember the name of the silly tree: and then he wanted to know why I put it down, and I had to say something or other. And after that he left off talking about it, and asked me how long I'd been here, and where my people lived, and things like that: and then I came away: but he wasn't looking a bit well.'

"I don't remember any more that was said by either of us about this. Next day McLeod took to his bed with a chill or something of the kind, and it was a week or more before he was in school again. And as much as a month went by without anything happening that was noticeable. Whether or not Mr. Sampson was really startled, as McLeod had thought, he didn't show it. I am pretty sure, of course, now that there was something very curious in his past history, but I'm not going to pretend that we boys were sharp enough to guess any such thing.

"There was one other incident of the same kind as the last which I told you. Several times since that day we had had to make up examples in school to illustrate different rules, but there had never been any row, except when we did them wrong. At last there came a day when we were going through those dismal things which people call conditional sentences, and we were told to make a conditional sentence expressing a future consequence. We did it, right or wrong, and showed up our bits of paper, and Sampson began looking through them. All at once he got up, made some odd sort of noise in his throat, and rushed out by a door that was just by his desk. We sat there for a minute or two and then—I suppose it was incorrect—but we went up, I and one or two others, to look at the papers on his desk. Of course, I thought someone must have put down some nonsense or other, and Sampson had gone off to report him. All the same, I noticed that he hadn't taken any of the papers with him when he ran out. Well, the top paper on the desk was written in red ink—which no one used—and it wasn't in anyone's hand who was in the class. They all looked at it—McLeod and all—and took their dying oaths that it wasn't theirs. Then I thought of counting the bits of paper. And of this I made quite certain: that there were seventeen bits of paper on the desk and sixteen boys in the form. Well, I bagged the extra paper and kept it, and I believe I have it now. And now you will want to know what was written on it. It was simple enough and harmless enough, I should have said.

" ' *Si tu non veneris ad me, ego veniam ad te,*'" which means, I suppose, 'If you don't come to me, I'll come to you'."

" Could you show me the paper?" interrupted the listener.

" Yes, I could: but there's another odd thing about it. That same afternoon I took it out of my locker—I know for certain it was the same bit, for I made a finger-mark on it—and no single trace of writing of any kind was there on it. I kept it, as I said, and since that time I have tried various experiments to see whether sympathetic ink had been used, but absolutely without result.

" So much for that. After about half an hour Sampson looked in again: said he had felt unwell, and told us we might go. He came rather gingerly to his desk, and gave just one look at the uppermost paper: and I suppose he thought he must have been dreaming ; anyhow, he asked no questions.

" That day was a half-holiday, and next day Sampson was in school again, much as usual. That night the third and last incident in my story happened.

" We—McLeod and I—slept in a dormitory at right-angles to the main building. Sampson slept in the main building on the first floor. There was a very bright full moon. At an hour which I can't tell exactly, but probably between one and two, I was woke up by somebody shaking me. It was McLeod, and a nice state of mind he seemed to be in. 'Come,' he said, 'come! There's a burglar getting in through Sampson's window.' As soon as I could speak, I said, 'Well, why not call out and wake everybody up?' 'No, no,' he said. 'I'm not sure who it is. Don't make a row, come and look.' Naturally, I came and looked, and naturally there was no one there. I was cross enough, and should have called McLeod plenty of names, only—I couldn't tell why —it seemed to me that there *was* something wrong, something that made me very glad I wasn't alone to face it. We were still at the window looking out, and as soon as I could, I asked him what he had heard or seen. 'I didn't hear anything at all,' he said, 'but about five minutes before I woke you, I found myself looking out of this window here, and there was a man sitting or kneeling on Sampson's window-sill, and looking in, and I thought he was beckoning.' 'What sort of man?' McLeod wriggled. 'I don't know,' he said, 'but I can tell you one thing—he was beastly thin, and he looked as if he was wet all over, and,' he said, looking round and whispering as if he hardly liked to hear himself, 'I'm not at all sure that he was alive.'

"We went on talking in whispers some time longer, and eventually crept back to bed. No one else in the room woke or stirred the whole time. I believe we did sleep a bit afterward, but we were very cheap next day.

"And next day Mr. Sampson was gone: not to be found: and I believe no trace of him has ever come to light since. In thinking it over, one of the oddest things about it all has seemed to me to be the fact that neither McLeod nor I ever mentioned what we had seen to any third person whatever. Of course, no questions were asked on the subject, and if they had been, I am inclined to believe that we could not have made any answer: we seemed unable to speak about it.

"That is my story," said the narrator. "The only approach to a ghost story connected with a school that I know, but still, I think, an approach to such a thing."

The sequel to this may perhaps be reckoned highly conventional; but a sequel there is, and so it must be produced. There had been more than one listener to the story, and, in the latter part of that same year, or of the next, one such listener was staying at a country house in Ireland.

One evening his host was turning over a drawer full of odds and ends in the smoking-room. Suddenly he put his hand upon a little box. "Now," he said, "you know about old things; tell me what that is." My friend opened the little box and found in it a thin gold chain with an object attached to it. He glanced at the object and then took off his spectacles to examine it more narrowly. "What's the history of this?" he asked. "Odd enough," was the answer. "You know the yew thicket in the shrubbery. Well, a year or two back we were cleaning out the old well that used to be in the clearing here, and what do you suppose we found?"

"Is it possible that you found a body?" said the visitor, with an odd feeling of nervousness.

"We did that; but, what's more, in every sense of the word, we found two."

"Good heavens! Two? Was there anything to show how they got there? Was this thing found with them?"

"It was. Amongst the rags of the clothes that were on one of the bodies. A bad business, whatever the story of it may have been. One body had the arms tight round the other. They must have been there thirty years or more —long enough before we came to this place. You may judge we filled the well up fast enough. Do you make anything of what's cut on that gold coin you have there?"

"I think I can," said my friend, holding it to the light (but he read it without much difficulty); "it seems to be 'G.W.S., July 24, 1865'."

THE WOLVES OF CERNOGRATZ

Saki

" Are there any old legends attached to the castle?" asked
Conrad of his sister. Conrad was a prosperous Hamburg
merchant, but he was the one poetically-dispositioned member
of an eminently practical family.

The Baroness Gruebel shrugged her plump shoulders.

" There are always legends hanging about these old places.
They are not difficult to invent and they cost nothing. In
this case there is a story that when anyone dies in the castle
all the dogs in the village and the wild beasts in the forest
howl the night long. It would not be pleasant to listen
to, would it?"

" It would be weird and romantic," said the Hamburg
merchant.

" Anyhow, it isn't true," said the Baroness complacently ;
" since we bought the place we have had proof that nothing of
the sort happens. When the old mother-in-law died last
spring-time we all listened, but there was no howling. It is
just a story that lends dignity to the place without costing
anything."

" The story is not as you have told it," said Amalie, the
grey old governess. Everyone turned and looked at her in
astonishment. She was wont to sit silent and prim and
faded in her place at table, never speaking unless someone
spoke to her, and there were few who troubled themselves
to make conversation with her. To-day a sudden volubility
had descended on her ; she continued to talk, rapidly and
nervously, looking straight in front of her and seeming to
address no one in particular.

" It is not when *anyone* dies in the castle that the howling is
heard. It was when one of the Cernogratz family died here
that the wolves came from far and near and howled at the
edge of the forest just before the death hour. There were
only a few couple of wolves that had their lairs in this
part of the forest, but at such a time the keepers say there
would be scores of them, gliding about in the shadows and

howling in chorus, and the dogs of the castle and the village and all the farms round would bay and howl in fear and anger at the wolf chorus, and as the soul of the dying one left its body a tree would crash down in the park. That is what happened when a Cernogratz died in his family castle. But for a stranger dying here, of course no wolf would howl and no tree would fall. Oh, no."

There was a note of defiance, almost of contempt, in her voice as she said the last words. The well-fed, much-too-well-dressed Baroness stared angrily at the dowdy old woman who had come forth from her usual and seemly position of effacement to speak so disrespectfully.

" You seem to know quite a lot about the von Cernogratz legends, Fräulein Schmidt," she said sharply; " I did not know that family histories were among the subjects you are supposed to be proficient in."

The answer to her taunt was even more unexpected and astonishing than the conversational outbreak which had provoked it.

"I am a von Cernogratz myself," said the old woman, " that is why I know the family history."

"You a von Cernogratz? You!" came in an incredulous chorus.

"When we became very poor," she explained, " and I had to go out and give teaching lessons, I took another name; I thought it would be more in keeping. But my grandfather spent much of his time as a boy in this castle, and my father used to tell me many stories about it, and of course, I knew all the family legends and stories. When one has nothing left to one but memories, one guards and dusts them with especial care. I little thought when I took service with you that I should one day come with you to the old home of my family. I could wish it had been anywhere else."

There was silence when she finished speaking, and then the Baroness turned the conversation to a less embarrassing topic than family histories. But afterwards, when the old governess had slipped away quietly to her duties, there arose a clamour of derision and disbelief.

" It was an impertinence," snapped out the Baron, his protruding eyes taking on a scandalised expression; " fancy the woman talking like that at our table. She almost told us we were nobodies, and I don't believe a word of it. She is just Schmidt and nothing more. She has been talking to some of the peasants about the old Cernogratz family, and raked up their history and their stories."

" She wants to make herself out of some consequence," said the Baroness; " she knows she will soon be past work and she wants to appeal to our sympathies. Her grandfather, indeed!"

The Baroness had the usual number of grandfathers, but she never, never boasted about them.

" I dare say her grandfather was a pantry boy or something of the sort in the castle," sniggered the Baron; " that part of the story may be true."

The merchant from Hamburg said nothing; he had seen tears in the old woman's eyes when she spoke of guarding her memories—or, being of an imaginative disposition, he thought he had.

" I shall give her notice to go as soon as the New Year festivities are over," said the Baroness; " till then I shall be too busy to manage without her."

But she had to manage without her all the same, for in the cold biting weather after Christmas, the old governess fell ill and kept to her room.

" It is most provoking," said the Baroness, as her guests sat round the fire on one of the last evenings of the dying year; " all the time that she has been with us I cannot remember that she was ever seriously ill, too ill to go about and do her work, I mean. And now, when I have the house full, and she could be useful in so many ways, she goes and breaks down. One is sorry for her, of course, she looks so withered and shrunken, but it is intensely annoying all the same."

" Most annoying," agreed the banker's wife sympathetically; " it is the intense cold, I expect, it breaks the old people up. It has been unusually cold this year."

" The frost is the sharpest that has been known in December for many years," said the Baron.

" And, of course, she is quite old," said the Baroness; " I wish I had given her notice some weeks ago, then she would have left before this happened to her. Why, Wappi, what is the matter with you?"

The small, woolly lap-dog had leapt suddenly down from its cushion and crept shivering under the sofa. At the same moment an outburst of angry barking came from the dogs in the castle-yard, and other dogs could be heard yapping and barking in the distance.

"What is disturbing the animals?" asked the Baron.

And then the humans, listening intently, heard the sound that had roused the dogs to their demonstrations of fear and rage; heard a long-drawn whining howl, rising and falling, seeming at one moment leagues away, at others sweeping across the snow until it appeared to come from the foot of the castle walls. All the starved, cold misery of a frozen world, all the relentless hunger-fury of the wild, blended with other forlorn and haunting melodies to which one could give no name, seemed concentrated in that wailing cry.

"Wolves!" cried the Baron.

Their music broke forth in one raging burst, seeming to come from everywhere.

"Hundreds of wolves," said the Hamburg merchant, who was a man of strong imagination.

Moved by some impulse which she could not have explained, the Baroness left her guests and made her way to the narrow, cheerless room where the old governess lay watching the hours of the dying year slip by. In spite of the biting cold of the winter night, the window stood open. With a scandalised exclamation on her lips, the Baroness rushed forward to close it.

"Leave it open," said the old woman in a voice that for all its weakness carried an air of command such as the Baroness had never heard before from her lips.

"But you will die of cold!" she expostulated.

"I am dying in any case," said the voice, "and I want to hear their music. They have come from far and wide to sing the death-music of my family. It is beautiful that they have come; I am the last von Cernogratz that will die in our old castle, and they have come to sing to me. Hark, how loud they are calling!"

The cry of the wolves rose on the still winter air and floated round the castle walls in long-drawn piercing wails; the old woman lay back on her couch with a look of long-delayed happiness on her face.

"Go away," she said to the Baroness; "I am not lonely any more I am one of a great old family. . . ."

"I think she is dying," said the Baroness when she had

F.G.G.S.   E rejoined her guests; "I suppose we must send for a doctor. And that terrible howling! Not for much money would I have such death-music."

"That music is not to be bought for any amount of money," said Conrad.

"Hark! What is that other sound?" asked the Baron, as a noise of splitting and crashing was heard.

It was a tree falling in the park.

There was a moment of constrained silence, and then the banker's wife spoke.

"It is the intense cold that is splitting the trees. It is also the cold that has brought the wolves out in such numbers. It is many years since we have had such a cold winter."

The Baroness eagerly agreed that the cold was responsible for these things. It was the cold of the open window, too, which caused the heart failure that made the doctor's ministrations unnecessary for the old Fräulein. But the notice in the newspapers looked very well——

"On December 29th, at Schloss Cernogratz, Amalie von Cernogratz, for many years the valued friend of Baron and Baroness Gruebel."

MAD MONKTON

William Wilkie Collins

CHAPTER I

The Monktons of Wincot Abbey bore a sad character for
want of sociability in our county. They held no friendly
intercourse with their neighbours; and, excepting my father,
and a lady and her daughter living near them, they never
received anyone under their own roof.

Proud as they all certainly were, it was not pride but
dread which kept them thus apart from their neighbours.
The family had suffered for generations past from the
horrible affliction of hereditary insanity, and the members of
it shrank from exposing their calamity to others, as they
must have exposed it if they had mingled with the busy
little world around them. There is a frightful story of a
crime committed in past time by two of the Monktons,
near relatives, from which the first appearance of the insanity
was always supposed to date, but it is needless for me to
shock anyone by repeating it. It is enough to say that at
intervals almost every form of madness appeared in the
family; monomania being the most frequent manifestation of
the affliction among them. I have these particulars, and
one or two yet to be related, from my father.

At the period of my youth but three of the Monktons were
left at the Abbey: Mr. and Mrs. Monkton, and their only
child, Alfred, heir to the property. The one other member of
this, the elder, branch of the family who was then alive, was
Mr. Monkton's younger brother, Stephen. He was an un-
married man, possessing a fine estate in Scotland; but he
lived almost entirely on the Continent, and bore the reputation
of being a shameless profligate. The family at Wincot held
almost as little communication with him as with their
neighbours.

I have already mentioned my father, and a lady and her

daughter, as the only privileged people who were admitted into Wincot Abbey.

My father had been an old school and college friend of Mr. Monkton, and accident had brought them so much together in later life, that their continued intimacy at Wincot was quite intelligible. I am not so well able to account for the friendly terms on which Mrs. Elmslie (the lady to whom I have alluded) lived with the Monktons. Her late husband had been distantly related to Mrs. Monkton, and my father was her daughter's guardian. But even these claims to friendship and regard never seemed to me strong enough to explain the intimacy between Mrs. Elmslie and the inhabitants of the Abbey. Intimate, however, they certainly were, and one result of the constant interchange of visits between the two families in due time declared itself—Mr. Monkton's son and Mrs. Elmslie's daughter became attached to each other.

I had no opportunities of seeing much of the young lady; I only remember her at that time as a delicate, gentle, lovable girl, the very opposite in appearance, and apparently in character also, to Alfred Monkton. But perhaps that was one reason why they fell in love with each other. The attachment was soon discovered, and was far from being disapproved by the parents on either side. In all essential points, except that of wealth, the Elmslies were nearly the equals of the Monktons, and want of money in a bride was of no consequence to the heir of Wincot. Alfred, it was well known, would succeed to thirty thousand a year on his father's death.

Thus, though the parents on both sides thought the young people not old enough to be married at once, they saw no reason why Ada and Alfred should not be engaged to each other, with the understanding that they should be united when young Monkton came of age, in two years' time. The person to be consulted in the matter, after the parents, was my father in his capacity of Ada's guardian. He knew that the family misery had shown itself many years ago in Mrs. Monkton, who was her husband's cousin. The *illness*, as it was significantly called, had been palliated by careful treatment, and was reported to have passed away. But my father was not to be deceived. He knew where the hereditary taint still lurked; he viewed with horror the bare possibility of its reappearing one day in the children of his

friend's only daughter; and he positively refused his consent
to the marriage engagement.

The result was that the doors of the Abbey and the doors of
Mrs. Elmslie's house were closed to him. This suspension of
friendly intercourse had lasted but a very short time, when
Mrs. Monkton died. Her husband, who was fondly attached
to her, caught a violent cold while attending her funeral. The
cold was neglected, and settled on his lungs. In a few
months' time, he followed his wife to the grave, and Alfred
was left master of the grand old Abbey, and the fair lands that
spread all around it.

At this period Mrs. Elmslie had the indelicacy to endeavour
a second time to procure my father's consent to the marriage
engagement. He refused it again more positively than
before. More than a year passed away. The time was
approaching fast when Alfred would be of age. I returned
from college to spend the long vacation at home, and made
some advances towards bettering my acquaintance with
young Monkton. They were evaded—certainly with perfect
politeness, but still in such a way as to prevent me from
offering my friendship to him again. Any mortification I
might have felt at this petty repulse, under ordinary circumstances, was dismissed from my mind by the occurrence of
a real misfortune in our household. For some months past my
father's health had been failing, and, just at the time of which
I am now writing, his sons had to mourn the irreparable
calamity of his death.

This event (through some informality or error in the
late Mr. Elmslie's will) left the future of Ada's life entirely at
her mother's disposal. The consequence was the immediate
ratification of the marriage engagement to which my father
had so steadily refused his consent. As soon as the fact was
publicly announced, some of Mrs. Elmslie's more intimate
friends, who were acquainted with the reports affecting the
Monkton family, ventured to mingle with their former
congratulations one or two significant references to the late
Mrs. Monkton, and some searching inquiries as to the
disposition of her son.

Mrs. Elmslie always met these polite hints with one bold
form of answer. She first admitted the existence of those
reports about the Monktons which her friends were unwilling
to specify distinctly; and then declared that they were

infamous calumnies. The hereditary taint had died out of
the family generations back. Alfred was the best, the
kindest, the sanest of human beings. He loved study and
retirement; Ada sympathised with his tastes, and had made
her choice unbiased; if any more hints were dropped about
sacrificing her by her marriage, those hints would be viewed
as so many insults to her mother, whose affection for her
it was monstrous to call in question. This way of talking
silenced people, but did not convince them. They began to
suspect, what was indeed the actual truth, that Mrs. Elmslie
was a selfish, worldly, grasping woman, who wanted to get
her daughter well married, and cared nothing for consequences
as long as she saw Ada mistress of the greatest establishment
in the whole county.

It seemed, however, as if there was some fatality at work to
prevent the attainment of Mrs. Elmslie's great object in life.
Hardly was one obstacle to the ill-omened marriage removed
by my father's death, before another succeeded it, in the
shape of anxieties and difficulties caused by the delicate state
of Ada's health. Doctors were consulted in all directions, and
the result of their advice was that the marriage must be
deferred, and that Miss Elmslie must leave England for a
certain time, to reside in a warmer climate; the South of
France, if I remember rightly. Thus it happened that just
before Alfred came of age, Ada and her mother departed for
the Continent, and the union of the two young people was
understood to be indefinitely postponed.

Some curiosity was felt in the neighbourhood as to what
Alfred Monkton would do under these circumstances. Would
he follow his lady-love? Would he go yachting? Would he
throw open the doors of the old Abbey at last, and endeavour
to forget the absence of Ada, and the postponement of his
marriage, in a round of gaieties? He did none of these
things. He simply remained at Wincot, living as suspiciously
strange and solitary a life as his father had lived before him.
Literally, there was now no companion for him at the
Abbey but the old priest (the Monktons, I should have
mentioned before, were Roman Catholics) who had held
the office of tutor to Alfred from his earliest years. He came
of age, and there was not even so much as a private dinner-
party at Wincot to celebrate the event. Families in the
neighbourhood determined to forget the offence which his

father's reserve had given them, and invited him to their houses. The invitations were politely declined. Civil visitors called resolutely at the Abbey, and were resolutely bowed away from the doors as soon as they had left their cards. Under this combination of sinister and aggravating circumstances, people in all directions took to shaking their heads mysteriously when the name of Mr. Alfred Monkton was mentioned, hinting at the family calamity, and wondering peevishly or sadly, as their tempers inclined them, what he could possibly do to occupy himself month after month in the lonely old house.

The right answer to this question was not easy to find. It was quite useless, for example, to apply to the priest for it. He was a very quiet, polite old gentleman; his replies were always excessively ready and civil, and appeared at the time to convey a reasonable amount of information; but when they were tested by after-reflection, it was universally observed that nothing tangible could be extracted from them. The housekeeper, a weird old woman, with a very abrupt and repelling manner, was too fierce and taciturn to be safely approached. The few indoor servants had all been long enough in the family to have learnt to hold their tongues in public as a regular habit. It was only from the farm-servants who supplied the table at the Abbey, that any information could be obtained; and vague enough it was when they came to communicate it.

Some of them had observed the "young master" walking about the library with heaps of dusty papers in his hands. Others had heard odd noises in the uninhabited parts of the Abbey, had looked up, and had seen him forcing open the old windows, as if to let light and air into rooms supposed to have been shut close for years and years; or had discovered him standing on the perilous summit of one of the crumbling turrets, never ascended before within their memories, and popularly considered to be inhabited by the ghosts of the monks who had once possessed the building. The result of these observations and discoveries, when they were communicated to others, was of course to impress everyone with a firm belief that "poor young Monkton was going the way that the rest of the family had gone before him": which opinion always appeared to be immensely strengthened in the popular mind by a conviction—founded on no particle of evidence—that the priest was at the bottom of all the mischief.

Thus far I have spoken from hearsay evidence mostly. What I have next to tell will be the result of my own personal experience.

CHAPTER II

About five months after Alfred Monkton came of age I left college, and resolved to amuse and instruct myself a little by travelling abroad.

At the time when I quitted England, young Monkton was still leading his secluded life at the Abbey, and was, in the opinion of everybody, sinking rapidly, if he had not already succumbed, under the hereditary curse of his family. As to the Elmslies, report said that Ada had benefited by her sojourn abroad, and that mother and daughter were on their way back to England to resume their old relations with the heir of Wincot. Before they returned, I was away on my travels, and wandered half over Europe, hardly ever planning whither I should shape my course beforehand. Chance, which thus led me everywhere, led me at last to Naples. There I met with an old school friend, who was one of the *attachés* at the British embassy; and there began the extraordinary events in connection with Alfred Monkton which form the main interest of the story I am now relating.

I was idling away the time one morning with my friend the *attaché*, in the garden of the Villa Reale, when we were passed by a young man, walking alone, who exchanged bows with my friend.

I thought I recognised the dark eager eyes, the colourless cheeks, the strangely-vigilant, anxious expression which I remembered in past times as characteristic of Alfred Monkton's face, and was about to question my friend on the subject, when he gave me unasked the information of which I was in search.

" That is Alfred Monkton," said he ; " he comes from your part of England. You ought to know him."

" I do know a little of him," I answered ; " he was engaged to Miss Elmslie when I was last in the neighbourhood of Wincot. Is he married to her yet?"

" No; and he never ought to be. He has gone the way of the rest of the family; or, in plainer words, he has gone mad."

" Mad! But I ought not to be surprised at hearing that, after the reports about him in England."

" I speak from no reports; I speak from what he has said and done here before me, and before hundreds of other people. Surely you must have heard of it?"

" Never. I have been out of the way of news from Naples or England for months past."

" Then I have a very extraordinary story to tell you. You know, of course, that Alfred had an uncle, Stephen Monkton. Well, some time ago, this uncle fought a duel in the Roman states, with a Frenchman, who shot him dead. The seconds and the Frenchman (who was unhurt) took to flight in different directions, as it is supposed. We heard nothing here of the details of the duel till a month after it happened, when one of the French journals published an account of it, taken from papers left by Monkton's second, who died at Paris of consumption. These papers stated the manner in which the duel was fought, and how it terminated, but nothing more. The surviving second and the Frenchman have never been traced from that time to this. All that any-body knows, therefore, of the duel is that Stephen Monkton was shot; an event which nobody can regret, for a greater scoundrel never existed. The exact place where he died, and what was done with his body, are still mysteries not to be penetrated."

" But what has all this to do with Alfred?"

" Wait a moment, and you will hear. Soon after the news of his uncle's death reached England, what do you think Alfred did? He actually put off his marriage with Miss Elmslie, which was then about to be celebrated, to come out here in search of the burial-place of his wretched scamp of an uncle. And no power on earth will now induce him to return to England and to Miss Elmslie, until he has found the body and can take it back with him to be buried with all the other dead Monktons, in the vault under Wincot Abbey Chapel. He has squandered his money, pestered the police, exposed himself to the ridicule of the men and the indigation of the women for the last three months, in trying to achieve his insane purpose, and is now as far from it as ever. He will not assign to anybody the smallest motive for his conduct. You can't laugh him out of it, or reason him out of it. When we met him just now, I happen to know that he was on his way to the office of the police minister, to send out fresh agents to search and inquire through the Roman states for the place where his uncle was shot. And mind, all this time he professes to be passionately in love with Miss Elmslie, and to be miserable at his separation from her. Just think of that! And then think of his self-imposed absence from her here, to hunt after the remains of a wretch who was a disgrace to the family, and whom he never saw but once or twice in his life. Of all the ' Mad Monktons,' as they used to call them in England, Alfred is the maddest. He is actually our principal excitement in this dull opera season, though, for my own part, when I think of the poor girl in England, I am a great deal more ready to despise him than to laugh at him."

" You know the Elmslies, then?"

" Intimately. The other day, my mother wrote to me from England, after having seen Ada. This escapade of Monkton's has outraged all her friends. They have been entreating her to break off the match, which it seems she could do if she liked. Even her mother, sordid and selfish as she is, has been obliged at last, in common decency, to side with the rest of the family; but the good faithful girl won't give Monkton up. She humours his insanity, declares he gave her a good reason, in secret, for going away; says she could always make him happy when they were together in the old Abbey, and can make him still happier when they are married; in short, she loves him dearly, and will therefore believe in him to the last. Nothing shakes her ; she has made up her mind to throw away her life on him, and she will do it."

" I hope not. Mad as his conduct looks to us, he may have some sensible reason for it that we cannot imagine. Does his mind seem at all disordered when he talks on ordinary topics?"

" Not in the least. When you can get him to say anything, which is not often, he talks like a sensible, well-educated man. Keep silence about his precious errand here, and you would fancy him the gentlest and most temperate of human beings. But touch the subject of his vagabond of an uncle, and the Monkton madness comes out directly. The other night a lady asked him, jestingly of course, whether he had ever seen his uncle's ghost. He scowled at her like a perfect fiend, and said that he and his uncle would answer her question together some day, if they came from hell to do it. We laughed at his words, but the lady fainted at his looks, and we had a scene of hysterics and hartshorn in consequence. Any other man would have been kicked out of the room for nearly frightening a pretty woman to death in that way; but 'Mad Monkton,' as we have christened him, is a privileged lunatic in Neapolitan society, because he is English, good-looking, and worth thirty thousand a year. He goes out everywhere, under the impression that he may meet with somebody who has been let into the secret of the place where the mysterious duel was fought. If you are introduced to him, he is sure to ask you whether you know anything about it; but beware of following up the subject after you have answered him, unless you want to make sure that he is out of his senses. In that case, only talk of his uncle, and the result will rather more than satisfy you."

A day or two after this conversation with my friend the *attaché*, I met Monkton at an evening party.

The moment he heard my name mentioned, his face flushed up; he drew me away into a corner, and referring to his cool reception of my advance, years ago, towards making his acquaintance, asked my pardon for what he termed his inexcusable ingratitude, with an earnestness and an agitation which utterly astonished me. His next proceeding was to question me, as my friend had said he would, about the place of the mysterious duel.

An extraordinary change came over him while he interrogated me on this point. Instead of looking into my face as they had looked hitherto, his eyes wandered away, and fixed themselves intensely, almost fiercely, either on the perfectly empty wall at our side, or on the vacant space between the wall and ourselves—it was impossible to say which. I had come to Naples from Spain by sea, and briefly told him so, as the best way of satisfying him that I could not assist his inquiries. He pursued them no further; and mindful of my friend's warning, I took care to lead the conversation to general topics. He looked back at me directly, and as long as we stood in our corner, his eyes never wandered away again to the empty wall or the vacant space at our side.

Though more ready to listen than to speak, his conversation, when he did talk, had no trace of anything the least like insanity about it. He had evidently read, not generally only, but deeply as well, and could apply his reading with singular felicity to the illustration of almost any subject under discussion, neither obtruding his knowledge absurdly, nor concealing it affectedly. His manner was in itself a standing protest against such a nickname as "Mad Monkton." He was so shy, so quiet, so composed and gentle in all his actions, that at times I should have been almost inclined to call him effeminate. We had a long talk together on the first evening of our meeting; we often saw each other afterwards, and never lost a single opportunity of bettering our acquaintance. I felt that he had taken a liking to me; and in spite of what I had heard about his behaviour to Miss Elmslie, in spite of the suspicions which the history of his family and his own conduct had arrayed against him, I began to like "Mad Monkton" as much as he liked me. We took many a quiet ride together in the country, and sailed often along the shores of the Bay on either side. But for two eccentricities in his conduct, which I could not at all understand, I should soon have felt as much at my ease in his society as if he had been my own brother.

The first of these eccentricities consisted in the reappearance on several occasions of the odd expression in his eyes, which I had first seen when he asked me whether I knew anything about the duel. No matter what we were talking about, or where we happened to be, there were times when he would suddenly look away from my face, now on one side of me, now on the other, but always where there was nothing to see, and always with the same intensity and fierceness in his eyes. This looked so like madness—or hypochondria, at the least—that I felt afraid to ask him about it, and always pretended not to observe him.

The second peculiarity in his conduct was that he never referred, while in my company, to the reports about his errand at Naples, and never once spoke of Miss Elmslie, or of his life at Wincot Abbey. This not only astonished me, but amazed those who had noticed our intimacy, and who had made sure that I must be the depositary of all his secrets. But the time was near at hand when this mystery, and some other mysteries of which I had no suspicion at that period, were all to be revealed.

I met him one night at a large ball, given by a Russian nobleman, whose name I could not pronounce then, and cannot remember now. I had wandered away from reception-room, ball-room, and card-room to a small apartment at one extremity of the palace, which was half conservatory, half boudoir, and which had been prettily illuminated for the occasion with Chinese lanthorns. Nobody was in the room when I got there. The view over the Mediterranean, bathed in the bright softness of Italian moonlight, was so lovely, that I remained for a long time at the window, looking out, and listening to the dance music which faintly reached me from the ball-room. My thoughts were far away with the relations I had left in England, when I was startled out of them by hearing my name softly pronounced.

I looked round directly, and saw Monkton standing in the room. A livid paleness overspread his face, and his eyes were turned away from me with the same extraordinary expression in them to which I have already alluded.

"Do you mind leaving the ball early to-night?" he asked, still not looking at me.

"Not at all," said I. "Can I do anything for you? Are you ill?"

"No, at least nothing to speak of. Will you come to my rooms?"

"At once, if you like."

"No, not at once. *I* must go home directly; but don't you come to me for half an hour yet. You have not been at my rooms before, I know; but you will easily find them out, they are close by. There is a card with my address. I *must* speak to you to-night; my life depends on it. Pray come! for God's sake come when the half hour is up!"

I promised to be punctual, and he left me directly.

Most people will be easily able to imagine the state of nervous impatience and vague expectation in which I passed the allotted period of delay, after hearing such words as those Monkton had spoken to me. Before the half hour had quite expired, I began to make my way out through the ball-room.

At the head of the staircase, my friend the *attaché* met me.

" What! going away already?" said he.

" Yes; and on a very curious expedition. I am going to Monkton's rooms, by his own invitation."

" You don't mean it! Upon my honour, you're a bold fellow to trust yourself alone with 'Mad Monkton' when the moon is at the full."

" He is ill, poor fellow. Besides, I don't think him half as mad as you do."

" We won't dispute about that; but mark my words, he has not asked you to go where no visitor has ever been admitted before, without a special purpose. I predict that you will see or hear something to-night which you will remember for the rest of your life."

We parted. When I knocked at the courtyard gate of the house where Monkton lived, my friend's last words on the palace staircase occurred to me; and though I had laughed at him when he had spoke then, I began to suspect even then that his prediction would be fulfilled.

CHAPTER III

The porter who let me into the house where Monkton lived, directed me to the floor on which his rooms were situated. On getting up stairs, I found his door on the landing ajar. He heard my footsteps, I suppose, for he called to me to come in before I could knock.

I entered, and found him sitting by the table, with some loose letters in his hand, which he was just tying together in a packet. I noticed, as he asked me to sit down, that his expression looked more composed, though the paleness had not yet left his face. He thanked me for coming; repeated that he had something very important to say to me; and then stopped short, apparently too much embarrassed to proceed. I tried to set him at his ease by assuring him that if my assistance or advice could be of any use, I was ready to place myself and my time heartily and unreservedly at his service.

As I said this, I saw his eyes beginning to wander away from my face—to wander slowly, inch by inch as it were, until they stopped at a certain point, with the same fixed stare into vacancy which had so often startled me on former occasions.

The whole expression of his face altered as I had never yet seen it alter; he sat before me, looking like a man in a death-trance.

"You are very kind," he said, slowly and faintly, speaking, not to me, but in the direction in which his eyes were still fixed.—" I know you can help me ; but——"

He stopped ; his face whitened horribly, and the perspiration broke out all over it. He tried to continue ; said a word or two ; then stopped again. Seriously alarmed about him, I rose from my chair, with the intention of getting him some water from a jug which I saw standing on a side table.

He sprang up at the same moment. All the suspicions I had ever heard whispered against his sanity flashed over my mind in an instant ; and I involuntarily stepped back a pace or two.

"Stop," he said, seating himself again; "don't mind me ; and don't leave your chair. I want—I wish, if you please, to make a little alteration, before we say anything more. Do you mind sitting in a strong light?"

"Not in the least."

I had hitherto been seated in the shade of his reading lamp, the only light in the room.

As I answered him, he rose again ; and going into another apartment, returned with a large lamp in his hand ; then took two candles from the side table, and two others from the chimney-piece ; placed them all, to my amazement, together, so as to stand exactly between us ; and then tried to light them. His hand trembled so, that he was obliged to give up the attempt, and allow me to come to his assistance. By his direction I took the shade off the reading lamp, after I had lit the other lamp and the four candles. When he sat down again, with this concentration of light between us, his better and gentler manner began to return: and while he now addressed me, he spoke without the slightest hesitation.

"It is useless to ask whether you have heard the reports about me," he said; "I know that you have. My purpose to-night is to give you some reasonable explanation of the conduct which has produced those reports. My secret has been hitherto confided to one person only ; I am now about to trust it to your keeping, with a special object which will appear as I go on. First, however, I must begin by telling you exactly what the great difficulty is which obliges me to be still absent from England. I want your advice and your help ; and, to conceal nothing from you, I want also to test your forbearance and your friendly sympathy, before I can venture on thrusting my miserable secret into your keeping. Will you pardon this apparent distrust of your frank and open character—this apparent ingratitude for your kindness towards me ever since we first met?"

I begged him not to speak of these things, but to go on.

" You know," he proceeded, " that I am here to recover the body of my Uncle Stephen, and to carry it back with me to our family-burial place in England; and you must also be aware that I have not yet succeeded in discovering his remains. Try to pass over for the present whatever may seem extraordinary and incomprehensible in such a purpose as mine is ; and read this newspaper article, where the ink-line is traced. It is the only evidence hitherto obtained on the subject of the fatal duel in which my uncle fell : and I want to hear what course of proceeding the perusal of it may suggest to you as likely to be best on my part."

He handed me an old French newspaper. The substance of what I read there is still so firmly impressed on my memory, that I am certain of being able to repeat correctly, at this distance of time, all the facts which it is necessary for me to communicate to the reader.

The article began, I remember, with editorial remarks on the great curiosity then felt in regard to the fatal duel between the Count St. Lo and Mr. Stephen Monkton, an English gentleman. The writer proceeded to dwell at great length on the extraordinary secrecy in which the whole affair had been involved from first to last ; and to express a hope that the publication of a certain manuscript, to which his introductory observations referred, might lead to the production of fresh evidence from other and better informed quarters. The manuscript had been found among the papers of Monsieur Foulon, Mr. Monkton's second, who had died at Paris of a rapid decline, shortly after returning to his home in that city from the scene of the duel. The document was unfinished, having been left incomplete at the very place where the reader would most wish to find it continued. No reason could be discovered for this, and no second manuscript bearing on the all-important subject had been found, after the strictest search among the papers left by the deceased.

The document itself then followed.

It purported to be an agreement privately drawn up between Mr. Monkton's second, Monsieur Foulon, and the Count St. Lo's second, Monsieur Dalville ; and contained a statement of all the arrangements for conducting the duel. The paper was dated " Naples, February 22nd " ; and was divided into some seven or eight clauses.

The first clause described the origin and nature of the quarrel—a very disgraceful affair on both sides, worth neither remembering nor repeating. The second clause stated that the challenged man having chosen the pistol as his weapon, and the challenger (an excellent swordsman) having, on his side, thereupon insisted that the duel should be fought in such a manner as to make the first fire decisive in its results, the seconds, seeing that fatal consequences must inevitably follow the hostile meeting, determined, first of all, that the duel should be kept a profound secret from everybody, and that the place where it was to be fought should not be made known beforehand, even to the principals themselves. It was added that this excess of precaution had been rendered absolutely necessary, in consequence of a recent address from the Pope to the ruling powers in Italy, commenting on the scandalous frequency of the practice of duelling, and urgently desiring that the laws against duellists should be enforced for the future with the utmost rigour.

The third clause detailed the manner in which it had been arranged that the duel should be fought.

The pistols having been loaded by the seconds on the ground, the combatants were to be placed thirty paces apart, and were to toss up for the first fire. The man who won was to advance ten paces—marked out for him beforehand —and was then to discharge his pistol. If he missed, or failed to disable his opponent, the latter was free to advance, if he chose, the whole remaining twenty paces before he fired in his turn. This arrangement ensured the decisive termination of the duel at the first discharge of the pistols, and both principals and seconds pledged themselves on either side to abide by it.

The fourth clause stated that the seconds had agreed that the duel should be fought *out* of the Neapolitan states, but left themselves to be guided by circumstances as to the exact locality in which it should take place. The remaining clauses, so far as I remember them, were devoted to detailing the different precautions to be adopted for avoiding discovery. The duellists and their seconds were to leave Naples in separate parties ; were to change carriages several times ; were to meet at a certain town, or, failing that, at a certain post-house on the highroad from Naples to Rome ; were to carry drawing-books, colour-boxes, and cap-stools, as if they had been artists out on a sketching tour ; and were to proceed to the place of the duel on foot, employing no guides, for fear of treachery. Such general arrangements as these, and other for facilitating the flight of the survivors after the affair was over, formed the conclusion of this extaordinary document, which was signed, in initials only, by both the seconds.

Just below the initials, appeared the beginning of a narrative, dated " Paris," and evidently intended to describe the duel itself with extreme minuteness. The handwriting was that of the deceased second.

Monsieur Foulon, the gentleman in question, stated his belief that circumstances might transpire which would render an account by an eye-witness of the hostile meeting between St. Lo and Mr. Monkton an important document. He proposed, therefore, as one of the seconds, to testify that the duel had been fought in exact accordance with the terms of the agreement, both the principals conducting themselves like men of gallantry and honour (!). And he further announced that, in order not to compromise anyone, he should place the paper containing his testimony in safe hands, with strict directions that it was on no account to be opened, except in a case of the last emergency.

After this preamble, Monsieur Foulon related that the duel had been fought two days after the drawing up of the agreement, in a locality to which accident had conducted the duelling party. (The name of the place was not mentioned, nor even the neighbourhood in which it was situated.) The men having been placed according to previous arrangement, the Count St. Lo had won the toss for the first fire, had advanced his ten paces, and had shot his opponent in the body. Mr. Monkton did not immediately fall, but staggered forward some six or seven paces, discharged his pistol ineffectually at the Count, and dropped to the ground a dead man. Monsieur Foulon then stated that he tore a leaf from his pocket-book, wrote on it a brief description of the manner in which Mr. Monkton had died, and pinned the paper to his clothes ; this proceeding having been rendered necessary by the peculiar nature of the plan organised on the spot for safely disposing of the dead body. What this plan was, or what was done with the corpse, did not appear, for at this important point the narrative abruptly broke off.

A footnote in the newspaper merely stated the manner in which the document had been obtained for publication, and repeated the announcement contained in the editor's introductory remarks, that no continuation had been found by the persons entrusted with the care of Monsieur Foulon's papers. I have now given the whole substance of what I read, and have mentioned all that was then known of Mr. Stephen Monkton's death.

When I gave the newspaper back to Alfred, he was too much agitated to speak ; but he reminded me by a sign that he was anxiously waiting to hear what I had to say. My position was a very trying and a very painful one. I could hardly tell what consequences might not follow any want of caution on my part, and could think at first of no safer plan than questioning him carefully before I committed myself either one way or the other.

" Will you excuse me if I ask you a question or two before I give you my advice?" I said.

He nodded impatiently.

" Yes, yes ; any questions you like."

" Were you at any time in the habit of seeing your uncle frequently?"

" I never saw him more than twice in my life ; on each occasion, when I was a mere child."

" Then you could have had no very strong personal regard for him?"

" Regard for him! I should have been ashamed to feel any regard for him. He disgraced us wherever he went."

" May I ask if any family motive is involved in your anxiety to recover his remains?"

" Family motives may enter into it among others—but why do you ask?"

" Because, having heard that you employ the police to assist your search, I was anxious to know whether you had stimulated their superiors to make them do their best in your service, by giving some strong personal reasons at headquarters for the very unusual project which has brought you here."

"I give no reasons. I pay for the work I want done, and in return for my liberality I am treated with the most infamous indifference on all sides. A stranger in the country, and badly acquainted with the language, I can do nothing to help myself. The authorities, both at Rome and in this place, pretend to assist me, pretend to search and inquire as I would have them search and inquire, and do nothing more. I am insulted, laughed at, almost to my face."

"Do you not think it possible—mind, I have no wish to excuse the misconduct of the authorities, and do not share in any such opinion myself—but do you not think it likely that the police may doubt whether you are in earnest?"

"Not in earnest!" he cried, starting up and confronting me fiercely, with wild eyes and quickened breath. "Not in earnest! *You* think I'm not in earnest, too. I know you think it, though you tell me you don't. Stop! before we say another word, your own eyes shall convince you. Come here—only for a minute—only for one minute!"

I followed him into his bedroom, which opened out of the sitting-room. At one side of his bed stood a large packing-case of plain wood, upwards of seven feet in length.

"Open the lid, and look in," he said, "while I hold the candle so that you can see."

I obeyed his directions, and discovered, to my astonishment, that the packing-case contained a leaden coffin, magnificently emblazoned with the arms of the Monkton family, and inscribed in old-fashioned letters with the name of "Stephen Monkton," his age and the manner of his death being added underneath.

"I keep his coffin ready for him," whispered Alfred, close at my ear. "Does that look like earnest?"

It looked more like insanity—so like, that I shrank from answering him.

"Yes! yes! I see you are convinced," he continued, quickly; "we may go back into the next room, and may talk without restraint on either side now."

On returning to our places, I mechanically moved my chair away from the table. My mind was by this time in such a state of confusion and uncertainty about what it would be best for me to say or do next, that I forgot for the moment the position he had assigned to me when we lit the candles. He reminded me of this directly.

"Don't move away," he said, very earnestly; "keep on sitting in the light; pray do! I'll soon tell you why I am so particular about that. But first give me your advice; help me in my great distress and suspense. Remember, you promised me you would."

I made an effort to collect my thoughts and succeeded. It was useless to treat the affair otherwise than seriously in his presence; it would have been cruel not to have advised him as I best could.

"You know," I said, "that two days after the drawing up of the agreement of Naples, the duel was fought out of the Neapolitan States. This fact has of course led you to the conclusion that all inquiries about localities had better be confined to the Roman territory?"

"Certainly: the search, such as it is, has been made there, and there only. If I can believe the police, they and their agents have inquired for the place where the duel was fought (offering a large reward in my name to the person who can discover it), all along the highroad from Naples to Rome. They have also circulated—at least, so they tell me—descriptions of the duellists and their seconds; have left an agent to superintend investigations at the post-house, and another at the town mentioned as meeting-points in the agreement; and have endeavoured by correspondence with foreign authorities to trace the Count St. Lo and Monsieur Dalville to their place or places of refuge. All these efforts, supposing them to have been really made, have hitherto proved utterly fruitless."

"My impression is," said I, after a moment's consideration, "that all inquiries made along the highroad, or anywhere near Rome, are likely to be made in vain. As to the discovery of your uncle's remains, that is, I think, identical with the discovery of the place where he was shot; for those engaged in the duel would certainly not risk detection by carrying a corpse any distance with them in their flight. The place, then, is all that we want to find out. Now, let us consider for a moment. The duelling-party changed carriages; travelled separately, two and two; doubtless took roundabout roads; stopped at the post-house and the town as a blind; walked, perhaps, a considerable distance unguided. Depend upon it, such precautions as these (which we know they must have employed) left them very little time out of the two days —though they might start at sunrise, and not stop at night-fall—for straightforward travelling. My belief therefore is, that the duel was fought somewhere near the Neapolitan frontier ; and if I had been the police agent who conducted the search, I should only have pursued it parallel with the frontier, starting from west to east till I got up among the lonely places in the mountains. That is my idea : do you think it worth anything?"

His face flushed all over in an instant. "I think it an inspiration!" he cried. " Not a day is to be lost in carrying out our plan. The police are not to be trusted with it. I must start myself, to-morrow morning ; and you——"

He stopped ; his face grew suddenly pale ; he sighed heavily; his eyes wandered once more into the fixed look at vacancy ; and the rigid, deathly expression fastened again upon all his features.

" I must tell you my secret before I talk of to-morrow," he proceeded, faintly. " If I hesitated any longer at confessing everything, I should be unworthy of your past kindness, unworthy of the help which it is my last hope that you will gladly give me when you have heard all."

I begged him to wait until he was more composed, until he was better able to speak ; but he did not appear to notice what I said. Slowly, and struggling as it seemed against himself, he turned a little away from me ; and bending his head over the table, supported it on his hand. The packet of letters, with which I had seen him occupied when I came in, lay just beneath his eyes. He looked down on it steadfastly when he next spoke to me.

CHAPTER IV

" You were born, I believe, in our county," he said ; " perhaps therefore you may have heard at some time of a curious old prophecy about our family, which is still preserved among the traditions of Wincot Abbey?"

" I have heard of such a prophecy," I answered ; " but I never knew in what terms it was expressed. It professed to predict the extinction of your family, or something of that sort, did it not?"

"No inquiries," he went on, "have traced back that prophecy to the time when it was first made; none of our family records tell us anything of its origin. Old servants and old tenants of ours remember to have heard it from their fathers and grandfathers. The monks, whom we succeeded in the Abbey in Henry the Eighth's time, got knowledge of it in some way; for I myself discovered the rhymes in which we know the prophecy to have been preserved from a very remote period, written on a blank leaf of one of the Abbey manuscripts. These are the verses, if verses they deserve to be called.

> When in Wincot vault a place
> Waits for one of Monkton's race;
> When that one forlorn shall lie
> Graveless under open sky,
> Beggared of six feet of earth,
> Though lord of acres from his birth—
> That shall be a certain sign
> Of the end of Monkton's line.
> Dwindling ever faster, faster,
> Dwindling to the last-left master;
> From mortal ken, from light of day,
> Monkton's race shall pass away.

"The prediction seems almost vague enough to have been uttered by an ancient oracle," said I, observing that he waited, after repeating the verses, as if expecting me to say something.

"Vague or not, it is being accomplished," he returned. "I am now the 'Last-left Master'—the last of that elder line of our family at which the prediction points; and the corpse of Stephen Monkton is not in the vaults of Wincot Abbey. Wait, before you exclaim against me! I have more to say about this. Long before the Abbey was ours, when we lived in the ancient manor-house near it (the very ruins of which have long since disappeared), the family-burying place was in the vault under the Abbey chapel. Whether in those remote times the prediction against us was known and dreaded or not, this much is certain: every one of the Monktons (whether living at the Abbey or on the smaller estate in Scotland) was buried in Wincot vault, no matter at what risk or what sacrifice. In the fierce fighting days of the olden time, the bodies of my ancestors who fell in foreign places were recovered and brought back to Wincot, though it often cost, not heavy ransom only but desperate bloodshed as well, to obtain them. This superstition, if you please to call it so, has never died out of the family from that time to the present day; for centuries the succession of the dead in the vault at the Abbey has been unbroken—absolutely unbroken—until now. The place mentioned in the prediction as waiting to be filled, is Stephen Monkton's place; the voice that cries vainly to the earth for shelter is the voice of the dead. As surely as if I saw it, I know that they have left him unburied on the ground where he fell!"

He stopped me before I could utter a word in remonstrance, by slowly rising to his feet, and pointing in the same direction towards which his eyes had wandered a short time since.

" I can guess what you want to ask me," he exclaimed, sternly and loudly; " you want to ask me how I can be mad enough to believe in a doggerel prophecy, uttered in an age of superstition to awe the most ignorant hearers. I answer " (at those words his voice sank suddenly to a whisper), " I answer, because *Stephen Monkton himself stands there at this moment, confirming me in my belief.*"

Whether it was the awe and horror that looked out ghastly from his face as he confronted me, whether it was that I had never hitherto fairly believed in the reports about his madness, and that the conviction of their truth now forced itself upon me on a sudden I know not; but I felt my blood curdling as he spoke, and I knew in my own heart, as I sat there speechless, that I dare not turn round and look where he was still pointing close at my side.

" I see there," he went on in the same whispering voice, " the figure of a dark-complexioned man, standing up with his head uncovered. One of his hands, still clutching a pistol, has fallen to his side; the other presses a bloody handkerchief over his mouth. The spasm of mortal agony convulses his features; but I know them for the features of a swarthy man, who twice frightened me by taking me up in his arms when I was a child, at Wincot Abbey. I asked the nurses at the time who that man was, and they told me it was my uncle, Stephen Monkton. Plainly, as if he stood there living, I see him now at your side, with the death-glare in his

great black eyes; and so have I ever seen him since the
moment when he was shot; at home and abroad, waking or
sleeping, day and night, we are always together wherever I
go!"

His whispering tones sank into almost inaudible murmuring
as he pronounced these last words. From the direction and
expression of his eyes, I suspected that he was speaking to
the apparition. If I had beheld it myself at that moment, it
would have been, I think, a less horrible sight to witness
than to see him, as I saw him now, muttering inarticulately
at vacancy. My own nerves were more shaken than I could
have thought possible by what had passed. A vague dread of
being near him in his present mood came over me, and
I moved back a step or two.

He noticed the action instantly.

"Don't go!—Pray, pray don't go! Have I alarmed you?
Don't you believe me? Do the lights make your eyes ache? I
only asked you to sit in the glare of the candles because
I could not bear to see the light that always shines from the
phantom there at dusk, shining over you as you sat in the
shadow. Don't go—don't leave me yet!"

There was an utter forlornness, an unspeakable misery in
his face as he said those words, which gave me back my
self-possession by the simple process of first moving me to
pity. I resumed my chair, and said that I would stay with
him as long as he wished.

"Thank you a thousand times! You are patience and
kindness itself," he said, going back to his former place, and
resuming his former gentleness of manner. "Now that I have
got over my first confession of the misery that follows me in
secret wherever I go, I think I can tell you calmly all that
remains to be told. You see, as I said, my uncle Stephen,"
—he turned away his head quickly, and looked down at the
table as the name passed his lips—" my uncle Stephen came
twice to Wincot while I was a child, and on both occasions
frightened me dreadfully. He only took me up in his arms,
and spoke to me—very kindly, as I afterwards heard, for *him*
—but he terrified me, nevertheless. Perhaps I was frightened
at his great stature, his swarthy complexion, and his thick
black hair and moustache, as other children might have been;
perhaps the mere sight of him had some strange influence on
me which I could not then understand, and cannot now

explain. However it was, I used to dream of him long after he had gone away; and to fancy that he was stealing on me to catch me up in his arms, whenever I was left in the dark. The servants who took care of me found this out, and used to threaten me with my uncle Stephen whenever I was perverse and difficult to manage. As I grew up, I still retained my vague dread and abhorrence of our absent relative. I always listened intently, yet without knowing why, whenever his name was mentioned by my father or my mother—listened with an unaccountable presentiment that something terrible had happened to him, or was about to happen to me. This feeling only changed when I was left alone in the Abbey; and then it seemed to merge into the eager curiosity which had begun to grow on me rather before that time, about the origin of the ancient prophecy predicting the extinction of our race. Are you following me?"

"I follow every word with the closest attention."

"You must know, then, that I had first found out some fragments of the old rhyme, in which the prophecy occurs, quoted as a curiosity in an antiquarian book in the library. On the page opposite this quotation, had been pasted a rude old woodcut, representing a dark-haired man, whose face was so strangely like what I remembered of my uncle Stephen, that the portrait absolutely startled me. When I asked my father about this—it was then just before his death—he either knew, or pretended to know, nothing of it; and when I afterwards mentioned the prediction he fretfully changed the subject. It was just the same with our chaplain when I spoke to him. He said the portrait had been done centuries before my uncle was born; and called the prophecy doggerel and nonsense. I used to argue with him on the latter point, asking why we Catholics, who believed that the gift of working miracles had never departed from certain favoured persons, might not just as well believe that the gift of prophecy had never departed either? He would not dispute with me; he would only say that I must not waste time in thinking of such trifles, that I had more imagination than was good for me, and must suppress instead of exciting it. Such advice as this only irritated my curiosity. I determined secretly to search through the oldest uninhabited part of the Abbey, and to try if I could not find out from forgotten family records what the portrait was, and when the prophecy had been first written or uttered. Did you ever pass a day alone in the long-deserted chambers of an ancient house?"

" Never ; such solitude as that is not at all to my taste."

" Ah! what a life it was when I began my search. I should like to live it over again! Such tempting suspense, such strange discoveries, such wild fancies, such enthralling terrors, all belonged to that life! Only think of breaking open the door of a room which no living soul had entered for nearly a hundred years! think of the first step forward into a region of airless, awful stillness, where the light falls faint and sick through closed windows and rotting curtains! think of the ghostly creaking of the old floor that cries out on you for treading on it, step as softly as you will! think of arms, helmets, weird tapestries of bygone days, that seem to be moving out on you from the walls as you first walk up to them in the dim light! think of prying into great cabinets and iron-clasped chests, not knowing what horrors may appear when you tear them open! of poring over their contents till twilight stole on you, and darkness grew terrible in the lonely place! of trying to leave it, and not being able to go, as if something held you ; of wind wailing at you outside ; of shadows darkening round you, and closing you up in obscurity within. Only think of these things, and you may imagine the fascination of suspense and terror in such a life as mine was in those past days!"

(I shrunk from imagining that life : it was bad enough to see its results, as I saw them before me now.)

" Well, my search lasted months and months ; then it was suspended a little, then resumed. In whatever direction I pursued it, I always found something to lure me on. Terrible confessions of past crimes, shocking proofs of secret wickedness that had been hidden securely from all eyes but mine, came to light. Sometimes these discoveries were associated with particular parts of the Abbey, which have had a horrible interest of their own for me ever since. Sometimes with certain old portraits in the picture-gallery, which I actually dreaded to look at, after what I had found out. There were periods when the results of this search of mine so horrified me, that I determined to give it up entirely ; but I never could persevere in my resolution, the temptation to go on seemed at certain intervals to get too strong for me, and then I yielded to it again and again. At last I found

the book that had belonged to the monks, with the whole of
the prophecy written in the blank leaf. This first success
encouraged me to get back further yet in the family records.
I had discovered nothing hitherto of the identity of the
mysterious portrait, but the same intuitive conviction which
had assured me of its extraordinary resemblance to my
uncle Stephen, seemed also to assure me that he must be more
closely connected with the prophecy, and must know more of
it than anyone else. I had no means of holding any communication with him, no means of satisfying myself whether
this strange idea of mine were right or wrong, until the
day when my doubts were settled for ever, by the same
terrible proof which is now present to me in this very room."

He paused for a moment, and looked at me intently and
suspiciously; then asked if I believed all he had said to me so
far. My instant reply in the affirmative seemed to satisfy his
doubts, and he went on:

" On a fine evening in February, I was standing alone in
one of the deserted rooms of the western turret at the Abbey
looking at the sunset. Just before the sun went down, I felt
a sensation stealing over me which it is impossible to explain.
I saw nothing, heard nothing, knew nothing. This utter
self-oblivion came suddenly; it was not fainting, for I did not
fall to the ground, did not move an inch from my place. If
such a thing could be, I should say it was the temporary
separation of soul and body, without death: but all description of my situation at that time is impossible. Call my state
what you will, trance or catalepsy, I know that I remained
standing by the window utterly unconscious—dead, mind and
body—until the sun had set. Then I came to my senses
again; and then, when I opened my eyes, there was the
apparition of Stephen Monkton standing opposite to me,
faintly luminous, just as it stands opposite me at this very
moment by your side."

" Was this before the news of the duel reached England?"
I asked.

" *Two weeks before* the news of it reached us at Wincot.
And even when we heard of the duel, we did not hear of
the day on which it was fought. I only found that out
when the document which you have read was published in the
French newspapers. The date of that document, you will remember, is February 22nd, and it is stated that the duel was

fought two days afterwards. I wrote down in my pocket-book, on the evening when I saw the phantom, the day of the month on which it first appeared to me. That day was the 24th of February."

He paused again, as if expecting me to say something. After the words he had just spoken, what could I say? what could I think?

" Even in the first horror of first seeing the apparition," he went on, " the prophecy against our house came to my mind, and with it the conviction that I behold before me, in that spectral presence, the warning of my own doom. As soon as I recovered a little, I determined, nevertheless, to test the reality of what I saw—to find out whether I was the dupe of my own diseased fancy, or not. I left the turret; the phantom left it with me. I made an excuse to have the drawing-room at the Abbey brilliantly lighted up—the figure was still opposite me. I walked out into the park—it was there in the clear starlight. I went away from home, and travelled many miles to the sea-side; still the tall dark man in his death agony was with me. After this, I strove against the fatality no more. I returned to the Abbey, and tried to resign myself to my misery. But this was not to be. I had a hope that was dearer to me than my own life; I had one treasure belonging to me that I shuddered at the prospect of losing, and when the phantom presence stood a warning obstacle between me and this one treasure, this dearest hope —then my misery grew heavier than I could bear. You must know what I am alluding to; you must have heard often that I was engaged to be married?"

" Yes, often. I have some acquaintance myself with Miss Elmslie."

" You never can know all she has sacrificed for me—never can imagine what I have felt for years and years past "—his voice trembled, and the tears came into his eyes—" but I dare not trust myself to speak of that: the thought of the old happy days in the Abbey almost breaks my heart now. Let me get back to the other subject. I must tell you that I kept the frightful vision which pursued me, at all times, and in all places, a secret from everybody; knowing the vile reports about my having inherited madness from my family, and fearing that an unfair advantage would be taken of any confession that I might make. Though the phantom always stood opposite to me, and therefore always appeared either before or by the side of any person to whom I spoke, I soon schooled myself to hide from others that I was looking at it, except on rare occasions—when I have perhaps betrayed myself to you. But my self-possession availed me nothing with Ada. The day of our marriage was approaching."

He stopped and shuddered. I waited in silence till he had controlled himself.

"Think," he went on, "think of what I must have suffered at looking always on that hideous vision, whenever I looked on my betrothed wife! Think of my taking her hand, and seeming to take it through the figure of the apparition! Think of the calm angel-face and the tortured spectre-face being always together, whenever my eyes met hers! Think of this, and you will not wonder that I betrayed my secret to her. She eagerly entreated to know the worst—nay more, she insisted on knowing it. At her bidding I told all; and then left her free to break our engagement. The thought of death was in my heart as I spoke the parting words—death by my own act, if life still held out after our separation. She suspected that thought; she knew it, and never left me till her good influence had destroyed it for ever. But for her, I should not have been alive now—but for her, I should never have attempted the project which has brought me here."

"Do you mean that it was at Miss Elmslie's suggestion that you came to Naples?" I asked in amazement.

"I mean that what she said, suggested the design which has brought me to Naples," he answered. "While I believed that the phantom had appeared to me as the fatal messenger of death, there was no comfort, there was misery rather in hearing her say that no power on earth should make her desert, and that she would live for me, and for me only, through every trial. But it was far different when we afterwards reasoned together about the purpose which the apparition had come to fulfil—far different when she showed me that its mission might be for good, instead of for evil; and that the warning it was sent to give, might be to my profit instead of to my loss. At those words, the new idea which gave the new hope of life came to me in an instant. I believed then, what I believe now, that I have a supernatural warrant for my errand here. In that faith I live; without it I should die. *She* never ridiculed it, never

scorned it as insanity. Mark what I say! The spirit that
appeared to me in the Abbey, that has never left me since,
that stands there now by your side, warns me to escape from
the fatality which hangs over our race, and commands me, if
I would avoid it, to bury the unburied dead. Mortal loves
and mortal interests must bow to that awful bidding. The
spectre-presence will never leave me till I have sheltered the
corpse that cries to the earth to cover it! I dare not return
—I dare not marry till I have filled the place that is empty in
Wincot vault."

His eyes flashed and dilated; his voice deepened; a fanatic
ecstasy shone in his expression as he uttered these words.
Shocked and grieved as I was, I made no attempt to re-
monstrate or to reason with him. It would have been useless
to have referred to any of the usual common-places about
optical delusions, or diseased imaginations—worse than
useless to have attempted to account by natural causes for any
of the extraordinary coincidences and events of which he
had spoken. Briefly as he had referred to Miss Elmslie, he had
said enough to show that the only hope of the poor girl who
loved him best and had known him longest of anyone, was
in humouring his delusions to the last. How faithfully she
still clung to the belief that she could restore him! How
resolutely was she sacrificing herself to his morbid fancies,
in the hope of a happy future that might never come! Little
as I knew of Miss Elmslie, the mere thought of her situation,
as I now reflected on it, made me feel sick at heart.

"They call me 'Mad Monkton'!" he exclaimed, suddenly
breaking the silence between us during the last few minutes.

"Here and in England everybody believes I am out of
my senses, except Ada and you. She has been my salvation;
and you will be my salvation too. Something told me that,
when I first met you walking in the Villa Reale. I struggled
against the strong desire that was in me to trust my secret
to you; but I could resist it no longer when I saw you
to-night at the ball—the phantom seemed to draw me on to
you, as you stood alone in the quiet room. Tell me more
of that idea of yours about finding the place where the duel
was fought. If I set out to-morrow to seek for it myself,
where must I go to first?—where?" He stopped; his strength
was evidently becoming exhausted, and his mind was growing
confused. "What am I to do? I can't remember. You know

everything—will you not help me? My misery has made me unable to help myself!"

He stopped, murmured something about failing if he went to the frontier alone, and spoke confusedly of delays that might be fatal; then tried to utter the name of "Ada"; but in pronouncing the first letter his voice faltered, and turning abruptly from me he burst into tears.

My pity for him got the better of my prudence at that moment, and without thinking of responsibilities, I promised at once to do for him whatever he asked. The wild triumph in his expression, as he started up and seized my hand, showed me that I had better have been more cautious; but it was too late now to retract what I had said. The next best thing to do was to try if I could not induce him to compose himself a little, and then to go away and think coolly over the whole affair by myself.

"Yes, yes," he rejoined, in answer to the few words I now spoke to try and calm him, "don't be afraid about me. After what you have said, I'll answer for my own coolness and composure under all emergencies. I have been so long used to the apparition that I hardly feel its presence at all except on rare occasions. Besides, I have here, in this little packet of letters, the medicine for every malady of the sick heart. They are Ada's letters; I read them to calm me whenever my misfortune seems to get the better of my endurance. I wanted that half hour to read them in to-night, before you came, to make myself fit to see you; and I shall go through them again after you are gone. So, once more, don't be afraid about me. I know I shall succeed with your help; and Ada shall thank you as you deserve to be thanked when we get back to England. If you hear the fools at Naples talk about my being mad, don't trouble yourself to contradict them: the scandal is so contemptible that it must end by contradicting itself."

I left him, promising to return early the next day.

When I got back to my hotel, I felt that any idea of sleeping, after all that I had seen and heard, was out of the question. So I lit my pipe, and sitting by the window—how it refreshed my mind just then to look at the calm moonlight!—tried to think what it would be best to do. In the first place, any appeal to doctors or to Alfred's friends in England was out of the question. I could not persuade myself that his intellect was sufficiently disordered to justify me, under existing circumstances, in disclosing the secret which he had entrusted to my keeping. In the second place, all attempts on my part to induce him to abandon the idea of searching out his uncle's remains would be utterly useless after what I had incautiously said to him. Having settled these two conclusions, the only really great difficulty which remained to perplex me was whether I was justified in aiding him to execute his extraordinary purpose.

Supposing that with my help he found Mr. Monkton's body, and took it back with him to England, was it right in me thus to lend myself to promoting the marriage which would most likely follow these events—a marriage which it might be the duty of everyone to prevent at all hazards? This set me thinking about the extent of his madness, or, to speak more mildly and more correctly, of his delusion. Sane he certainly was on ordinary subjects; nay, in all the narrative parts of what he had said to me on this very evening he had spoken clearly and connectedly. As for the story of the apparition, other men, with intellects as clear as the intellects of their neighbours, had fancied themselves pursued by a phantom, and had even written about it in a high strain of philosophical speculation. It was plain that the real hallucination in the case now before me, lay in Monkton's conviction of the truth of the old prophecy, and in his idea that the fancied apparition was a supernatural warning to him to evade its denunciations. And it was equally clear that both delusions had been produced, in the first instance, by the lonely life he had led, acting on a naturally excitable temperament, which was rendered further liable to moral disease by a hereditary taint of insanity.

Was this curable? Miss Elmslie, who knew him far better than I did, seemed by her conduct to think so. Had I any reason or right to determine off-hand that she was mistaken? Supposing I refused to go to the frontier with him, he would then most certainly depart by himself, to commit all sorts of errors, and perhaps to meet with all sorts of accidents; while I, an idle man, with my time entirely at my own disposal, was stopping at Naples, and leaving him to his fate after I had suggested the plan of his expedition, and had encouraged him to confide in me. In this way I kept turning the subject over and over again in my mind—being quite free, let me add, from looking at it in any other than a practical point of view. I firmly believed, as a derider of all ghost stories, that Alfred was deceiving himself in fancying that he had seen the apparition of his uncle, before the news of Mr. Monkton's death reached England; and I was on this account therefore uninfluenced by the slightest infection of my unhappy friend's delusions, when I at last fairly decided to accompany him in his extraordinary search. Possibly my harum-scarum fondness for excitement at that time, biased me a little in forming my resolution; but I must add, in common justice to myself, that I also acted from motives of real sympathy for Monkton, and from a sincere wish to allay, if I could, the anxiety of the poor girl who was still so faithfully waiting and hoping for him far away in England.

Certain arrangements preliminary to our departure, which I found myself obliged to make after a second interview with Alfred, betrayed the object of our journey to most of our Neapolitan friends. The astonishment of everybody was of course unbounded, and the nearly universal suspicion that I must be as mad in my way as Monkton himself, showed itself pretty plainly in my presence. Some people actually tried to combat my resolution by telling me what a shameless profligate Stephen Monkton had been—as if I had a strong personal interest in hunting out his remains! Ridicule moved me as little as any arguments of this sort; my mind was made up, and I was as obstinate then as I am now.

In two days' time I had got everything ready, and had ordered the travelling carriage to the door some hours earlier than we had originally settled. We were jovially threatened with " a parting cheer " by all our English acquaintances, and I thought it desirable to avoid this on my friend's account; for he had been more excited, as it was, by the preparations for the journey than I at all liked. Accordingly, soon after sunrise, without a soul in the street to stare at us, we privately left Naples.

Nobody will wonder, I think, that I experienced some difficulty in realising my own position, and shrank instinctively from looking forward a single day into the future when I now found myself starting, in company with " Mad Monkton," to hunt for the body of a dead duellist all along the frontier line of the Roman states!

CHAPTER V

I had settled it in my own mind that we had better make the town of Fondi, close on the frontier, our headquarters, to begin with; and I had arranged, with the assistance of the Embassy, that the leaden coffin should follow us so far, securely nailed up in its packing case. Besides our passports, we were well furnished with letters of introduction to the local authorities at most of the important frontier towns, and to crown all, we had money enough at our command (thanks to Monkton's vast fortune) to make sure of the services of anyone whom we wanted to assist us, all along our line of search. These various resources ensured us every facility for action—provided always that we succeeded in discovering the body of the dead duellist. But, in the very probable event of our failing to do this, our future prospects—more especially after the responsibility I had undertaken—were of anything but an agreeable nature to contemplate. I confess I felt uneasy, almost hopeless, as we posted, in the dazzling Italian sunshine, along the road to Fondi.

We made an easy two days' journey of it; for I had insisted, on Monkton's account, that we should travel slowly.

On the first day the excessive agitation of my companion a little alarmed me; he showed, in many ways, more symptoms of a disordered mind than I had yet observed in him. On the second day, however, he seemed to get accustomed to contemplate calmly the new idea of the search on which we were bent, and, except on one point, he was cheerful and composed enough. Whenever his dead uncle formed the subject of conversation, he still persisted—on the strength of the old prophecy, and under the influence of the apparition which he saw, or thought he saw, always—in asserting that the corpse of Stephen Monkton, wherever it was, lay yet unburied. On every other topic he deferred to me with the utmost readiness and docility; on this, he maintained his strange opinion with an obstinacy which set reason and persuasion alike at defiance.

On the third day we rested at Fondi. The packing case with the coffin in it, reached us, and was deposited in a safe place under lock and key. We engaged some mules, and found a man to act as guide who knew the country thoroughly. It occurred to me that we had better begin by confiding the real object of our journey only to the most trustworthy people we could find among the better-educated classes. For this reason we followed, in one respect, the example of the duelling-party, by starting, early on the morning of the fourth day, with sketch-books and colour-boxes, as if we were only artists in search of the picturesque.

After travelling some hours in a northerly direction within the Roman frontier, we halted to rest ourselves and our mules at a wild little village, far out of the track of tourists in general.

The only person of the smallest importance in the place was the priest, and to him I addressed my first inquiries, leaving Monkton to await my return with the guide. I spoke Italian quite fluently and correctly enough for my purpose, and was extremely polite and cautious in introducing my business ; but, in spite of all the pains I took, I only succeeded in frightening and bewildering the poor priest more and more with every fresh word I said to him. The idea of a duelling-party and a dead man seemed to scare him out of his senses. He bowed, fidgeted, cast his eyes up to heaven, and piteously shrugging his shoulders, told me, with rapid Italian circumlocution, that he had not the faintest idea of what I was talking about. This was my first failure. I confess I was weak enough to feel a little dispirited when I joined Monkton and the guide.

After the heat of the day was over, we resumed our journey.

About three miles from the village, the road, or rather cart-track, branched off in two directions. The path to the right, our guide informed us, led up among the mountains to a convent about six miles off. If we penetrated beyond the convent, we should soon reach the Neapolitan frontier. The path to the left led far inwards on the Roman territory, and would conduct us to a small town where we could sleep for the night. Now the Roman territory presented the first and fittest field for our search, and the convent was always within reach, supposing we returned to Fondi unsuccessful. Besides, the path to the left led over the wildest part of the country we were starting to explore ; and I was

lways for vanquishing the greatest difficulty first—so we
lecided manfully on turning to the left. The expedition in
vhich this resolution involved us lasted a whole week, and
▪roduced no results. We discovered absolutely nothing, and re-
urned to our headquarters at Fondi so completely baffled
hat we did not know whither to turn our steps next.

I was made much more uneasy by the effect of our failure
▪n Monkton than by the failure itself. His resolution ap-
▪eared to break down altogether as soon as we began to
etrace our steps. He became first fretful and capricious, then
ilent and desponding. Finally, he sank into a lethargy of
▪ody and mind that seriously alarmed me. On the morning
fter our return to Fondi, he showed a strange tendency to
leep incessantly, which made me suspect the existence of
ome physical malady in his brain. The whole day he hardly
xchanged a word with me, and seemed to be never fairly
.wake. Early the next morning I went into his room, and
ound him as silent and lethargic as ever. His servant, who
▪as with us, informed me that Alfred had once or twice
▪efore exhibited such physical symptoms of mental exhaustion
s we were now observing, during his father's lifetime at
Vincot Abbey. This piece of information made me feel
asier, and left my mind free to return to the consideration
▪f the errand which had brought us to Fondi.

I resolved to occupy the time until my companion got better
n prosecuting our search by myself. That path to the right
.and which led to the convent, had not yet been explored. If
set off to trace it, I need not be away from Monkton more
han one night; and I should at least be able on my return to
ive him the satisfaction of knowing that one more uncer-
ainty regarding the place of the duel had been cleared up.
hese considerations decided me. I left a message for my
riend, in case he asked where I had gone, and set out
nce more for the village at which we had halted when
tarting on our first expedition.

Intending to walk to the convent, I parted company with
he guide and the mules where the track branched off, leaving
hem to go back to the village and await my return.

For the first four miles the path gently ascended through an
▪pen country, then became abruptly much steeper, and led me
eeper and deeper among thickets and endless woods. By the
me my watch informed me that I must have nearly walked

my appointed distance, the view was bounded on all sides,
and the sky was shut out overhead, by an impervious screen
of leaves and branches. I still followed my only guide, the
steep path ; and in ten minutes, emerging suddenly on a
plot of tolerably clear and level ground, I saw the convent
before me.

It was a dark, low, sinister-looking place. Not a sign of
life or movement was visible anywhere about it. Green stains
streaked the once white façade of the chapel in all directions.
Moss clustered thick in every crevice of the heavy scowling
wall that surrounded the convent. Long lank weeds grew out
of the fissures of roof and parapet, and drooping far down-
ward, waved wearily in and out of the barred dormitory
windows. The very cross opposite the entrance-gate, with
a shocking life sized figure in wood nailed to it, was so beset
at the base with crawling creatures, and looked so slimy,
green, and rotten all the way up, that I absolutely shrank
from it.

A bell-rope with a broken handle hung by the gate. I
approached it—hesitated, I hardly knew why—looked up at
the convent again, and then walked round to the back of
the building, partly to gain time to consider what I had better
do next ; partly from an unaccountable curiosity that urged
me, strangely to myself, to see all I could of the outside of the
place before I attempted to gain admission at the gate.

At the back of the convent I found an out-house, built on
to the wall—a clumsy, decayed building, with the greater
part of the roof fallen in, and with a jagged hole in one of
its sides, where in all probability a window had once been.
Behind the outhouse the trees grew thicker than ever. As I
looked towards them, I could not determine whether the
ground beyond me rose or fell—whether it was grassy, or
earthy, or rocky. I could see nothing but the all-pervading
leaves, brambles, ferns, and long grass.

Not a sound broke the oppressive stillness. No bird's note
rose from the leafy wilderness around me ; no voices spoke
in the convent garden behind the scowling wall; no clock
struck in the chapel-tower ; no dog barked in the ruined
out-house. The dead silence deepened the solitude of the
place inexpressibly. I began to feel it weighing on my
spirits—the more because woods were never favourite places
with me to walk in. The sort of pastoral happiness which

oets often represent, when they sing of life in the woods,
ever, to my mind, has half the charm of life on the mountain
r in the plain. When I am in a wood, I miss the boundless
oveliness of the sky, and the delicious softness that distance
ives to the earthly view beneath. I feel oppressively the
hange which the free air suffers when it gets imprisoned
mong leaves ; and I am always awed, rather than pleased,
y that mysterious still light which shines with such a strange
im lustre in deep places among trees. It may convict me of
ant of taste and absence of due feeling for the marvellous
eauties of vegetation, but I must frankly own that I never
enetrate far into a wood without finding that the getting
ut of it again is the pleasantest part of my walk—the
etting out on to the barest down, the wildest hill-side,
he bleakest mountain-top—the getting out anywhere so that
can see the sky over me and the view before me as far as
y eye can reach.

After such a confession as I have now made, it will appear
urprising to no one that I should have felt the strongest
ossible inclination, while I stood by the ruined out-house,
 retrace my steps at once, and make the best of my way out
f the wood. I had indeed actually turned to depart, when
he remembrance of the errand which had brought me to the
onvent suddenly stayed my feet. It seemed doubtful whether
should be admitted into the building if I rang the bell ; and
ore than doubtful, if I were let in, whether the inhabitants
ould be able to afford me any clue to the information of
hich I was in search. However, it was my duty to Monkton
 leave no means of helping him in his desperate object
ntried ; so I resolved to go round to the front of the
onvent again, and ring the gate-bell at all hazards.

By the merest chance I looked up as I passed the side of
e out-house where the jagged hole was, and noticed that
was pierced rather high in the wall.

As I stopped to observe this, the closeness of the atmosphere
 the wood seemed to be affecting me more unpleasantly
an ever.

I waited a minute and untied my cravat.

Closeness?—Surely it was something more than that. The
ir was even more distasteful to my nostrils than to my lungs.
here was some faint, indescribable smell loading it—some
nell of which I had never had any previous experience

—some smell which I thought (now that my attention wa
directed to it) grew more and more certainly traceable t
its source the nearer I advanced to the out-house.

By the time I had tried the experiment two or three time
and had made myself sure of this fact, my curiosity becam
excited. There were plenty of fragments of stone and bric
lying about me. I gathered some of them together, an
piled them up below the hole, then mounted to the top, and
feeling rather ashamed of what I was doing, peeped into th
out-house.

The sight of horror that met my eyes the instant I looke
through the hole, is as present to my memory now as if I ha
beheld it yesterday. I can hardly write of it at this distanc
of time without a thrill of the old terror running through m
again to the heart.

The first impression conveyed to me, as I looked in, was o
a long recumbent object, tinged with a lightish blue colou
all over, extended on trestles, and bearing a certain hideou
half-formed resemblance to the human face and figure.
looked again, and felt certain of it. There were the promin
ences of the forehead, nose, and chin, dimly shown as under
veil—there, the round outline of the chest, and the hollov
below it—there, the points of the knees, and the stiff, ghastl
upturned feet. I looked again, yet more attentively. My eye
got accustomed to the dim light streaming in through th
broken roof; and I satisfied myself, judging by the grea
length of the body from head to foot, that I was lookin
at the corpse of a man—a corpse that had apparently once ha
a sheet spread over it—and that had lain rotting on th
trestles under the open sky long enough for the linen t
take the livid, light-blue tinge of mildew and decay whicl
now covered it.

How long I remained with my eyes fixed on that drea
sight of death, on that tombless, terrible wreck of humanity
poisoning the still air, and seeming even to stain the fain
descending light that disclosed it, I know not. I remember
dull, distant sound among the trees, as if the breeze wer
rising—the slow creeping on of the sound to near the plac
where I stood—the noiseless, whirling fall of a dead leaf o
the corpse below me, through the gap in the out-house roc
—and the effect of awakening my energies, of relaxing th
heavy strain on my mind, which even the slight chang

wrought in the scene I beheld by the falling leaf, produced in me immediately. I descended to the ground, and, sitting down on the heap of stones, wiped away the thick perspiration which covered my face, and which I now became aware of for the first time. It was something more than the hideous spectacle unexpectedly offered to my eyes which had shaken my nerves, as I felt that they were shaken now. Monkton's prediction that, if we succeeded in discovering his uncle's body, we should find it unburied, recurred to me the instant I saw the trestles and their ghastly burden. I felt assured on the instant that I had found the dead man—the old prophecy recurred to my memory—a strange yearning sorrow, a vague foreboding of ill, an inexplicable terror, as I thought of the poor lad who was awaiting my return in the distant town, struck through me with a chill of superstitious dread, robbed me of my judgment and resolution, and left me, when I had at last recovered myself, weak and dizzy, as if I had just suffered under some pang of overpowering physical pain.

I hastened round to the convent gate, and rang impatiently at the bell—waited a little while, and rang again—then heard footsteps.

In the middle of the gate, just opposite my face, there was a small sliding panel, not more than a few inches long; this was presently pushed aside from within. I saw, through a bit of iron grating, two dull, light grey eyes staring vacantly at me, and heard a feeble, husky voice saying:—

" What may you please to want?"

" I am a traveller——" I began.

" We live in a miserable place. We have nothing to show travellers here."

" I don't come to see anything. I have an important question to ask, which I believe someone in this convent will be able to answer. If you are not willing to let me in, at least come out and speak to me here."

" Are you alone?"

" Quite alone."

" Are there no women with you?"

" None."

The gate was slowly unbarred; and an old Capuchin, very infirm, very suspicious, and very dirty, stood before me. I was far too excited and impatient to waste any time in prefatory phrases; so telling the monk at once how I had

looked through the hole in the out-house, and what I had
seen inside, I asked him in plain terms who the man had been
whose corpse I had beheld, and why the body was left
unburied?

The old Capuchin listened to me with watery eyes that
twinkled suspiciously. He had a battered tin snuff-box in his
hand ; and his finger and thumb slowly chased a few scattered
grains of snuff round and round the inside of the box all the
time I was speaking. When I had done, he shook his head,
and said, " that was certainly an ugly sight in their out-house ;
one of the ugliest sights, he felt sure, that ever I had seen
in all my life! "

" I don't want to talk of the sight," I rejoined impatiently ;
" I want to know who the man was, how he died, and why he
is not decently buried. Can you tell me? "

The monk's finger and thumb having captured three or
four grains of snuff at last, he slowly drew them into his
nostrils, holding the box open under his nose the while, to
prevent the possibility of wasting even one grain, sniffed
once or twice, luxuriously—closed the box—then looked at
me again, with his eyes watering and twinkling more suspiciously than before.

" Yes," said the monk, " that's an ugly sight in our out-
house—a very ugly sight, certainly! "

I never had more difficulty in keeping my temper in my
life, than at that moment. I succeeded, however, in repressing
a very disrespectful expression on the subject of monks in
general, which was on the tip of my tongue, and made
another attempt to conquer the old man's exasperating reserve.
Fortunately for my chances of succeeding with him, I was a
snuff-taker myself ; and I had a box full of excellent English
snuff in my pocket, which I now produced as a bribe. It was
my last resource.

" I thought your box seemed empty just now," said I ;
" will you try a pinch out of mine? "

The offer was accepted with an almost youthful alacrity of
gesture. The Capuchin took the largest pinch I ever saw
held between any man's finger and thumb, inhaled it slowly,
without spilling a single grain—half closed his eyes—and,
wagging his head gently, patted me paternally on the back.

" Oh! my son! " said the monk, " what delectable snuff!

Oh, my son and amiable traveller, give the spiritual father who loves you yet another tiny, tiny pinch!"

"Let me fill your box for you. I shall have plenty left for myself."

The battered tin snuff-box was given to me before I had done speaking—the paternal hand patted my back more approvingly than ever—the feeble, husky voice grew glib and eloquent in my praise. I had evidently found out the weak side of the old Capuchin; and, on returning him his box, I took instant advantage of the discovery.

"Excuse my troubling you on the subject again," I said, "but I have particular reasons for wanting to hear all that you can tell me in explanation of that horrible sight in the out-house."

"Come in," answered the monk.

He drew me inside the gate, closed it, and then leading the way across the grass-grown courtyard, looking out on a weedy kitchen garden, showed me into a long room with a low ceiling, a dirty dresser, a few rudely-carved stall seats, and one or two grim mildewed pictures for ornaments. This was the sacristy.

"There's nobody here, and it's nice and cool," said the old Capuchin. It was so damp that I actually shivered. "Would you like to see the church?" said the monk; "a jewel of a church, if we could only keep it in repair; but we can't. Ah! malediction and misery, we are too poor to keep our church in repair!"

Here he shook his head, and began fumbling with a large bunch of keys.

"Never mind the church now!" said I. "Can you, or can you not, tell me what I want to know?"

"Everything, from beginning to end—absolutely everything! Why, I answered the gate bell—I always answer the gate bell here," said the Capuchin.

"What, in heaven's name, has the gate bell to do with the unburied corpse in your out-house?"

"Listen, son of mine, and you shall know. Some time ago —some months—ah, me, I'm old; I've lost my memory; I don't know how many months—ah! miserable me, what a very old, old monk I am!" Here he comforted himself with another pinch of my snuff.

" Never mind the exact time," said I. " I don't care about that."

" Good," said the Capuchin. " Now I can go on. Well, let us say, it is some months ago—we in this convent are all at breakfast—wretched, wretched breakfasts, son of mine in this convent!—we are at breakfast, and we hear *bang! bang!* twice over. ' Guns,' says I. ' What are they shooting for?' says brother Jeremy. ' Game,' says brother Vincent. ' Aha! game,' says brother Jeremy. ' If I hear more, I shall send out and discover what it means,' says the father superior. We hear no more, and we go on with our wretched breakfasts."

" Where did the report of fire-arms come from?" I inquired.

" From down below, beyond the big trees at the back of the convent, where there's some clear ground—nice ground, if it wasn't for the pools and puddles. But, ah, misery! how damp we are in these parts! how very, very damp!"

" Well, what happened after the report of fire-arms?"

" You shall hear. We are still at breakfast, all silent—for what have we to talk about here? What have we but our devotions, our kitchen garden, and our wretched, wretched bits of breakfasts and dinners? I say we are all silent, when there comes suddenly such a ring at the bell as never was heard before—a very devil of a ring—a ring that caught us all with our bits—our wretched, wretched bits!—in our mouths, and stopped us before we could swallow them. ' Go, brother of mine!' says the father superior to me—' go, it is your duty—go to the gate.' I am brave—a very lion of a Capuchin. I slip out on tiptoe—I wait—I listen—I pull back our little shutter in the gate—I wait, I listen again—I peep through the hole—nothing, absolutely nothing, that I can see. I am brave—I am not to be daunted. What do I do next? I open the gate. Ah! Sacred Mother of Heaven, what do I behold lying all along our threshold? A man—dead!—a big man; bigger than you, bigger than me, bigger than anybody in this convent—buttoned up tight in a fine coat, with black eyes, staring, staring up at the sky; and blood soaking through and through the front of his shirt. What do I do? I scream once—I scream twice—and run back to the father superior!"

All the particulars of the fatal duel which I had gleaned from the French newspaper in Monkton's room at Naples, recurred vividly to my memory. The suspicion that I had felt when I looked into the out-house, became a certainty as I listened to the old monk's last words.

"So far I understand," said I. "The corpse I have just seen in the out-house, is the corpse of the man whom you found dead outside your gate. Now tell me why you have not given the remains decent burial?"

"Wait—wait—wait," answered the Capuchin. "The father superior hears me scream, and comes out; we all run together to the gate; we lift up the big man, and look at him close. Dead! dead as this" (smacking the dresser with his hand). "We look again, and see a bit of paper pinned to the collar of his coat. Aha! son of mine, you start at that. I thought I should make you start at last."

I had started indeed. That paper was doubtless the leaf mentioned in the second's unfinished narrative as having been torn out of his pocket-book, and inscribed with the statement of how the dead man had lost his life. If proof positive were wanted to identify the dead body, here was such proof found.

"What do you think was written on the bit of paper?" continued the Capuchin. "We read, and shudder. This dead man has been killed in a duel—he, the desperate, the miserable, has died in the commission of mortal sin; and the men who saw the killing of him, ask us Capuchins, holy men, servants of Heaven, children of our lord the pope—they ask *us* to give him burial! Oh! but we are outraged when we read that; we groan, we wring our hands, we turn away, we tear our beards, we——"

"Wait one moment," said I, seeing that the old man was heating himself with his narrative, and was likely, unless I stopped him, to talk more and more fluently to less and less purpose—"wait a moment. Have you preserved the paper that was pinned to the dead man's coat; and can I look at it?"

The Capuchin seemed on the point of giving me an answer, when he suddenly checked himself. I saw his eyes wander away from my face, and at the same moment heard a door softly opened and closed behind me.

Looking round immediately, I observed another monk in the sacristy—a tall, lean, black-bearded man, in whose presence my old friend with the snuff-box suddenly became quite decorous and devotional to look at. I suspected I was in the presence of the father superior; and I found that was right the moment he addressed me.

"I am the father superior of this convent," he said in quiet, clear tones, and looking me straight in the face while he spoke, with coldly attentive eyes. "I have heard th latter part of your conversation, and I wish to know why you are so particularly anxious to see the piece of paper tha was pinned to the dead man's coat?"

The coolness with which he avowed that he had been listening, and the quietly imperative manner in which he pu his concluding questions, perplexed and startled me. I hardly knew at first what tone I ought to take in answering him. He observed my hesitation, and attributing it to the wrong cause, signed to the old Capuchin to retire. Humbly stroking his long grey beard, and furtively consoling himself with a private pinch of the "delectable snuff," my venerable friend shuffled out of the room, making a profound obeisance at the door just before he disappeared.

"Now," said the father superior, as coldly as ever; "I am waiting, sir, for your reply."

"You shall have it in the fewest possible words," said I, answering him in his own tone. "I find, to my disgust and horror, there is an unburied corpse in an out-house attached to this convent. I believe that corpse to be the body of an English gentleman of rank and fortune, who was killed in a duel. I have come into this neighbourhood, with the nephew and only relation of the slain man, for the express purpose of recovering his remains; and I wish to see the paper found on the body, because I believe that paper will identify it to the satisfaction of the relative to whom I have referred. Do you find my reply sufficiently straightforward? And do you mean to give me permission to look at the paper?"

"I am satisfied with your reply, and see no reason for refusing you a sight of the paper," said the father superior, "but I have something to say first. In speaking of the impression produced on you by beholding the corpse, you used the words 'disgust' and 'horror.' This licence of expression in relation to what you have seen in the precincts of a convent, proves to me that you are out of the pale of the Holy Catholic Church. You have no right, therefore, to expect any explanation; but I will give you one, never theless, as a favour. The slain man died, unabsolved, in the commission of mortal sin. We infer so much from the paper which we found on his body; and we know, by the evidence of our own eyes and ears, that he was killed on the territories of the church, and in the act of committing direct violation of those special laws against the crime of duelling, the strict enforcement of which the Holy Father himself has urged on the faithful throughout his dominions, by letters signed with his own hand. Inside this convent the ground is consecrated; and we Catholics are not accustomed to bury the outlaws of our legion, the enemies of our Holy Father, and the violators of our most sacred laws, in consecrated ground. Outside this convent, we have no rights and no power; and, if we had both, we should remember that we are monks, not gravediggers, and that the only burial with which *we* can have any concern, is burial with prayers of the church. That is all the explanation I think it necessary to give. Wait for me here, and you shall see the paper." With those words the father superior left the room as quietly as he had entered it.

I had hardly time to think over this bitter and ungracious explanation, and to feel a little piqued by the language and manner of the person who had given it to me, before the father superior returned with the paper in his hand. He placed it before me on the dresser; and I read, hurriedly traced in pencil, the following lines:

"This paper is attached to the body of the late Mr. Stephen Monkton, an Englishman of distinction. He has been shot in a duel, conducted with perfect gallantry and honour on both sides. His body is placed at the door of this convent, to receive burial at the hands of its inmates, the survivors of the encounter being obliged to separate and secure their safety by immediate flight. I, the second of the slain man, and the writer of this explanation, certify, on my word of honour as a gentleman, that the shot which killed my principal on the instant, was fired fairly, in the strictest accordance with the rules laid down beforehand for the conduct of the duel.

(Signed) "F."

"F." I recognised easily enough as the initial letter of

Monsieur Foulon's name, the second of Mr. Monkton, who had died of consumption at Paris.

The discovery and the identification were now complete. Nothing remained but to break the news to Alfred, and to get permission to remove the remains in the out-house. I began almost to doubt the evidence of my own senses, when I reflected that the apparently impracticable object with which we had left Naples was already, by the merest chance, vitrually accomplished.

"The evidence of the paper is decisive," I said, handing it back. "There can be no doubt that the remains in the out-house are the remains of which we have been in search. May I inquire if any obstalces will be thrown in our way, should the late Mr. Monkton's nephew wish to remove his uncle's body to the family burial-place in England?"

"Where is this nephew?" asked the father superior.

"He is now waiting my return at the town of Fondi."

"Is he in a position to prove his relationship?"

"Certainly; he has papers with him which will place it beyond a doubt."

"Let him satisfy the civil authorities of his claim, and he need expect no obstacle to his wishes from anyone here."

I was in no humour for talking a moment longer with my sour-tempered companion than I could help. The day was wearing on fast; and, whether night overtook me or not, I was resolved never to stop on my return till I got back to Fondi. Accordingly, after telling the father superior that he might expect to hear from me again immediately, I made my bow, and hastened out of the sacristy.

At the convent gate stood my old friend with the tin snuff-box, waiting to let me out.

"Bless you, my son," said the venerable recluse, giving me a farewell pat on the shoulder; "come back soon to your spiritual father who loves you; and amiably favour him with another tiny, tiny pinch of the delectable snuff."

CHAPTER VI

I returned at the top of my speed to the village where I had left the mules, had the animals saddled immediately, and succeeded in getting back to Fondi a little before sunset.

While ascending the stairs of our hotel, I suffered under the most painful uncertainty as to how I should best communicate the news of my discovery to Alfred. If I could not succeed in preparing him properly for my tidings, the results—with such an organisation as his—might be fatal. On opening the door of his room, I felt by no means sure of myself ; and when I confronted him, his manner of receiving me took me so much by surprise that, for a moment or two, I lost my self-possession altogether.

Every trace of the lethargy in which he was sunk when I had last seen him, had disappeared. His eyes were bright, his cheeks deeply flushed. As I entered, he started up, and refused my offered hand.

"You have not treated me like a friend," he said passionately; "you had no right to continue the search unless searched with you—you had no right to leave me here alone. I was wrong to trust you: you are no better than all the rest of them."

I had by this time recovered a little from my first astonishment, and was able to reply before he could say anything more. It was quite useless, in his present state, to reason with him, or to defend myself. I determined to risk everything, and break my news to him at once.

"You will treat me more justly, Monkton, when you know that I have been doing you good service during my absence," I said. "Unless I am greatly mistaken, the object for which we have left Naples may be nearer attainment by both of us than——"

The flush left his cheeks almost in an instant. Some expression in my face, or some tone in my voice, of which I was not conscious, had revealed to his nervously-quickened perception more than I had intended that he should know at first. His eyes fixed themselves intently on mine ; his hand grasped my arm ; and he said to me in an eager whisper:

" Tell me the truth at once. Have you found him?"

It was too late to hesitate. I answered in the affirmative.

" Buried or unburied?"

His voice rose abruptly as he put the question, and hi
unoccupied hand fastened on my other arm.

" Unburied."

I had hardly uttered the word before the blood flew bacl
into his cheeks ; his eyes flashed again as they looked int
mine, and he burst into a fit of triumphant laughter, whicl
shocked and startled me inexpressibly.

" What did I tell you? What do you say to the old prophecy
now?" he cried, dropping his hold on my arms, and pacing
backwards and forwards in the room. " Own you wer
wrong. Own it, as all Naples shall own it, when once I have
got him safe in his coffin!"

His laughter grew more and more violent. I tried to
quiet him in vain. His servant and the landlord of the inr
entered the room ; but they only added fuel to the fire, and
I made them go out again. As I shut the door on them,
observed lying on a table near at hand, the packet of letter
from Miss Elmslie, which my unhappy friend preserved witl
such care, and read and re-read with such unfailing devotior
Looking towards me just when I passed by the table, th
letters caught his eyes. The new hope for the future, it
connection with the writer of them, which my news wa
already awakening in his heart, seemed to overwhelm hin
in an instant at sight of the treasured memorials that reminde
him of his betrothed wife. His laughter ceased, his fac
changed, he ran to the table, caught the letters up in hi
hand, looked from them to me for one moment with ar
altered expression which went to my heart, then sank down o
his knees at the table, laid his face on the letters, and burs
into tears. I let the new emotion have its way uninterruptedly
and quitted the room, without saying a word. When
returned, after a lapse of some little time, I found him sittin
quietly in his chair, reading one of the letters from the packe
which rested on his knee.

His look was kindness itself ; his gesture almost womanl
in its gentleness as he rose to meet me, and anxiously held ou
his hand.

He was quite calm enough now to hear in detail all that

had to tell him. I suppressed nothing but the particulars of the state in which I had found the corpse. I assumed no right of direction as to the share he was to take in our future proceedings, with the exception of insisting beforehand that he should leave the absolute superintendence of the removal of the body to me, and that he should be satisfied with a sight of M. Foulon's paper, after receiving my assurance that the remains placed in the coffin were really and truly the remains of which we had been in search.

"Your nerves are not so strong as mine," I said, by way of apology for my apparent dictation; "and for that reason I must beg leave to assume the leadership in all that we have now to do, until I see the leaden coffin soldered down and safe in your possession. After that, I shall resign all my functions to you."

"I want words to thank you for your kindness," he answered. "No brother could have borne with me more affectionately, or helped me more patiently, than you."

He stopped, and grew thoughtful, then occupied himself in tying up slowly and carefully the packet of Miss Elmslie's letters, and then looked suddenly towards the vacant wall behind me, with that strange expression the meaning of which I knew so well. Since we had left Naples, I had purposely avoided exciting him by talking on the useless and shocking subject of the apparition by which he believed himself to be perpetually followed. Just now, however, he seemed so calm and collected—so little likely to be violently agitated by any allusion to the dangerous topic—that I ventured to speak out boldly.

"Does the phantom still appear to you," I asked, "as it appeared at Naples?"

He looked at me, and smiled.

"Did I not tell you that it followed me everywhere?" His eyes wandered back again to the vacant space, and he went on speaking in that direction, as if he had been continuing the conversation with some third person in the room. "We shall part," he said slowly and softly, "when the empty place is filled in Wincot vault. Then I shall stand with Ada before the altar in the Abbey chapel; and, when my eyes meet hers, they will see the tortured face no more."

Saying this, he leaned his head on his **hand, sighed,**

and began repeating softly to himself the lines of the old prophecy:

> " *When in Wincot vault a place*
> *Waits for one of Monkton's race:*
> *When that one forlorn shall lie*
> *Graveless under open sky,*
> *Beggared of six feet of earth,*
> *Though lord of acres from his birth—*
> *That shall be a certain sign*
> *Of the end of Monkton's line.*
> *Dwindling ever faster, faster,*
> *Dwindling to the last-left master;*
> *From mortal ken, from light of day,*
> *Monkton's race shall pass away."*

Fancying that he pronounced the last lines a little incoherently, I tried to make him change the subject. He took no notice of what I said, and went on talking to himself.

" Monkton's race shall pass away!" he repeated ; " but not with *me*. The fatality hangs over *my* head no longer. I shall bury the unburied dead ; I shall fill the vacant place in Wincot vault. And then—then the new life, the life with Ada!" —That name seemed to recall him to himself. He drew his travelling desk towards him, placed the packet of letters in it, and then took out a sheet of paper. " I am going to write to Ada," he said, turning to me, " and tell her the good news. Her happiness, when she knows it, will be even greater than mine."

Worn out by the events of the day, I left him writing, and went to bed. I was, however, either too anxious or too tired to sleep. In this waking condition, my mind naturally occupied itself with the discovery at the convent, and with the events to which that discovery would in all probability lead. As I thought on the future, a depression for which I could not account weighed on my spirits. There was not the slightest reason for the vaguely melancholy forebodings that oppressed me. The remains, to the finding of which my unhappy friend attached so much importance, had been traced ; they would certainly be placed at his disposal in a few days ; he might take them to England by the first merchant vessel that sailed from Naples ; and, the gratification of his strange caprice thus accomplished, there was at least some reason to hope that his mind might recover its tone, and that the new life he would lead at Wincot might result in making him a happy man. Such considerations as these were, in themselves, certainly not calculated to exert any melancholy influence over me; and yet, all through the night, the same inconceivable, unaccountable depression weighed heavily on my spirits—heavily through the hours of darkness—heavily, even when I walked out to breathe the first freshness of the early morning air.

With the day came the all-engrossing business of opening negotiations with the authorities.

Only those who have had to deal with Italian officials can imagine how our patience was tried by everyone with whom we came in contact. We were bandied about from one authority to the other, were stared at, cross-questioned, mystified—not in the least because the case presented any special difficulties or intricacies, but because it was absolutely necessary that every civil dignitary to whom we applied should assert his own importance by leading us to our object in the most roundabout manner possible. After our first day's experience of official life in Italy, I left the absurd formalities, which we had no choice but to perform, to be accomplished by Alfred alone, and applied myself to considering the really serious question of how the remains in the convent out-house were to be safely removed.

The best plan that suggested itself to me was to write to a friend at Rome, where I knew that it was a custom to embalm the bodies of high dignitaries of the church, and where, I consequently inferred, such chemical assistance as was needed in our emergency might be obtained. I simply stated in my letter that the removal of the body was imperative, then described the conditions in which I had found it, and engaged that no expense on our part should be spared if the right person or persons could be found to help us. Here again more difficulties interposed themselves, and more useless formalities were to be gone through; but, in the end, patience, perseverance, and money triumphed, and two men came expressly from Rome to undertake the duties we required of them.

It is unnecessary that I should shock the reader by entering into any detail in this part of my narrative. When I have said

that the progress of decay was so far suspended by chemical
means as to allow of the remains being placed in the
coffin, and to ensure their being transported to England with
perfect safety and convenience, I have said enough. After
ten days had been wasted in useless delays and difficulties, I
had the satisfaction of seeing the convent outhouse empty at
last; passed through a final ceremony of snuff-taking, or
rather, of snuff-giving, with the old Capuchin; and ordered
the travelling carriage to be ready at the inn door. Hardly a
month had elapsed since our departure, when we entered
Naples successful in the achievement of a design which
had been ridiculed as wildly impracticable by every friend of
ours who had heard of it.

The first object to be accomplished on our return was
to obtain the means of carrying the coffin to England—
by sea, as a matter of course. All inquiries after a merchant
vessel on the point of sailing for any British port, led to the
most unsatisfactory results. There was only one way of
ensuring the immediate transportation of the remains to
England, and that was to hire a vessel. Impatient to return,
and resolved not to lose sight of the coffin till he had seen
it placed in Wincot vault, Monkton decided immediately on
hiring the first ship that could be obtained. The vessel in
port which we were informed could soonest be got ready for
sea, was a Sicilian brig; and this vessel my friend accordingly
engaged. The best dockyard artisans that could be got were
set to work, and the smartest captain and crew to be picked
up on an emergency in Naples, were chosen to navigate the
brig.

Monkton, after again expressing in the warmest terms his
gratitude for the services I had rendered him, disclaimed any
intention of asking me to accompany him on the voyage to
England. Greatly to his surprise and delight, however, I
offered of my own accord to take passage in the brig. The
strange coincidences I had witnessed, the extraordinary
discovery I had hit on, since our first meeting in Naples, had
made his one great interest in life my one great interest for
the time being, as well. I shared none of his delusions,
poor fellow; but it is hardly an exaggeration to say that my
eagerness to follow our remarkable adventure to its end, was
as great as his anxiety to see the coffin laid in Wincot
vault. Curiosity influenced me, I am afraid, almost as strongly

s friendship, when I offered myself as the companion of his
voyage home.

We set sail for England on a calm and lovely afternoon.

For the first time since I had known him, Monkton seemed
to be in high spirits. He talked and jested on all sorts of
subjects, and laughed at me for allowing my cheerfulness to
be affected by the dread of sea-sickness. I had really no
such fear; it was my excuse to my friend for a return of
that unaccountable depression under which I had suffered at
Fondi. Everything was in our favour; everybody on board
the brig was in good spirits. The captain was delighted with
the vessel; the crew, Italians and Maltese, were in high glee
at the prospect of making a short voyage on high wages in
well-provisioned ship. I alone felt heavy at heart. There
was no valid reason that I could assign to myself for the
melancholy that oppressed me, and yet I struggled against
it in vain.

Late on our first night at sea, I made a discovery which
was by no means calculated to restore my spirits to their
usual equilibrium. Monkton was in the cabin, on the floor of
which had been placed the packing-case containing the
coffin; and I was on deck. The wind had fallen almost to
a calm, and I was lazily watching the sails of the brig as they
flapped from time to time against the masts, when the captain
approached, and, drawing me out of hearing of the man at the
helm, whispered in my ear:

"There's something wrong among the men forward. Did
you observe how suddenly they all became silent just before
sunset?"

I had observed it, and told him so.

"There's a Maltese boy on board," pursued the captain,
"who is a smart lad enough, but a bad one to deal with. I
have found out that he has been telling the men there is
a dead body inside that packing-case of your friend's in the
cabin."

My heart sank as he spoke. Knowing the superstitious
irrationality of sailors—of foreign sailors especially—I had
taken care to spread a report on board the brig, before
the coffin was shipped, that the packing-case contained a
valuable marble statue which Mr. Monkton prized highly, and
was unwilling to trust out of his own sight. How could this
Maltese boy have discovered that the pretended statue was

a human corpse? As I pondered over the question, my suspicions fixed themselves on Monkton's servant, who spoke Italian fluently, and whom I knew to be an incorrigible gossip. The man denied it when I charged him with betraying us, but I have never believed his denial to this day.

" The little imp won't say where he picked up this notion of his about the dead body," continued the captain. " It's not my place to pry into secrets; but I advise you to call the crew aft and contradict the boy, whether he speaks the truth or not. The men are a parcel of fools, who believe in ghosts, and all the rest of it. Some of them say they would never have signed our articles if they had known they were going to sail with a dead man; others only grumble; but I'm afraid we shall have some trouble with them all, in case of rough weather, unless the boy is contradicted by you or the other gentleman. The men say that if either you or your friend tell them on your words of honour that the Maltese is a liar, they will hand him up to be rope's ended accordingly; but that if you won't, they have made up their minds to believe the boy."

Here the captain paused, and awaited my answer. I could give him none. I felt hopeless under our desperate emergency. To get the boy punished by giving my word of honour to support a direct falsehood, was not to be thought of even for a moment. What other means of extrication from his miserable dilemma remained? None that I could think of. I thanked the captain for his attention to our interests, told him I would take time to consider what course I should pursue, and begged that he would say nothing to my friend about the discovery he had made. He promised to be silent, sulkily enough, and walked away from me.

We had expected the breeze to spring up with the morning, but no breeze came. As it wore on towards noon, the atmosphere became insufferably sultry, and the sea looked as smooth as glass. I saw the captain's eye turn often and anxiously to windward. Far away in that direction, and alone in the blue heaven, I observed a little black cloud, and asked if it would bring us any wind.

" More than we want," the captain replied shortly; and then, to my astonishment, ordered the crew aloft to take in sail. The execution of this manœuvre showed but too plainly the temper of the men; they did their work sulkily and slowly, grumbling and murmuring among themselves. The captain's manner, as he urged them on with oaths and threats, convinced me we were in danger. I looked again to windward. The one little cloud had enlarged to a great bank of murky vapour, and the sea at the horizon had changed in colour.

"The squall will be on us before we know where we are," said the captain. "Go below; you will be only in the way here."

I descended to the cabin, and prepared Monkton for what was coming. He was still questioning me about what I had observed on deck, when the storm burst on us. We felt the little brig strain for an instant as if she would part in two, then she seemed to be swinging round with us, then to be quite still for a moment, trembling in every timber. Last, came a shock which hurled us from our seats, a deafening crash, and a flood of water pouring into the cabin. We clambered, half-drowned, to the deck. The brig had, in the nautical phrase, "broached to," and she now lay on her beam ends.

Before I could make out anything distinctly in the horrible confusion, except the one tremendous certainty that we were entirely at the mercy of the sea, I heard a voice from the fore part of the ship which stilled the clamouring and shouting of the rest of the crew in an instant. The words were in Italian, but I understood their fatal meaning only too easily. We had sprung a leak, and the sea was pouring into the ship's hold like the race of a mill-stream. The captain did not lose his presence of mind in this fresh emergency. He called for his axe to cut away the foremast, and ordering some of the crew to help him, directed the others to rig out the pumps.

The words had hardly passed his lips, before the men broke into open mutiny. With a savage look at me, their ringleader declared that the passengers might do as they pleased, but that he and his messmates were determined to take the boat, and leave the accursed ship, and *the dead man in her*, to go to the bottom together. As he spoke there was a shout among the sailors, and I observed some of them pointing derisively behind me. Looking round, I saw Monkton, who had hitherto kept close at my side, making his way back to the cabin. I followed him directly, but the water and confusion on deck, and the impossibility, from the position of the brig, of moving the feet without the slow assistance of the hands, so impeded my progress that it was impossible for me to overtake him. When I had got below, he was crouched upon the coffin, with the water on the cabin floor whirling and splashing about him, as the ship heaved and plunged. I saw a warning brightness in his eyes, a warning flush on his cheeks, as I approached and said to him:

"There is nothing left for it, Alfred, but to bow to our misfortune, and do the best we can to save our lives."

"Save yours," he cried, waving his hand to me, "for *you* have a future before you. Mine is gone when this coffin goes to the bottom. If the ship sinks, I shall know that the fatality is accomplished, and shall sink with her."

I saw that he was in no state to be reasoned with or persuaded, and raised myself again to the deck. The men were cutting away all obstalces, so as to launch the long boat, placed amidships, over the depressed bulwark of the brig, as she lay on her side; and the captain, after having made a last vain exertion to restore his authority, was looking on at them in silence. The violence of the squall seemed already to be spending itself, and I asked whether there was really no chance for us if we remained by the ship. The captain answered that there might have been the best chance if the men had obeyed his orders, but that now there was none. Knowing that I could place no dependence on the presence of mind of Monkton's servant, I confided to the captain, in the fewest and plainest words, the condition of my unhappy friend, and asked if I might depend on his help. He nodded his head, and we descended together to the cabin. Even at this day, it costs me pain to write of the terrible necessity to which the strength and obstinacy of Monkton's delusion reduced us, in the last resort. We were compelled to secure his hands, and drag him by main force to the deck. The men were on the point of launching the boat, and refused at first to receive us into it.

"You cowards!" cried the captain, "have we got the dead man with us this time? Isn't he going to the bottom along with the brig? Who are you afraid of when we get into the boat?"

This sort of appeal produced the desired effect; the men became ashamed of themselves, and retracted their refusal.

Just as we pushed off from the sinking ship, Alfred made

an effort to break from me, but I held him firm, and he never repeated the attempt. He sat by me, with drooping head, still and silent, while the sailors rowed away from the vessel: still and silent, when with one accord they paused at a little distance off, and we all waited and watched to see the brig sink: still and silent, even when that sinking happened, when the labouring hull plunged slowly into a hollow of the sea—hesitated, as it seemed, for one moment—rose a little again—then sank to rise no more.

Sank with her dead freight: sank, and snatched for ever from our power the corpse which we had discovered almost by a miracle—those jealously-preserved remains on the safe keeping of which rested so strangely the hopes and the love-destinies of two living beings! As the last signs of the ship disappeared in the depths of the waters, I felt Monkton trembling all over as he sat close at my side, and heard him repeating to himself, sadly, and many times over, the name of " Ada."

I tried to turn his thoughts to another subject, but it was useless. He pointed over the sea to where the brig had once been, and where nothing was left to look at but the rolling waves.

" The empty place will now remain empty for ever in Wincot vault."

As he said those words, he fixed his eyes for a moment sadly and earnestly on my face, then looked away, leant his cheek upon his hand, and spoke no more.

We were sighted long before nightfall by a trading-vessel, were taken on board, and landed at Cartagena in Spain. Alfred never held up his head, and never once spoke to me of his own accord, the whole time we were at sea in the merchantman. I observed, however, with alarm, that he talked often and incoherently to himself—constantly muttering the lines of the old prophecy—constantly referring to the fatal place that was empty in Wincot vault—constantly repeating in broken accents which it affected me inexpressibly to hear, the name of the poor girl who was awaiting his return to England. Nor were these the only causes for the apprehension that I now felt on his account. Towards the end of our voyage he began to suffer from alternations of fever fits and shivering fits, which I ignorantly imagined to be attacks of ague. I was soon undeceived. We had hardly been a day on shore before he became to much worse that I secured the best medical assistance Cartagena could afford. For a day or two the doctors differed, as usual, about the nature of his complaint, but ere long alarming symptoms displayed themselves. The medical men declared that his life was in danger, and told me that his disease was brain fever.

Shocked and grieved as I was, I hardly knew how to act at first under the fresh responsibility now laid upon me. Ultimately, I decided on writing to the old priest who had been Alfred's tutor, and who, as I knew, still resided at Wincot Abbey. I told this gentleman all that had happened, begged him to break my melancholy news as gently as possible to Miss Elmslie, and assured him of my resolution to remain with Monkton to the last.

After I had despatched my letter, and had sent to Gibraltar to secure the best English medical advice that could be obtained, I felt that I had done my best, and that nothing remained but to wait and hope.

Many a sad and anxious hour did I pass by my poor friend's bedside. Many a time did I doubt whether I had done right in giving any encouragement to his delusion. The reasons for doing so which had suggested themselves to me, after my first interview with him, seem, however, on reflection, to be valid reasons still. The only way of hastening his return to England and to Miss Elmslie, who was pining for that return, was the way I had taken. It was not my fault that a disaster which no man could foresee, had overthrown all his projects and all mine. But now that the calamity had happened, and was irretrievable, how, in the event of his physical recovery, was his moral malady to be combated?

When I reflected on the hereditary taint in his mental organisation, on that childish fright of Stephen Monkton from which he had never recovered, on the perilously secluded life that he had led at the Abbey, and on his firm persuasion of the reality of the apparition by which he believed himself to be constantly followed, I confess I despaired of shaking his superstitious faith in every word and line of the old family prophecy. If the series of striking coincidences which appeared to attest its truth had made a strong and lasting impression on *me* (and this was assuredly the case), how could I wonder that they had produced the effect of absolute conviction on *his* mind, constituted as it was? If I argued with him, and he answered me, how could I rejoin? If he said, " The prophecy points at the last of the family: *I* am the last of the family. The prophecy mentions an empty place in Wincot vault: there is such an empty place there at this moment. On the faith of the prophecy I told you that Stephen Monkton's body was unburied, and you found that it was unburied."—if he said this, of what use would it be for me to reply, " These are only strange coincidences, after all?"

The more I thought of the task that lay before me, if he recovered, the more I felt inclined to despond. The oftener the English physician who attended on him said to me, " He may get the better of the fever, but he has a fixed idea, which never leaves him night or day, which has unsettled his reason, and which will end in killing him, unless you or some of his friends can remove it."—the oftener I heard this, the more acutely I felt my own powerlessness, the more I shrank from every idea that was connected with the hopeless future.

I had only expected to receive my answer from Wincot in the shape of a letter. It was consequently a great surprise, as well as a great relief, to be informed one day that two gentlemen wished to speak with me, and to find that of these two gentlemen the first was the old priest, and the second a male relative of Mrs. Elmslie.

Just before their arrival the fever symptoms had disappeared, and Alfred had been pronounced out of danger. Both the priest and his companion were eager to know when the sufferer would be strong enough to travel. They had come to Cartagena expressly to take him home with them, and felt far more hopeful than I did of the restorative effects of his native air. After all the questions connected with the first important point of the journey to England had been asked and answered, I ventured to make some inquiries after Miss Elmslie. Her relative informed me that she was suffering both in body and in mind from excess of anxiety on Alfred's account. They had been obliged to deceive her as to the dangerous nature of his illness, in order to deter her from accompanying the priest and her relation on their mission to Spain.

Slowly and imperfectly, as the weeks wore on, Alfred regained something of his former physical strength, but no alteration appeared in his illness as it affected his mind.

From the very first day of his advance towards recovery, it had been discovered that the brain fever had exercised the strangest influence over his faculties of memory. All recollection of recent events was gone from him. Everything connected with Naples, with me, with his journey to Italy, had dropped in some mysterious manner entirely out of his remembrance. So completely had all late circumstances passed from his memory, that, though he recognised the old priest and his own servant easily on the first days of his convalescence, he never recognised me, but regarded me with such a wistful, doubting expression, that I felt inexpressibly pained when I approached his bedside. All his questions were about Miss Elmslie and Wincot Abbey; and all his talk referred to the period when his father was yet alive.

The doctors augured good rather than ill from this loss of memory of recent incidents, saying that it would turn out to be temporary, and that it answered the first great healing purpose of keeping his mind at ease. I tried to believe them —tried to feel as sanguine, when the day came for his departure, as the old friends felt who were taking him home. But the effort was too much for me. A foreboding that I should never see him again oppressed my heart, and the tears came into my eyes as I saw the worn figure of my poor friend half helped, half lifted into the travelling carriage, and borne away gently on the road towards home.

He had never recognised me, and the doctors had begged that I would give him, for some time to come, as few opportunities as possible of doing so. But for this request I should have accompanied him to England. As it was, nothing better remained for me to do than to change the scene, and recruit as I best could my energies of body and mind, depressed of late by much watching and anxiety. The famous cities of Spain were not new to me, but I visited them again, and revived old impressions of the Alhambra and Madrid. Once or twice I thought of making a pilgrimage to the East, but late events had sobered and altered me. That yearning unsatisfied feeling which we call "home-sickness," began to prey upon my heart, and I resolved to return to England.

I went back by way of Paris, having settled with the

priest that he should write to me at my banker's there, as soon as he could after Alfred had returned to Wincot. If I had gone to the East, the letter would have been forwarded to me. I wrote to prevent this; and, on my arrival at Paris, stopped at the banker's before I went to my hotel.

The moment the letter was put into my hands, the black border on the envelope told me the worst. He was dead.

There was but one consolation—he had died calmly, almost happily, without once referring to those fatal chances which had wrought the fulfilment of the ancient prophecy. "My beloved pupil," the old priest wrote, "seemed to rally a little the first few days after his return, but he gained no real strength, and soon suffered a slight relapse of fever. After this he sank gradually and gently day by day, and so departed from us on the last dread journey. Miss Elmslie (who knows that I am writing this) desires me to express her deep and lasting gratitude for all your kindness to Alfred. She told me when we brought him back, that she had waited for him as his promised wife, and that she would nurse him now as a wife should; and she never left him. His face was turned towards her, his hand was clasped in hers, when he died. It will console you to know that he never mentioned events at Naples, or the shipwreck that followed them, from the day of his return to the day of his death."

Three days after reading the letter I was at Wincot, and heard all the details of Alfred's last moments from the priest. I felt a shock which it would not be very easy for me to analyse or explain, when I heard that he had been buried, at his own desire, in the fatal Abbey vault.

The priest took me down to see the place—a grim, cold, subterranean building, with a low roof, supported on heavy Saxon arches. Narrow niches, with the ends only of coffins visible within them, ran down each side of the vault. The nails and silver ornaments flashed here and there as my companion moved past them with a lamp in his hand. At the lower end of the place he stopped, pointed to a niche, and said: "He lies here, between his father and mother." I looked a little further on, and saw what appeared at first like a long dark tunnel. "That is only an empty niche," said the priest, following me. "If the body of Mr. Stephen Monkton had been brought to Wincot, his coffin would have been placed there."

A chill came over me, and a sense of dread which I am ashamed of having felt now, but which I could not combat then. The blessed light of day was pouring down gaily at the other end of the vault through the open door. I turned my back on the empty niche, and hurried into the sunlight and the fresh air.

As I walked across the grass glade leading down to the vault, I heard the rustle of a woman's dress behind me, and, turning round, saw a young lady advancing, clad in deep mourning. Her sweet, sad face, her manner as she held out her hand, told me who it was in an instant.

"I heard that you were here," she said, "and I wished"—her voice faltered a little. My heart ached as I saw how her lip trembled, but before I could say anything, she recovered herself, and went on—"I wished to take your hand, and thank you for your brotherly kindness to Alfred; and I wanted to tell you that I am sure, in all you did, you acted tenderly and considerately for the best. Perhaps you may be soon going away from home again, and we may not meet any more. I shall never, never forget that you were kind to him when he wanted a friend, and that you have the greatest claim of anyone on earth to be gratefully remembered in my thoughts as long as I live."

The inexpressible tenderness of her voice, trembling a little all the while she spoke, the pale beauty of her face, the artless candour in her sad, quiet eyes, so affected me that I could not trust myself to answer her at first, except by gesture. Before I recovered my voice, she had given me her hand once more and had left me.

I never saw her again. The chances and changes of life kept us apart. When I last heard of her, years and years ago, she was faithful to the memory of the dead, and was Ada Elmslie still, for Alfred Monkton's sake.